I0619399

Blood Debt

James Mathews

DISTANT LANDS BOOKS
Text copyright © 2010 by James Mathews
Jacket art copyright © 2010 by Kevin Lee
Copyright © 2007 by James Mathews
ISBN-10:061553368X
ISBN-13:978-0615533681

For Heather, my beautiful bride, the wind beneath my wings; for your encouragement, your patience, and your ability to urge me forward.

I don't understand myself at all, for I really want to do what is right, but I don't do it. Instead, I do the very thing I hate... There is another law at work within me that is at war with my mind... Oh, what a miserable person I am! Who will save me from this life of death?

--- Paul of Tarsus

One

1887
Fallen Oak, California

A drop of sweat trickled down the face of eight-year old John as he sat in the front pew. He didn't bother to wipe it off, knowing that another would quickly replace it. The California sun beamed through the dirty windows of Fallen Oak Methodist Assembly.

It was an especially hot day, even compared to normal summer temperatures in California. There hadn't been much rain in the past months. The almost non-existent farming economy of Briar County was crippled. Fret was inscribed on the faces of the congregation, ever present in the form of upside down smiles and heavy brows. No one's mind was on the sermon or the country preacher that paced back and forth in front of the church. The West was a hard and unforgiving place. A person's grandest dreams and worst nightmares were all possible in this land.

The Grady family had moved from Tennessee when John was four years old. Ma hadn't really wanted to leave the South, but Pa had said, "He was being called by God."

That's how God works. The saying was Pa's way of explaining things that didn't make sense. There's not much you can say against a statement like that. So, the family had packed up and moved to a little church in Fallen Oak, a small town about twenty miles east of San Francisco.

On the front pew, John stared at the floor between his feet. The aging wood had become worn and smooth. The planks ran in ancient rows from the front to the back of the little building. For the ant that scurried in front of him, it must have been a vast, unexplored territory. He watched as the ant crawled over ripples and around cracks.

Fallen Oak was dying.

John stepped on the ant and began twisting his shoe on the dusty floor.

"Uh-umm," boomed a voice from above.

John looked up to find the preacher looking down at him. He was a tall, rugged man, not soft like most ministers. His strong, tanned hands gripped the top of the pulpit. Round spectacles were pulled down to the tip of his nose. The preacher's large brown eyes peered over them. He drew in a breath, then after a pause released it. His eyes looked powerful and domineering from the pulpit. They always did. His Pa always took on a different persona when he stepped up to preach. He had to. The West was a cruel place. People had to have a minister who was solid and confident. They *wanted* discipline.

John pushed the mop of black hair off of his forehead. He looked toward his Pa and cracked a smile. Pa tried to keep a straight face as he turned back to the congregation, but he couldn't. Despite his best efforts, the corners of his mouth crept upward. The expression probably seemed like a grimace or a look of frustration to the congregation, but John knew what it was. His father loved him. And he could always make Pa smile.

* * *

The Sunday evening service had gone just as usual. It had started with the singing of three hymns, followed by the message, and ended with an invitation. The gathering was always the same. The program had lasted about an hour. No one walked down the aisle or stepped forward with some life-changing discovery. Nobody admitted any deep, hidden sin.

An hour later, John found himself standing in the doorway of the little church, shaking the hands of the parishioners... as was custom. His Ma stood outside talking to a couple of other ladies. They were dressed in their Sunday best with their bonnets tied neatly under their chins. Their flower print dresses flowed in the strong noonday breeze. The wind was sporadic today and kept the ladies on their guard. When a big gust would come along, they would have to hold their skirts down. John chuckled. He didn't really see what the big deal was, but that was the way with women. They seemed to make a "big-to-do" out of everything. Pa had explained to him how one day he would appreciate it.

Behind the ladies, in the distance, a cloud of dust blew across the center of town. John was struck by a curious white glow from within. What at first seemed to be a result of the strange wind, slowly took the form of two men on horseback. The riders had stopped in the middle of the town square and stared toward the church. One of them tipped his hat to the crowd and pulled his horse away, back into town. He wore a white derby hat, like the ones men wore in the city. The other rider followed him as he rode toward the opposite side of town. Fallen Oak received a lot of visitors who stopped by on their way to San Francisco. People were always passing through, staying only long enough to rest from their journey to the city.

Inside the church, Pa talked with two men, both members of the congregation. One of them was Joe, an Apache Indian. He was an older man and had rough hands. John loved to shake Joe's hand on Sundays. He would try to squeeze harder than Joe. Sometimes Joe would act like his hand was hurt. His tanned, wrinkled face would contort with pain and he would make a noise like he was in agony. John knew he hadn't really hurt Joe.

The other man was a new member. John didn't know much about him. The man seemed nice enough, though, and he dressed well. There was something about him that didn't feel quite right, though. John couldn't put his finger on it. The man seemed edgy, like he was always worried about something. Ma wasn't very fond of him. He had overheard his parents arguing about him before. He was a young, dark complected man with fine black hair, which he wore in a neat part down the center. John thought his name was Ragone. The pronunciation sounded funny, like there was a letter 'A' on the end of it. He couldn't understand why Ma didn't like the man.

The threesome ended their conversation and sauntered toward the front of the church. John politely moved from the doorway to accommodate them. Joe offered John his hand and the boy took it with his smaller hand.

"Put-her there partner," said Joe in his broken English-Apache.

Joe looked him in the eye and squinted as if exerting all of his strength. John dropped his elbow, pulled his arm close to his body, and returned the gesture with everything he had.

"Ah…" Joe moaned with an over exaggerated grimace on his face.

"You'd better let Joe go, son," Pa said. "He's still got to make a living with that hand."

Joe put his hand on John's shoulder. "You have the grip of a warrior."

John smiled. He liked Joe.

Joe patted him on his head and shuffled heavily out the door, then hobbled down the stairs with his characteristic limp. He tipped his hat to the ladies. Joe was a gentleman.

Ragone slipped by John without a word. He looked at Pa again and extended his hand. Pa replied with a hearty shake. John noticed something in their eyes… something private.

"Thank you, Preacher."

"Remember, God can lead our lives, but only if we choose to let Him," said Pa.

"I'll remember that."

"We'll be praying. Now, you'd better hurry up and get going."

He nodded a courtesy farewell to John, then turned and walked down the steps of Fallen Oak Methodist Assembly.

* * *

The wagon ride home had been relaxing and uneventful. The Grady family lived out in the country, about a mile from town. Pa liked it out there. The seclusion allowed him to think.

Their home was simple. It was a small one; nevertheless, it had all the comforts one could need. It came complete with a front porch, two rocking chairs, and the white picket fence that Ma had wanted since childhood. The porch was the best part, though. It was a cozy retreat where the family liked to finish off the day.

John sat between his mother and father. Pa rocked in his chair, gently puffing on his pipe. John loved the smell of Pa's pipe. It was one of the earliest memories he had of his father. A soft tune floated from his opposite side as Ma hummed and flipped through the pages of the newest Sears & Roebuck catalog. The magazine was as much a tradition as the evenings on the porch. She always looked, but never bought anything.

The days were getting shorter. On the horizon, the sun was drawing close to the ground, casting strong shadows with its harsh light. The rays felt nice and warm as they tickled the hair on John's bare arms. Ma's tune drifted into the air and intermingled with the sounds of birds and cicadas as they prepared for the night. John's eyelids began to grow heavy.

"Honey," said Pa, breaking the serenity.

He rose from his chair and placed a hand on his forehead to shield his eyes from the sun. "Why don't you make two more glasses of lemonade? It looks like we have some visitors."

John squinted hard into the setting sun. The light burned his eyes, so he placed his hand over his brow just as Pa had done. He could barely make out two dark figures on horseback, emerging from the descending circle of the sun. One of the riders looked odd. There seemed to be something glowing above his head... almost like a halo. The horses seemed to float, their dark legs disappearing in the light as they cantered closer. John could've been dreaming.

A sound behind him broke the mood. Ma was returning with two glasses of lemonade in her hands. She crossed the porch and handed the cups to Pa.

"Who are they, James?"

"I don't know. I can't imagine who'd be coming out here this time of evening."

The riders drew close to the front gate. Their horses panted heavily. Their hooves beat the ground with a heavy thud, as if they were nearly too tired to lift their legs. The riders stopped at the gate and one of the horses let out a heavy sigh. Pa, with lemonade in hand, stepped off the porch and walked out to greet them. John followed behind him.

As they walked closer, still squinting against the sun, John began to make out more details of the riders. They looked like young men. The one on the left was slightly younger and wore a tattered leather hat with a feather protruding from the band. His face was youthful and smooth and looked as though he could have been in his late teens.

Next to him, was the rider with the halo. Now, John could see that it wasn't a halo at all, but that the rider was wearing a bright, white derby — *the kind worn in the big city*. He was the rider from town, the same one he had seen after church. A pistol was tied to his leg.

"Good evening gentleman," said Pa.

"You the preacher?" asked the rider wearing the derby. He spoke with a funny accent. John had heard some of the railroad workers use it. It was Irish.

"I am. Would you care for something cool to drink?"

"We don't have time for drinks. We're here to talk about a mutual friend we share... a Mr. Ragone. You know the man I'm talkin' about?"

"I do."

"Has he ever mentioned anything about a Mr. Saietta?"

"I don't recall."

"Oh, I think you do recall," the younger rider replied.

"I'm sorry, but what goes on between a pastor and his laity is confidential," explained Pa. "It's a trust issue."

"No, I'm the one that's sorry," the man replied. "Truly, I am. I'm sorry that Mr. Ragone didn't feel the same way. You see... Mr. Ragone spilled his guts about everything... right before I put a bullet between his eyes. I know what he told you."

Pa's body grew rigged.

"Don't think me a heathen, Preacher... but business is business."

Boom!! The sound of hell filled the air. The blast was deafening. Glasses of lemonade exploded into a million pieces, transforming their sweet contents into a fine mist that filled the air. Because of the sun, John had never seen the double-barrel shotgun that was snaked around the saddle horn of the derby man's horse. Today, the light that gives life to all the earth had been used to conceal death.

John stared at the derby man as a sickening void filled his heart. Images of his Pa swirled through his head. He remembered fishing at Corn Creek, walks in the meadow, catching rabbits in homemade traps, and the scent of pipe smoke tickling his nose. The killer grinned with evil satisfaction.

Through the ringing in his ears, a shrill scream sounded in some distant world. Behind him, Ma began to stumble

8

down the steps of the porch. The only thing John could think to do was to gather the shattered pieces of the drinking glasses. He began to fumble for one of the bigger pieces, but his treasure hunt was cut short when he discovered a large figure resting behind the shard. *It* was his Pa. He hadn't recognized his face.

John looked up at the riders. The murderer tipped his white derby.

"See ya 'round, kid."

He pulled his horse hard left and the younger rider followed. In a cloud of dust, they galloped away into the sun... back to the fiery inferno that birthed them.

Reality began to set in with a cruelty John had never experienced. The screaming that was once distant began to envelop him. Ma collapsed into the dirt beside him and lifted Pa's torn body into her arms. All of the pain her heart felt wailed out into the evening air. John wanted to help, but he had no idea where to begin. So he prayed. He prayed with all his might that God would spare his Pa. He prayed that this moment had never happened... that he had fallen asleep in his rocking chair... that this was all a dream.

Tears of confusion poured from his eyes. Of all the things he had ever learned... of all the things he had ever heard his Pa preach on, one thought stood out above the rest.

That's how God works.

Two

1915
New York City

Tim O'Hare smoothed his thinning, gray hair to the side. He could remember when he'd had trouble running his hands through it. Now, he barely even noticed it was there.

It was early. He had awakened at sunrise. He'd never been one to roll around in bed, but adhered to an old proverb that went something like, *don't turn in your bed like a door on a rusty hinge or poverty will overtake you.* There was enough poverty going around without adding another old man to the lot. Looking into his tall, swivel mirror, he adjusted his white collar and smoothed his black shirt. He inhaled a deep breath and released it with a heavy sigh.

The cool, morning air felt crisp on his already flushed cheeks. It was late September and autumn was beginning to sneak into the city. Each morning was growing progressively colder. This morning was particularly cooler than it had been lately. Breath floated from his mouth in billows of steam. The change in weather reinvigorated him after a long, muggy summer.

These days, Tim needed all of the reinvigoration he could get for his aging body. At sixty-two years old, his instrument of life wasn't what it used to be. His walks weren't as long as they once were and his feet grew sore a little faster now along with every other body part. But, he could deal with a little pain for the sense of fulfillment a walk through his neighborhood brought. It was so nice to get out and visit his people.

Tim O'Hare watched his feet as they impacted the sidewalk one at a time. He'd shined his black, leather shoes only a few days ago, but they were already dusty and fading. He wondered what the point was in shining shoes anyway. Who decided that having shiny shoes was the proper thing to do? Did shiny shoes do something that dull shoes couldn't? Well, what did it matter? Shiny shoes were the accepted norm. He guessed the idiosyncrasy was just like any other courtesy that gentlemen showed—such as opening doors for ladies, and keeping your elbows off of the supper table. There were a lot of things Tim had to get used to when he had moved from the West. Sometimes, he couldn't help but wonder why he'd ever come to this city.

"Reverend O'Hare," said a crackly voice.

A hunched, older lady peeked around the corner of a doorway to his right. She made a hard effort at a grin with the few teeth she still owned.

"Good mornin' to you," she continued.

"Top of the mornin' to you, Mrs. Ryan," replied Tim in a broken, Irish accent. "Aren't you looking chipper this mornin'?"

"Well I may be lookin' it, but I'm not feelin' it," she managed to pronounce between her remaining teeth. "This weather ain't the best for elder people you know."

"I'm beginnin' to understand that more and more everyday, Mrs. Ryan. Good day to you."

He tipped his hat to her, exercising another one of those gentlemanly fashions and continued on his stroll. He knew it wouldn't be long until his walk was interrupted again. It didn't matter. After all, it wasn't the walk that kept him doing this day after day; it was the people.

So many pastors were unconnected to their people. As of late, more and more ministers were settling for the Sunday routine of seeing their congregation come into the church and leave two hours later. They never got involved in any other aspect of their parishioners' lives. They never knew the people's children, their work, or their families. It was so easy to forget that a congregation was made of people and people were always different. There were never two alike.

Getting to know his people had been no easy task. Human beings could be hard to love, especially in *this* city. Life was tough here.

"Reverend O'Hare! Good morning to you, sir."

"Good mornin', Charles."

Charles Kell was a good man… a hard worker. Tim was pleased to see him. He loved talking to men who were hard workers. They never wasted time with cheap talk. They didn't have the time to spare. Charles was an especially hard worker; he had eight children… all girls. *God help the man.*

Charles was standing in front of his butcher's shop. His hands were planted on the waist of his bloody, leather apron. He was a tall, lean man with black, thinning hair. Tim thought he looked a little young to be missing so much hair.

But then again, he supposed eight daughters could do that to a man.

"How are we this morning my good minister?" asked Charles.

"We are doin' excellent," replied Tim. "How about your young army?"

"Take a look for yourself," Charles replied.

Charles moved out of the way and motioned for Tim to look inside. He obliged and peeked into the doorway. The butcher shop was full of hustle and bustle, not to mention a battalion of young girls carrying meat, wrapping packages, and cleaning the floor of blood and other leftovers of the butcher business.

Tim laughed to himself. Most men would be upset that they hadn't been given any boys, but Charles hadn't let that slow him down at all.

"Not bad Charles!" said O'Hare. "Not bad at all. Now what are you goin' to do when these ladies become inclined to follow the company of some young gentlemen? Or rather, the gentlemen become inclined to follow after them?" asked O'Hare, chuckling.

"I know you like marrying folks, Reverend, but don't be getting ahead of yourself!" Charles' eyes grew wide. "I've already considered the situation. There are some finer points to being a butcher, you know."

Tim slammed his hands onto his knees, and let out a hearty laugh. Charles seemed amused that his joke had gone over so well. But the truth was, Tim needed it, and would have laughed at most anything. Tim loved to laugh, especially with good people… people like Charles Kell.

As the needed release tapered to an end, Tim already began to miss it. If only life could be like a laugh… *if only*.

13

"It was good to see you this mornin', Charles," said Tim, giving the man a jovial slap on the shoulder.

Charles winced in pain, and then forced a quick grin on his face in an attempt to hide it. He nodded his head to Tim, suggesting he was all right. Tim couldn't ignore it.

"Have you hurt yourself, Charles?"

"Oh... I'm fine Reverend... just not as young as I used to be."

Tim nodded and smirked in agreement. "Sure, I've noticed a lot of that this mornin'. Have you had visitors recently, then?" Tim didn't mean just anyone. Charles knew that.

Charles sighed and rubbed his shoulder. "Yes. But, it's nothing for you to worry about."

Charles was a good man... and brave.

"How often?" Tim asked.

"Often enough, I suppose. Some weeks are better than others."

"By that, you mean, the weeks when you have more money?"

"It's all right. After all, they do give us protection."

Tim was about to say something when Charles interrupted him.

"Really, it's all right. Look, I have my girls to look after. There's no need to stir up any trouble. I can't afford to."

"I understand." Tim dropped his head and sighed. "Will I see you Sunday?"

"Oh... of course."

"Good! Take care, Charles. Be careful with that arm. Don't mess up and cut off the wrong thing."

They both laughed, but this time it was different. The innocence was no longer there. Brooklyn was like that. The city hated to leave anything pure... even a laugh.

Charles ducked into his shop. He was a good man. Most of Tim's people were good. They deserved better. He'd nearly forgotten. That's the reason he'd taken a pastorate in this city... *for the people.*

Brooklyn had been a frightened town with a lot of promise and had been the perfect place for Tim to make a difference. These people needed him. They needed guidance... a minister who cared.

But as of late, the load had begun to weigh too heavily on his shoulders. Tim had to sit back and watch in agony as the people struggled. He knew the truth. Too many of them ached. Too many had missing teeth, bruised faces... broken arms... too many closed businesses. But, the people kept quiet. There was no one to turn to.

Thank God help was coming.

But, helping a new minister adapt to this city was going to put a strain on Tim. He'd trained younger men before, and it was a trying process. Still, this young minister would bring with him a breath of fresh air. Hopefully, he would take some of the pressure off of Tim. He would be an ally, someone to confide in, and someone to share his hopes and hurts with. The man would be a friend... another soldier. And, now more than ever, Tim O'Hare needed a partner.

The gangs were growing.

Three

The room was dark. Anders McCain had never grown comfortable with the fact that he preferred the dark. So he reasoned that there was a method to the nuance, something that he'd picked up in his youth. The habit had everything to do with survival. Survival, after all, was the most important thing in a man's life. It was the most essential skill to the continuation of the human species. Why should he feel silly? Why should he question himself?

Hadn't the dark saved his life more than a few times? How many dark rooms had he hidden in during his life? How many times had he sat nervously, waiting, concealed in the shadows like a cougar awaiting his prey? The dark had always been his ally. Wrapped in the cocoon of darkness, he felt untouchable. It wasn't an addiction… it was a choice.

A knock at the door interrupted his thoughts. McCain straightened at his desk. His hand moved to his thigh, searching for an object long retired. Old habits die hard.

"Yes?" McCain asked.

"Mr. McCain," said a young voice. The silhouette of a man stood amidst the light which spilled through his office doors.

The young man was his new assistant. He was in his early twenties... someone's cousin or something. McCain could never keep up with all of the assistants. They came and went so often. The rascals were almost never trustworthy enough to survive. And, the ones who were dependable were always needed elsewhere.

"Mr. Thompson is here to see you, sir," Jennings continued.

"He's early," replied McCain.

"You have an appointment at three o'clock, sir."

McCain looked at the grandfather clock on the wall of his office. The timepiece read two minutes 'til the hour of three. He looked back to Jennings. Was there something this kid didn't understand?

"He's early," said McCain, repeating himself.

"Yes, sir."

Jennings pulled himself out of the cracked doorway he'd been residing in for the last thirty seconds of McCain's valuable time. The kid had understood. *Good for him. He might go a long way, if he keeps learning.*

Mr. Thompson was early. Promptness was a good trait. That didn't mean, however, that his appointment would be any sooner. *That* was reality. Life was dependent upon timing. Time could give you everything you ever wanted or take away everything you had. You simply had to be in the right place at the right or wrong time. Too bad more people didn't understand that.

He looked at the clock again. The timepiece was crafted of a beautiful cherry colored wood. The hand of a master had carved it. The gold rim shone around its dimly lit face. A heavy pendulum swung back and forth, counting every second of its existence. The clock understood. It counted every moment.

Three chimes interrupted the solitude of his thoughts. The music echoed through the lightly adorned office.

Knuckles rapped against the door for a second time.

"Yes?" McCain asked.

The door cracked and Jennings poked his head in once again.

"Sir, Mr. Thompson is here."

"He's late," replied McCain.

"Sir, I'm sorry… I don't understand."

"Mr. Jennings…" McCain said, as he gestured toward the clock. "Do you see that?"

"It says three o'clock, sir," replied Jennings.

"Take another look, Mr. Jennings. What time is it?"

Jennings started to speak but the words got jumbled as they came off of his tongue. He was quickly interrupted.

"The time is currently one minute past three," explained McCain. "Do you know what that means?"

"I'm late, sir?"

"No. Mr. Thompson is late *because* of you. Time is *everything*. Do you understand that Mr. Jennings?"

"Yes, sir," replied Jennings. "Time is everything."

"Send Mr. Thompson in, please."

"Yes, sir."

Jennings retreated from the door. There was some mumbling outside. Within moments, a short, balding man stepped through the doorway. He adjusted his spectacles as he left the brighter lobby area.

As Ronald Thompson's eyes adjusted, he could make out the form of a man seated behind the desk. Sunlight crept through the closed curtains behind McCain, leaving features hidden in shadow.

"Good afternoon, Mr. McCain," said Thompson, unsure if he should have spoken first.

"Have a seat, Mr. Thompson," instructed a voice in a subdued Irish dialect.

The seats were farther away from the desk than normal. The entire meeting felt extremely odd to Ronald Thompson. The office seemed too dark and the chairs were so far from the desk. Why had McCain disapproved of his early arrival time? Oh, yes, he had heard some of the discussion even though the young assistant had tried to hide it. The meeting was off to a strange start. But, then again, Anders McCain was no normal businessman.

Thompson eased into one of the high backed, leather seats. The chair was comfortable, but not enough to make him relax. He placed his document carrier to the right of his chair and crossed his legs. Thompson grinned politely and craned his head to get a clearer picture of the face in the shadows.

"Are you alright, Mr. Thompson?" asked McCain.

"Yes," replied Thompson, worried that McCain had noticed his curiosity. The move had been stupid of him. He'd better remember with whom he was dealing.

"I'm fine," replied Thompson. "I was just trying to see... it's a..." He remembered what his informant had said about Mr. McCain. *Don't comment on the darkness.*

"It's what?" asked McCain.

"Uh… nothing," Thompson replied. "I hope that my early arrival didn't inconvenience you too much?"

Had McCain detected the sarcasm in that question? Thompson hadn't intended the inference; nevertheless, it had escaped. He couldn't help himself. The whole episode had been ridiculous. Just the same, he had better be more wary of his mouth while in the presence of McCain.

"It didn't inconvenience me at all," McCain explained. "I merely seized the opportunity to make a point."

"May I ask, to whom?" replied Thompson.

"To you… my assistant… to anyone who finds out about it, really. Timing is everything."

"Yes, you're right," agreed Thompson. "In business, timing is essential."

"No, Mr. Thompson. In *everything*, timing is essential," said McCain, hammering each word.

Thompson shifted uneasily in his chair. This was insane. He was having a conversation about time with one of the most feared men in New York. How had he gotten to this place?

"Of course," replied Thompson. "How is it that I can be of service to you, Mr. McCain?"

"You are an accountant, correct?"

"Yes, that is my occupation, and if I may be so bold as to say, I'm rather good at what I do."

"You may. I like boldness in a man so long as it's kept in its place."

"Well, thank you."

"I've been told that you are at the top of your field, Mr. Thompson, which is why I have asked you here today. I have also been told that you are trustworthy and are good at keeping secrets. Trustworthiness is a very important trait, don't you think, Mr. Thompson?"

"Oh yes, to be sure. A man's business is, after all, his own business. I simply manage his assets."

"Well, I have to be straightforward with you. I am a very secretive man and my business is no less secretive. You might say my very life depends on it. Should you accept my job offer, your life will also depend on those secrets remaining just that. Do you understand?"

"Yes, I think we understand each other," replied Thompson.

"Excellent," said McCain.

McCain extended his hand toward a small lamp on his desk. With a click of the switch, the atmosphere of the room brightened with a soft glow. It was amazing how a small amount of light could make so much difference.

For the first time, Thompson could see McCain. The man behind the desk looked to be in his fifties. He had a round, soft face and dark hair that was graying at the temples. He didn't seem to be very tall from what Thompson could see. Actually, he was slightly on the plump side. By no means was he the imposing figure his legend conjured. McCain's appearance put Thompson at ease. Muscles relaxed and he leaned back into his chair.

McCain pulled a sheet of paper from his desk drawer. After dipping a pen into a small vile of ink, he quickly scribbled on the paper and pushed the note toward the end of his desk.

Thompson did nothing.

With a nod of his head, McCain motioned for him to retrieve the paper.

Unsure of the move he was making, Thompson rose from his chair and covered the distance to the desk, stopping just within arms' reach. He felt as if he were approaching holy ground or a forbidden place of some kind. Getting no closer than was necessary, Thompson stretched over and picked up the slip of paper.

What was on it? Should he read it now or sit back down? *Quit thinking so much you idiot!*

He eased back to his chair and sat down, then leaned forward with both feet planted on McCain's expensive rug.

McCain watched Thompson's expression. His eyes opened wide and bulged. The small man inhaled deeply and shifted his weight in his chair. A long held breath released suddenly, causing Thompson's cheeks to inflate.

"I take it the amount is sufficient for a year's salary under my employment," asked McCain with an air of extreme confidence.

Thompson was at a loss for words. Of course the figure was sufficient. He was a recently fired New York City accountant. McCain knew that he'd never seen a salary figure like that.

"Mr. Thompson?"

"Yes, sir," Thompson finally replied. "The amount is sufficient."

"Good. Before we go any farther, I need to know if you intend to work for me."

"Yes, Mr. McCain. I do. Although, I'm not very clear about what it is I'll be doing."

"In a year's time, Mr. Thompson… you may wish you still didn't."

Four

John Grady's fingers traced the smooth surface of a golden ring. The trinket hung around his neck on a rawhide cord. The habit was an unconscious one and he had decided on numerous occasions to get rid of the object. Some things were hard to leave behind... some were impossible.

The train ride seemed to take an eternity. John couldn't remember why he'd decided to take the train. He preferred long treks through the outdoors... always had. But, it was late September, and the nights were growing cooler, especially in the northern states.

New York City was a long way from Seminary, Missouri. There would be a lot of differences. He'd heard about the living conditions in the city. Most of the families in the inner city lived in small, cramped apartments, which were stacked on top of each other, story upon story. Sometimes, several families might live in the same room, where they would eat, sleep, and live all cramped together in the tiny space. *And don't forget about the trees. What trees?* There probably wouldn't be too many of those where he was going. How could there be? John had seen pictures of New York City before and he couldn't remember seeing any trees.

Riding to New York on horseback could have made for an interesting trip. Folks were doing that less and less these days. It seemed unthinkable that horses were soon to be replaced by automobiles. People used to scoff at the idea. Back when automobiles were first showing up, they were always breaking down. People used to joke that a man with an automobile would tow his horse along so that the horse could tow the car later.

But, now, with the introduction of an auto that could carry a family, it seemed that the change might actually be happening. He'd even heard that earlier this month, a car set a speed record of over a hundred miles per hour.

Yes, the world was changing. Travel was changing. The old order was slowly passing away only to be replaced by a new world that couldn't keep up with itself. John wasn't sure how he would fit into the scheme of this new age.

But, he would, nonetheless. He would adapt. He would overcome. He had always beaten adversity, and he supposed he always would. It was his nature to be a survivor. At this point in his life, he would need that trait more than ever. From what he'd heard, New York would chew a man up and spit him out. He'd *have* to be strong, make hard choices.

But wasn't he supposed to be weak? Isn't that what the Bible says to be? Didn't God show his strength through weak people?

No. He'd seen what happens to the weak. Too many times he saw lives destroyed because of the refusal or inability to act.   How often had the weak prospered?   How often had they survived?

The Bible could be confusing.   John had concluded that some of its content wasn't to be taken literally.   How could it have been?

No, he would choose to be strong.   John Grady was a fighter.   He had been taught to take care of himself.   He was a man who could get the job done… *the only man willing*.

He knew that it would be no simple feat.   Ministering to the broken inhabitants of this cursed city was not a task for a weakling.   No, these people needed his strength.   They needed his confidence.   *This* was the real reason he had come to New York.

But, that wasn't the complete truth.   There was another reason, another motive that drove his life.   This was where *the end* was, wasn't it… in New York City?   All the clues led here, to this place.   All the clues pointed to one man. *Don't fool yourself. You're not here to serve God.*

But, there were many things he would be able to accomplish here.   Just think of all the good things that he would be able to do.   What about all of the people he would be able to help, to comfort, even… *to love?*   Could he do that?   Was John Grady even capable of love anymore?

His shortcomings weren't the issue.   The point was that he could do something positive with his life here.   God needed him to be here… if for more than one reason.

So, here he was, on a train only a few hours from the largest city in America, in the world, as far as he knew.   This was his destiny and nothing would stop him.

The whistle sounded, breaking the jumble of thoughts.   The noise erupted in a low moaning howl and rose steadily until ending in a shrill pitch. He'd always liked the sound of a train. He had ridden many trains in his life.

John opened his collar and tucked the golden band into his shirt, then scanned the crowded coach car. There were so many different faces, all headed toward this city that so many people were trying to escape. The search for the American dream lured so many immigrants to this country.

He supposed some of them would be able to make something of their lives, if they were lucky. But, how many dreams had been dashed upon the rocks of New York's harbor? How many dreams lost to the West like dust scattered in the wind? It was all a false hope.

Time trickled past at a snail's pace. John thought he would never hear the sound of the brakes grinding — that long awaited screech signaling the end of his journey. But, at last, the end came. The engine pulled into New York's Union Station, none too soon.

John stepped from the hanging stairway of the passenger car. The rest of the travelers had not unloaded as quickly as he had imagined they would. There was fear in their eyes... hesitation in their bodies. For them, this was the final destination, in many ways. New York was either the last place for them to find hope or the only place where they knew how to survive. He figured that most of the passengers were returning to the city rather than visiting for the first time. Many of them had packed their families and headed west for land and fortune, only to find out that most of the land was taken and it took a fortune to make one. Crushed and disillusioned, they were returning here, to the one place they could survive — the one place they fit in. He knew that as soon as they stepped out of the aging coach car, they would disappear into the sea of ethnicity in which he was now standing.

The whole world seemed to be represented in the station. He had never been to New York, but he had been studying about it. He knew the city as well as anyone could know something without direct experience. He'd read many books on the great city over the last several years. New York was one gigantic puzzle of nationalities. If America was considered the "melting pot" of the world, New York was the kettle from which the ingredients were poured. There were literally hundreds of different faces mingling around the bustling boardwalks of the station. The noise of the crowd was an indistinguishable jumble of dialects, but there were a few accents he recognized.

There was a German man yelling for his two children who had been separated by a mob of Irish immigrants. The family had been pushing their way toward the train when the children had been swept away in the madness. An Italian woman passed by screaming angrily into her husband's ear. Every direction he turned, he was bombarded by different languages, some of which he recognized and some that he had *never* heard.

Chaos.

If Union Station were any indication of the hurriedness of the rest of the city, it would require a patient adjustment. Just figuring out what people were trying to say would be enough of a problem.

John began pushing his way through the crowd of travelers. He needed to get to the freight cars. There was someone he needed to visit.

At first, he tried being as cordial as possible, saying "excuse me" and "sorry". Sometimes it seemed that he was losing a step for every two he took forward. It was too much... too soon. What had he gotten himself into? The world was falling in on him. His chest tightened as the mob pressed inward. The stench from all of the people and animals saturated his senses. Why did everyone have to be so cramped together? Why didn't they just get out of the way? Couldn't they see that they could back away from the tracks? There was ample room deeper in the station. Did they really have to squeeze in so close to the cars?

He began nudging a little harder as he moved. Within moments, he was plowing through the bodies, pushing people out of the way. *Control yourself, John.*

"Hey! Watch it you bloody yank," yelled a small guy who stepped back and glared.

A voice came from somewhere in the back of his mind. It was telling him to show the man how they did things in America. At six feet and two inches tall, John Grady towered over the small Englishman.

"Excuse me," replied John. "I'm sorry... I'm in a hurry."

"Well, aren't we all now," said the Englishman.

John turned and walked away. That's how it always went; give a little guy an inch and he'd take a mile.

Exercising a little more courtesy, he walked towards the animal cars at the rear of the train. The small guy was still behind him, jabbering some words that drifted into the jumble of voices in the station. Sometimes, he wished that he wasn't a minister.

At last, he found the car he had been looking for. The green paint flecked off in large areas and a strong odor seeped from the freight car. The smell wasn't pleasant, but it wasn't necessarily bad either... a familiar aroma that reminded him of home.

White letters stenciled on the side read: 'Livestock'. About six feet up from the base of the car was a long, rectangular window that wrapped around the entire length of the car. The opening was about a foot in height and was supported by rusty, iron bars. Several long noses protruded from within. A pale, gray chin, covered in whiskers, reached out to meet his hand.

"Hey boy," said John, comforting the animal.

The horse shifted his weight and stomped nervously. It had been a long ride.

"Easy…"

Ash's hair felt smooth against his palm as he gently stroked the bridge of the horse's nose.

"We're here. It's gonna be all right."

They *were* here. Tomorrow was going to be a long day. But, the most important part was that they had arrived. John was in New York City. And there was work to do.

It was time to start picking up the pieces.

* * *

Anders McCain was standing at the back of his office, staring out of the window at the rainy, dismal evening, when Jennings stumbled in. In the blink of an eye, the doors had burst open, exposing his room with a flood of light. There had been no warning, no cordial knock. Anders McCain had been caught off guard.

He whipped around to face the figure that was intruding through his door. McCain's hand grasped for the object that should have been on his thigh, but there was nothing.

"Mr. McCain!" said Jennings in an excited state.

"This had better be good," McCain replied. The kid's life was counting on it.

"S...s...sir there's been a problem with one of our deliveries," Jennings stammered.

Weren't there always?

"Spit it out," ordered McCain.

"We don't know what happened exactly," replied the kid, "but there was an explosion."

"Where?"

"Jersey."

"How much did we lose?"

The assistant hesitated. "Everything."

McCain paced the floor, his hands clasped behind his back. His nephew had been on that crew. He had just put the boy in charge of it. He wasn't a very bright kid, but...

"And the men?" asked McCain.

The assistant struggled for courage. "Most of them killed... some by gunshots."

McCain's head snapped upright and he glared at Jennings.

"Nobody saw anything," Jennings stammered. "But the attackers left this."

Jennings extended a shaky hand. In his trembling fingertips was a piece of paper. McCain took the note and turned on his desk lamp.

On the top of the note appeared his last name, scribbled in handwriting. Under it read three words.

See you around.

Five

ohn Grady wasn't what Tim O'Hare had expected. Most ministers were softer and talked more. John didn't talk much at all, and he certainly didn't appear to be soft. Piercing gray eyes hinted at a deep sadness within the man. His tall, lean figure, tanned, weathered features, and dark hair made him look more like a cowboy. Well, he *had* originated from California. So, Tim supposed he looked exactly like westerners were supposed to look. Who was he to say what a preacher could or couldn't look like, anyway?

But, John *was* quiet, a trait not many ministers possessed. Most pastors he knew had been given the "gift of gab". Getting a preacher to shut up could be a monumental feat in itself. But, John liked to stay to himself most of the time. If not gauged properly, his solitude could become a big hindrance to his ministry. Tim couldn't blame the man, though. A few years in the ministry was enough to send any man seeking solace, including himself.

The art of ministering was built around relationships. It could be said that *relationships* were a minister's primary job. People were always expecting guidance, even on seemingly trivial issues. Tim could have never predicted the amount of time he would be required to invest in his congregation. And, after having to interact with so many people throughout the week, it was nice to be alone and enjoy a little peace and quiet. In his solitude, he didn't have to be Reverend O'Hare. He was just plain ole' Tim.

To a certain degree, that was a good thing. *Tim* was fun and lighthearted. He allowed nuisances to roll off his sleeve and still treasured an idealistic outlook on life. The problem was that sooner or later plain ole' Tim started to think like bad ole' Tim. If allowed to roam freely, bad ole' Tim could find himself in trouble. Old Tim would do whatever it took to have his way or to prove his case. Other people and their opinions didn't matter, nor did their welfare. Everything else took second place to what *he* wanted. Bad ole' Tim could never be the man that these people needed. So, Tim kept that part of himself tucked far away.

Despite John's odd ways, he'd had been a welcomed addition to Tim's life. He was a hard worker, and within the few weeks he had been at Mount Zion Methodist Assembly, he'd adapted very well. New York City was a hard place to adjust to, especially for someone who had been accustomed to the space of the sparsely settled West. Nevertheless, Grady carried out his duties like he had lived in the city his entire life. There was never a complaint.

There was one thing that bothered him about John, though. There was something that he couldn't quite put his finger on. What was it? It seemed as if he was... *preoccupied...* as if another force were driving him.

Sometimes, Tim couldn't help but feel that Grady had to force himself to interact with people. It was as if his mind was always focused somewhere else while his body carried out the work at hand.

How can you say that? You hardly know the man. Who are you to judge?

What he did know, was that John Grady had come *here*. John had been sent to *him*. And, he was going to do the best job he could at mentoring this young preacher. *God has entrusted him to you.*

Light footsteps padded the carpet behind him. Tim pulled away from his thoughts and prepared for a warm wind to fill his spirit. Mary had a way of spreading joy wherever she went.

"Now I'm bettin' that you've been wearin' that same suit ever since I left," said a delicate voice from behind him. A beautiful girl, with strawberry-blonde hair, stood behind him in a cleaning smock. Blue eyes beamed at him. "Now don't go lyin' to me."

"I have not," Tim replied. "This is the second one, thank you very much. I finally had to put it on yesterday when my other one sprouted legs and ran off," he laughed. "It's good to have you back, Mary. How is your sister doin'?"

"As well as can be after deliverin' a ten pound babe," Mary replied. "How would you be doin'?"

"A little sore I suppose," replied Tim. "Although I don't think I would have been in her predicament to begin with."

"I should hope not," retorted Mary as she placed her hands onto her hips. "Now, about those suits! You promised that you would be able to handle the washin' without me around."

The girl played a pretty good "old biddy" considering how young she was.

"I *was* able to handle it," Tim explained. "I just chose to wear the same suit. It's been cool lately and I haven't been sweatin' much at all."

"A respectable minister ain't got no business runnin' around in the same britches for a month," she fussed at O'Hare. "They start smellin'."

"They don't smell at all," he replied, slightly offended.

"That's what you think," she retorted.

Mary was a sweet girl. She reminded him of his older daughter. But even more, she brought back peaceful memories of Rosalyn. Her hair... her ways... her smile... She filled a void in his life. His reasoning for taking her in had gone beyond compassion. Was there anything wrong with that? Wasn't it all right to *need* someone in your life? Was it abnormal to desire companionship? He'd grown to love her. She had become like a daughter to him.

"I'm going to go and fetch the rest of your suits and catch up on some washin'," said Mary.

"No. Please... You've had a long trip. I know you... and I know you worked the entire time you were away. Why don't you just rest today?"

"There's work to be done," she replied.

"Really... Just relax. You look tired."

She did look tired. She must have been exhausted. She had been taking care of her sister for nearly a month and Tim knew she hadn't taken a break in all that time. Mary was one of the hardest workers he'd ever seen. The girl never stopped working. *What a rare trait.* She would make someone an incredible wife someday, if she would ever marry at all. She didn't care too much for men. It's been said that time is the best doctor, but not even time can heal all wounds.

"Let me just get your suits, then?" She insisted. "That's all I'll do. I promise."

"All right then, girl," he conceded with a wave of his hand.

She turned to walk away, but stopped, remembering something. "Reverend Grady," she inquired, "have things been goin' well with him?"

"Oh yes... very well. It's been nice to have him around. He's out visitin' right now. I can't wait for you to meet him. I think you'll like him. He's a little like you... enjoys to work. He's been doin' a lot of repairs in the basement since he arrived. He's a little loud sometimes, but a man could have greater faults."

"Well, he sounds like a good man then. What about everythin' else?"

"Things are going well, I suppose."

"Good," she said. "I'll just go and tidy up a bit."

Tim had lied. Things weren't well. The Irish and Italian gangs were at it again. They were fighting over territory, which always involved innocent people. Conquering territory meant collecting from local businessmen. It was a painful process, of which there was a lot going around. To make matters worse, there had been a hit on the Irish mob. Tim had heard through certain people that one of Anders McCain's storage houses had been destroyed. Several of his men were killed, including McCain's own nephew. It was suspected that the Italians were behind the attack. Whatever or whomever the cause, the result was always the same.

35

Innocent people got caught in the crossfire. Why was it that the ones who deserved pain always escaped it?

Anyway, Mary didn't need to be bothered with the depressing details. She would find out soon enough.

Mary strolled away from the front of the sanctuary and headed toward the living quarters. She was an interesting young lady. Tim didn't know how he'd ever gotten along without her.

"It's good to have you back Mary," yelled O'Hare.

"It's nice to be back," she shouted, without turning around.

Tim knew that she wouldn't rest after she'd finished the laundry.

* * *

The bowels of the church were filled with a dim, yellow light. Mary walked, dragging her fingertips along the faded wallpaper. The decor had been pretty at one time. Golden vases with matching flowers were imprinted onto the paper. Unlike real flowers, these were meant to last. Time, however, catches up with everything. If life had taught Mary anything, it was that *nothing* lasts.

Floorboards creaked under her small feet as she drew near to the stairs. She was greeted by a familiar, musty odor before descending to the boarding rooms.

The basement was vast, spreading underneath the entire area of the building. It contained a few rooms, but most of it was uninhabited. The undeveloped area was dark and dusty, an urban cave that frightened Mary. She rarely ventured into the uninhabited section. Because the open area couldn't be seen from the developed section, very few people even knew it existed.

The stairs came to rest at the apex of an L-shaped hallway. The first section ran away to her left, ending at a door that led into the vacant part of the basement. There were two doors on the right side of the hallway. The closest door opened into one of the two boarding rooms, which were rooms the church had built to house people who were down on their luck. There was never any shortage of unlucky people in New York.

The other section of the hall ran directly away from the foot of the stairs. Mary left the last step and walked into the second corridor. The walls were made of a dark golden, finished wood, whose grains swirled throughout. The rooms had been built with beautiful craftsmanship, in keeping with the quality of the rest of the church. She was amazed that among the poverty and bad circumstances that plagued this area, people still gave their best when it came to building God's house.

The construction had been a large project that started several years ago when Reverend O'Hare accepted the pastorate at Mount Zion. Originally, the pastors had lived on the first floor behind the sanctuary. But as the congregation grew, the original living quarters needed to be used for Sunday school rooms. Reverend O'Hare had suggested that they begin furnishing the large, unused basement. The construction also provided an opportunity to supply the community with a housing mission. The idea had worked, and many people, who had been ravaged by the claws of life, benefited from the project, including Mary.

Halfway down the corridor, another hallway broke away to her left. She turned and headed toward the wall at the end. On her right was a doorway into the second boarding room. She could hear Mattie Turner speaking to her daughter. Mattie had recently lost her husband and had been living in the basement for about three months.   Towards the end of the hallway, were two more doors. The one on the right opened into Reverend O'Hare's room, and the one directly across had been vacant until John Grady arrived.

Mary turned the knob of Tim O'Hare's door and pushed it open. She walked in and looked around the room. It was exactly as she expected. The room was a complete mess. There was a dull layer of dust on all of the wooden furniture. Papers lay upon the desk scattered around, as if a gust of wind had ripped through the place. The bed looked as though it had been ransacked by a shipload of pirates.

"He probably hasn't made that bed since I've been gone," she said, aloud. "I suppose I knew better than to trust a man to be able to take care of himself." She shook her head before bending down to pick up the discarded pieces of paper.

She made her way toward the laundry hamper, which was a simple cutout in the wall. She opened the waist high cabinet door to find one dirty suit and several pairs of long underwear. "Good gracious, Reverend," she grimaced.

The fact that he hadn't realized that the pants were starting to smell was inconceivable. *How do men survive without us?*

She picked up his clothing and placed it into a cloth bag that she was carrying. Then, she left the room and headed across the hall to the room of John Grady.

Her thoughts were still focused on the folly of Tim O'Hare when she burst into John's room. The bag of laundry dropped from her hand and she covered her mouth. She hadn't expected to see what her eyes beheld. Tim had said that Reverend Grady was out visiting, but he wasn't.

She was taken aback. There was a man seated at the desk on the right side of the wall and she hadn't thought to knock.

"Oh… I'm sorry. Excuse me. I'll come back later," she apologized as she started to back out of the door.

"No. That's alright… really," replied John.

Without looking away from Mary, he reached down to a journal he had been writing in and closed the cover. He stood up from the desk and pushed the chair away.

"I'm very embarrassed," she said. "Reverend O'Hare said that you'd be out visitin'. So I just…"

"It's all right. I *was* out visiting," he replied while offering his hand. "I'm John Grady."

She accepted it as he bowed his head slightly.

"You must be Mary," he added.

"Yes… Reverend Grady. Again, I *am* sorry. I was just pickin' up the laundry. I do that durin' the day… pick up the laundry that is… to wash…" She was obviously flustered from the unexpected meeting. "Do you have any laundry?"

"No, I don't," he replied, smiling.

"Oh… well, that's alright then… neither did Reverend O'Hare. He didn't see any need in changin' clothes while I was gone," she laughed. The gesture hadn't been a real laugh, but an uncomfortable chuckle. She stood in front of the door with her hands clasped and twiddled her thumbs.

"I wash my own clothes," he said breaking the silence.

"Oh… you don't have to do that," she replied. "I do the washin' 'round here."

"Well… there's no need for you to have to add mine to your load."

"No… really I don't mind," she said biting her bottom lip. "I enjoy it… cleanin' and the like."

"Thank you. But, if it's all the same, I think I'll just do my own cleaning."

"Of course... I'm sorry again for bargin' in. I'll just go now and wash Reverend O'Hare's things." She turned into the hallway and began to close the door. "It was nice to meet you," she said peeking through the narrowing crack between the door and jamb.

"Likewise," he offered in return.

The door shut and Mary hurried away.

"That was real stupid," she said to herself. "You're an idiot Mary Lyles... a real baboon."

The meeting hadn't been the most ideal way to meet the new pastor. She would have preferred a formal introduction, one less awkward... one in which she hadn't appeared as an idiot.

He hadn't been what she'd expected. Reverend Grady didn't look like a minister. But, what had she expected him to look like? Soft and pudgy?

One thing perturbed her. He didn't want her to do any kind of work for him. Did he not understand that she got paid to clean up after the men? Perhaps he had been taken off guard and didn't know how to react. The man hadn't seemed very warm, though. *I don't think he liked me. It's going to be hard to work with this man, I'll wager. I hope I didn't bother his Royal Highness too much.*

Funny girl. John opened the journal that lay closed in front of him. Things were going well here, so far. Mount Zion was a good church. The people were friendly. They seemed to be warming up to him. But, there was a lot of work to do.

Tim had told him all about the gangs and their "protection" insurance. The idea had been around since humans learned to oppress other humans. John had seen it in many places and in many forms. The scheme always came down to the same bottom line. The "protection" insurance protected the businessmen from the insurers themselves. The racket was a farce. Everyone knew it. You'd pay off one man only to protect you from another enforcer from the same gang. And if you missed a payment, your insurer reminded you to never miss another one.

What could one do? The law was just as much apart of it as anyone was. Either the policemen's hands were in the gangs' pockets or they were too afraid to do anything. It was a tough world and one had to *choose* to survive.

Something had been happening recently, though. Tim had tried to stay quiet about it at first, but there was talk going around.

The main Irish group in the city was getting a taste of its own medicine. One of their bootlegging crews had been hit. The rumor was that one of the main bosses lost a nephew. *What comes around goes around.* He savored the irony.

The best part of the story, however, was in the making. The Irish groups were blaming the Italians. The families were on the brink of war... *too bad.* God willing, they would wipe each other off the face of the earth.

Families destroying families, gangs ripping each other to shreds... it was a nice thought, but probably too ideal to be reality, at this point anyway. But it could happen... if only someone could push the chess pieces in the right direction...

...if a rider was pulling the reins.

Six

Moonlight trickled down through the opaque skylight of the warehouse on Flatbush Avenue. The resulting shadows were menacing and deep. Electrical lights weren't standard for most warehouses. Electricity was a valuable and hard to come by commodity. Instead, the spacious buildings used skylights. The large windows worked well enough during the daylight hours, but proved insufficient at night. This night was especially dark.

"Hey Mac," yelled Tom Reigny from inside the warehouse. "Here they are, over here."

"Keep your voice down, you moron," replied John McGregor.

The crates were stacked on top of each other not far from the warehouse entrance. They were picking up thirteen of them tonight. McGregor didn't like that number. *Why not twelve of them*, he thought... *or fourteen?* The feeling was only superstition, of course. Numbers were just numbers... *aren't they? Of course they are.* Still, the coincidence did make him feel a little uncomfortable.

"Make sure these are the right ones," said McGregor.

"They're the right ones. They've got *Nostrand* written on them," replied an aggravated Reigny, motioning toward the crates. "Check for yourself."

McGregor would have checked, but he couldn't read. There *were* worse travesties in life. Many people in the city lacked the ability to read. Life in the city was tough. John McGregor had learned that first hand. As a boy he hadn't enjoyed the liberty of attending school. After the death of his father, he and his three brothers were forced to provide a living for the rest of his family. So, his lack of reading skills was the result of a noble act.

"I don't need to check," replied McGregor. "Just open the bay doors and get this stuff loaded."

Reigny was ambitious. He wanted to be at the top and he was moving quickly. The last thing McGregor needed was to give him an edge, like allowing him to know that he couldn't read.

The old days were different. Back when he'd started in the business, everyone was Irish. If a man weren't related to the "old country" somehow, he just didn't get in. Times were changing. The organization was expanding. There was opportunity for new people... people with ideas. Mr. McCain thought differently than other bosses. His loyalties lay with whomever and whatever expanded his empire. If a man could follow orders and think on his feet, he had a shot at making something of himself. Opportunity was knocking and ambitious men like Reigny were always too willing to answer. These were hard times. A man either climbed on board the ship as it left, or stood on the dock, poor and hungry.

Well, Tom Reigny had better remember his place on this ship.

Reigny stepped through the smaller entrance door that stood ajar. His hand brushed over the aging wood of the doorframe. In the alley, two men sat on the back of a flatbed truck.

"Get this rig in here," ordered Reigny. "We're late and we've gotta get this stuff on the road... yesterday! We gotta load thirteen crates and get em' moved over to Nostrand Avenue by ten o'clock!"

"Slow down darlin'," replied one of the two men. "We got all night. The joint ain't movin' before we get there."

"Besides," replied the second man. "We haven't tested the product yet."

"Yea! We don't want to go sendin' bad stuff to Mr. McCain's number one joint, now do we?" said the first man with a chuckle.

"If you knew Mr. McCain, you wouldn't be sittin' here on your tails," explained Reigny. "This isn't some late night outing you idiots! Mr. McCain isn't one to be playin' with. If you know what's good for you... you'll get this truck in gear."

Reigny started to walk inside, but stopped.

"Another thing," he continued. "If you ever question me again, I may introduce you to Mr. McCain, personally. I'm sure he'd appreciate the part about you 'testing the merchandise'. Let's get this show on the road."

Reigny disappeared into the shadows of the doorway. McGregor was waiting for him next to the crates. His shadow cast an eerie figure on the moonlit floor.

"What's the problem?" whispered McGregor. "We're falling behind."

"Hold your horses," replied Reigny. "I've got this under control."

"This isn't your operation, Tom."

"Well, maybe…"

"Keep your voice down!" McGregor whispered forcefully. He looked around nervously.

"Well maybe it's about time for you to pick up a different line of work," Reigny retorted.

McGregor scowled at the man under his breath. "Just help me so we can get out of here." He begins to maneuver a large crate on top of the stack. "I promised my kid we'd catch the game at Ebett's Field tomorrow."

"Well isn't that sweet," mocked Reigny. "What are those guys doin'? I told them to get those doors open!"

Reigny removed his hands from the crate and stuck a finger of his work glove in his mouth. He pulled the glove off with his teeth then stormed towards the door. He yelled at the men outside. "Hey, what are you fellas doing? Didn't I tell you to get in here? What are you… morons!?"

Outside, the engine fired, struggled to life, and purred for a moment. Someone gunned the accelerator and sent the motor revving up and down.

"Where do they find these guys?" Reigny chuckled.

Reigny walked back toward Mac where he struggled with the crate.

"If you want to get anything done, you've gotta do it yourself," said Reigny.

Bang!

The enormous bay doors exploded. Chaos echoed throughout the warehouse as splinters and nails whizzed past them, followed by the flatbed truck.

Reigny managed to dive just as the machine clipped his leg and spun him into a crate. Pain raced through his torso as his ribs caught the corner of the box. Bones cracked. Reigny screamed in agony.

With a powerful crash, the remains of McCain's crates stopped the runaway truck. The pungent smell of bourbon filled the air as the liquid dripped and ran from the bed of the vehicle. Gallons of the precious beverage soaked into the dirt floor.

The engine continued to sputter.

"What are you idiots doing?!" winced Reigny, now rising to his knees. "I'm going to kill you, Robins!"

Reigny's heart skipped a beat. A form slipped from the passenger side of the wrecked vehicle. Something... or someone... It couldn't have been a person.

Settle down, Tom.

"Mac?!" yelled Reigny. "You all right?"

For the first time tonight, he truly hoped that McGregor was alive.

"Fellas, are you over there?" he asked.

The truck struggled to stay alive.

"This ain't funny! We got a mess to fix!"

Reigny's bottom lip quivered. He reached under his jacket and touched the butt of his pistol. The gun was still there. His hand found surety as it wrapped around the handle of the weapon. He slid the gun from its holster. The resulting pain caused a puff of air to leave his lips.

There was blood on the gun. Reigny was confused. Then he realized… he'd punctured his side on the corner of the crate. A frightened emptiness radiated from the pit of his stomach.

"Guys… I'm hurt! It's all right. We'll figure this out… just come help me."

But the only reply was the sputtering of the truck's motor as it stalled out. The ensuing silence was ominous. Nothing stirred in the room. Reigny slowly became aware of a low rasping sound. It took him a moment to realize that the noise was his breathing. The gasps were fast and labored. His heart was beating out of his chest. The sickening taste of copper filled his mouth. Reigny was bleeding internally. Fear replaced any rational thought.

He ground his teeth and struggled to his feet, then wobbled toward the back of the truck. The ground was saturated with a mixture of whiskey and gasoline that produced a nauseating aroma. One spark from the engine and the whole place could go up in flames.

But, fire was the least of his worries. Outside in the alley, he saw two new problems. Robins was on his back, sprawled out on the pavement. The other crewman was in a half sitting position, propped against the wall of the far building. Neither man was moving.

A boot scuffed on the floor. Reigny froze. Every muscle tensed. *Someone's in here.* And wherever *it* was, it was watching Reigny. He racked his brain, searching for an idea, but a thick fog suffocated it.

"What do you want?!" he yelled into the darkness.

Something moved to his right, far away in the shadows. Reigny fired his revolver wildly in the direction. Another noise followed. This time, a shadowy figure moved across

47

the nearest wall. Reigny fired again. With a zing, the bullet ricocheted off of a metal object.

"Who are you?!" screamed Reigny.

More footsteps. The thing moved left. Reigny's gun sounded twice more, this time the bullets connected with wood.

"Come out!" yelled Reigny, accidentally discharging his fifth shot into the ground. *Stupid!*

Reigny was stuck in the middle of the bay where the moonlight revealed his every move. Somehow, he had to get to cover. The last place he'd heard the intruder was to his left. So, Reigny began backing to his right. If he could just make it to the next set of crates and slip into the shadows, he might be able to get a look at the *thing* that hunted him.

Then, from behind him, two footsteps grated on the dirt floor. Reigny turned slowly.

"Stop," said a voice barely higher than a whisper.

Reigny froze. At this point, he nearly faced the apparition. From the corner of his eye, he could see a figure. The man was tall, but there wasn't much more to see. He didn't *seem* to be holding a weapon. Reigny shifted his weight.

"You've got one shot left," the figure informed.

I could do it, he reasoned. *I could take him.* Reigny considered himself a good shot. It's not as if he made his living as a hired killer, but he'd always been able to handle a gun.

Was there any chance this assassin would let him walk? What did the dark man want? Reigny could surrender. He could take a chance and throw himself at the mercy of this man. *No.* He couldn't. There was Anders McCain. What would he do if Reigny were the only one who left this warehouse alive? His life would be over… worthless.

A light crept into the eyes of Tom Reigny. What if *he* delivered this man to McCain? *Yeah….* What if this were the same person who attacked the Jersey crew? Reigny had already drawn his gun. He was a full step ahead of the man. All he would have to do is make half a turn and fire. The man was no farther than fifteen paces. He could do this. He *had* to do this. What other choice did he have? *Better to die shooting.* With finality, Reigny planted his feet.

His thoughts must have broadcast a move because the man spoke again.

"Don't…"

An inner voice told Reigny to obey, but his pride refused to listen. With all the strength he could muster, Reigny lowered his body, wheeled and swung his gun toward the target. As his eyes locked on the tall figure, a piece of clothing opened. He saw the slightest gleam of light reflected from a metallic surface, then a bright flash. In an instant, the air was slammed out of Reigny's body and he floundered back.

The crack of the gun bounced from wall to wall in the vast building. Reigny wavered and fell to his knees. Millions of stars swarmed before his eyes. He searched for the shadowy figure, but found nothing. He'd never seen anyone move so fast. It couldn't have been human.

Reigny clutched his chest and pulled away hands covered in a red liquid. He blinked his eyes, fighting the sleep that was overtaking him. But he was powerless to stop the stars which moved and grew, and swirled in and out of each other in a myriad of colors. Tom Reigny had never seen anything so mesmerizing. He longed to be a part of the event, and to experience the transformation himself. Then, in an instant, the lights faded to nothing… blackness… and Tom Reigny collapsed.

John McGregor had witnessed the gunfight. After the impact, he had managed to pull himself up against the wheel of an old wagon that had been stored in the bay. That accomplishment had been the last movement he was physically able to make. From the wagon, he'd seen the figure gun Reigny down then, disappear. If he didn't get out of this warehouse, he'd be next. McGregor reached into the depths of his body and attempted to muster some strength. He only found pain. His body was broken. He had been maneuvering the top crate when the truck slammed through the door. By the time he'd turned around to see what was happening, the bed of the truck had caught him in his pelvis and driven him through the stack of heavy crates. McGregor had never felt pain of such intensity, as if an elephant had stepped on his mid-section. Movement was impossible. He was, in effect, stuck to the floor. Breathing was exhausting in itself. But he knew he had to do something. He knew the shadow would be coming for him.

McGregor's hand managed to find the holster under his left arm. The gun was still there. He fumbled the weapon out of its leather sheath. But the weight of the gun was too great, and his hand fell to the ground beside him with a metallic clank.

Footsteps. Someone was approaching… directly in front of him. A form began to emerge from a cocoon of darkness, but he could not tell what *it* was.

Despite intense pain, McGregor tried to raise his gun from the floor. A boot stomped down on his hand and crushed his knuckles between the floor and the heavy gun.

"Oh... God!" McGregor winced. "What do you want?"

Out of the darkness, the shadow began to take shape. The man in dark clothing eased down onto one knee and leaned toward McGregor. There was no face. His head was covered in some type of black cloth, like that of a... *executioner.* From within the nothing, two eyes emerged... lifeless.

"What?" repeated McGregor.

"I want information," the man said in a gentle voice.

"What kind of information?"

"I need to know about McCain."

"Are you crazy?" he managed. "He'd kill me."

The man looked McGregor over. "Nothing can stop that now," he replied with a hint of sympathy.

"Oh... God... You've killed me," whimpered McGregor. "You've killed me. I'm supposed to take my son to a ball game tomorrow. It was going to be our first time to go to Ebett Field." He began to struggle for air.

"I'm sorry," the man replied. "You've lived your life doing what was wrong. Die doing something right. You *know* what kind of man McCain is..."

McGregor thought about it for a moment. "What do you want to know?" he conceded.

"Anything... Everything..."

* * *

Mr. Robertshaw had walked to his window after the first shot was fired around nine-thirty. He'd heard several more afterward, but all had been quiet for the last half hour. The

51

police hadn't responded yet. That wasn't surprising. They probably wouldn't. The police were all too "informed" about how to respond to certain situations in this neighborhood. And, gunshots were a fairly normal occurrence around this area of Brooklyn.

Mr. Robertshaw turned from the windowpane. The glass was covered in moisture from his breath, providing evidence of the time he had spent there. As he walked back to his bed, the explosion caused him to yelp aloud. There had been no warning.

Mr. Robertshaw quickly ran to the window and wiped it clean with his hand. He pressed his forehead to the cold surface. Outside, a cloud of dust rolled into the air above an adjacent building. Within moments, an orange glow illuminated the rising smoke.

Mr. Robertshaw was absorbed with the hellish landscape when a delicate hand grasped his shoulder. "Henry, what's happening?!" asked Mrs. Robertshaw.

"I don't know," the man replied, unable to tear his gaze away from the carnage. But he did know one thing. That warehouse belonged to Anders McCain.

Somebody had found trouble.

Seven

Streams of rain poured from the gray sky as the long Cadillac pulled into the alleyway from Flatbush Avenue. The automobile was an elegant royal blue with black fenders and running boards that extended along its length. Narrow, white-walled tires, mounted on their matching blue wagon-spoke wheels, cut easily through the puddles of water.

Anders McCain observed the drops of rain as they ran and danced along the rear passenger-side window of the car. It was a typical late September morning in the Northeast. Old Man Winter was finding his way into the city according to no one's schedule but his own. Rainy weather wasn't so bad, but cold, rainy weather was downright depressing. This part of the year, a transition period, was McCain's least favorite season. He preferred snow to the cold rain, any day. Snow was cold, but you could brush it off. And, it did leave the city in a somewhat beautiful condition, if you could use the adjective "beautiful" in the same sentence with "New York". A horizon, blanketed in white, always seemed to lift his spirits, despite the frigid temperatures.

Good weather was the one thing he missed the most from his days spent working out West. He particularly enjoyed California. If the weather did turn wet, it would be over within a day or two.

He would love to retire in a place like that one day. But, retirement was only a dream. He couldn't stop working. Even the idea of such a thing was foolishness at best. He was at the top of his game. He was the boss of one of the three largest gangs in New York. He was the head of the Irish family and thousands of people were subject to him.

Steam rose from the remains of McCain's warehouse, making it hard to tell where the fog of the nasty New York morning ended and the smoke from the building began. There wasn't much left of the building, but not because it had burned to the ground. As a matter of fact, the warehouse hadn't burned that much at all. Yet, everything was destroyed. *Interesting.*

Whoever caused this destruction knew what they were doing. Debris was scattered everywhere. The explosion had obviously been powerful... strong enough to blow out any fire that may have started. There had been *some* burning, but not enough to do any damage to the surrounding buildings. With the assistance of the late night rain, the firemen had easily handled the small blaze that had occurred.

Did the bombers have a conscience?

Even more curious, was the issue of *whom* this person or persons was working *for.* Would the Jewish gangs have the gusto for such an attack? Could someone be uniting them? Or, was it an Italian job?

McCain's thoughts were interrupted by the approach of a short, stocky man, wearing a long yellow slicker. He knew that underneath the man's overcoat, he wore the "navy blue" of a police uniform.

McCain rolled down his window. Cold droplets of rain sprayed his cheeks as water bounced from the windowpane.

"Good mornin', Mr. McCain," said Captain Douglas Adams.

"What's so *good* about it?" replied McCain.

"Well, I have seen worse in this city."

"Are you referring to the weather or my warehouse?"

"Both," Adams replied.

"What's the damage look like?" asked McCain.

"Bad," Adams replied. "Whoever did it, set out to destroy everything... not just the liquor... all of your supplies—fruit, clothing, kerosene... everything. They did a pretty good job of it, too."

"I can see that."

Adams was a good man to have on the payroll. Cops were fairly easy to "buy off", but, loyalty was an entirely different thing. Adams was a loyal man. He wouldn't work for the other families. He was of Irish blood, and his loyalties lay with his own people. He'd helped McCain with other situations in the past. There were some things that you just couldn't get done on your own, especially when you were on the wrong side of the law. Douglas Adams was well worth his price.

"Well," said Adams, "I've managed to get this situation settled down. We're going to be labeling it an accident. The explosion will be attributed to the kerosene distribution you were running out of this particular building. Kerosene is explosive, you know."

"So, I've heard," replied McCain, playing along.

"You might want to be more careful in your storage practices next time. There are city regulations."

"Thank you, officer. I'll keep that in mind."

Adams wasn't foolish. He wasn't chiding McCain on the proper handling of flammable liquids. Adams was too smart to do something so stupid. He feared McCain. He was simply covering his trail. Adams was doing what any police officer would have done. He was creating a façade for the relationship. Captain Adams was a police officer. McCain was a citizen.

"Do you have any idea what happened to my workers?" asked McCain.

"I think the question is did your workers have any idea?"

"Explain." replied McCain.

"Let me show you." Adams motioned with a turn of his head.

McCain fastened the top button of his raincoat, placed a wide-brimmed hat on his head, then pulled the door latch and stepped out. The rain was cold. Within moments, he could feel the nastiness of it running down the back of his neck. This day was getting worse and worse.

He walked beside Adams as they made their way down the alley. The destroyed warehouse loomed against the backdrop of the Brooklyn skyline. Inside the collapsed building, he could see the remains of a burned-out truck. Cold water seeped through his shoes and into his socks.

"All of your men were killed, Mr. McCain."

That was the second crew in two weeks. *This is getting expensive.* Who, in their right mind, was stupid enough to go to war with Anders McCain?

The two men stepped inside the open door of a storage building across the alley from the warehouse. Water dripped from holes in the roof and formed numerous puddles on the concrete floor. The sound of the rain striking the street made it hard to hear inside the building.

Inside the structure, several police paddy wagons were parked. Behind the vehicles, four covered figures lay upon the chilled concrete. Adams bent down and pulled the tarp off of one of the men.

McCain recognized him immediately. The man was Tom Reigny. *Just as well. Too ambitious.* McCain always figured that he would have had to do the job himself. There was a single bullet hole to his chest. *Strange.* Reigny hadn't been gunned down by the typical barrage of bullets, but by one well-placed shot.

"Italians," whispered McCain. "It has to be. The shot is too perfect. Only professionals could take out four men like that."

"There's more," replied Adams. He pulled the cover off of two other bodies. The wounds were bad, but McCain had seen worse.

"Only one of them was shot," said Adams. "These were killed at close range. Whoever did it used some kind of cutting weapon."

"Like a big knife?" clarified McCain.

"Heavier... like a meat cleaver or hatchet."

"Maybe he could kill one man like that," reasoned McCain. "But the other would have reacted. The other man would have taken a shot. How did he kill both?"

That was the question. How could someone have approached and killed two armed men at such close range? *Why* would someone do it? *Why not just shoot them?*

"What about the other man?" asked McCain.

"It looks like he died from internal injuries," Adams replied. McCain lifted the tarp himself. *John McGregor.* The man had been one of McCain's most trusted foremen.

Internal injuries… That meant that McGregor would have died slowly instead of being killed in the heat of battle. He could have been questioned. But, what information could a peon like McGregor know that could hurt McCain? *Plenty.* It was time for McCain to start asking some questions of his own.

"Do you *still* think it was the Italians?" asked Adams, breaking McCain's train of thought.

"I don't know," he replied. "But, I'm going to… soon."

* * *

By the time McCain arrived at the empty warehouse on Twenty-First Street in Manhattan, Vincent Barboni was already bound to a chair. He sat in the middle of the room, his hands tied behind his back, surrounded by four of McCain's men.

Barboni was a street thug. He was always "in the know". He knew anything and everything about whatever was happening in the gangs… especially the Italians. The rumor was that Vincent had been one of Ignacio Saietta's most trusted employees at the turn of the century. The last fifteen years had been bad. With the imprisonment of his boss, Saietta, and the organization of the Italian families by Giuseppe Masseria, Barboni had found himself without loyalties. He had turned into a street informant who could give whatever information was needed… for the right price, of course. McCain knew that if Barboni had loyalties, they would lie with the Italians. They were, after all, his people.

Barboni had obviously been uncooperative up to the present time. McCain's boys had been forced to take different measures.

Nick Rocci approached McCain.

"He ain't sayin' much boss... clammed up like a parrot with a cracker in his beak."

Nicholas, "The Fist" Rocci, was McCain's number one man. He was an Italian, but it didn't matter. He was the fiercest and most loyal person McCain had ever worked with. Nick was the only person in the world that McCain trusted. He sometimes wondered if it was foolish to have faith in anyone, but Rocci had proven himself time and time again. He had immigrated to America in the eighteen-nineties as a teenager. Being unskilled and uneducated, Rocci had turned to boxing. He became one of the most notorious and vicious prizefighters the slums of New York had ever seen. Opponents said he was so fast that all they could see was a blaze of fists before they were beaten senseless. Nick Rocci was of medium height and muscular. He was deceivingly powerful and one of the strongest men McCain had ever been around. The Italian was intimidating to look at as well. With his square jaw and acne-scarred face, Nick had the stereotypical look of a mob enforcer.

Nick had set out earlier that morning to find some information on the two recent attacks.

Barboni was a man for hire. Normally, he would talk for a price. But there were some things that not even Barboni would divulge. Today, Vincent wasn't selling.

No matter, thought McCain. *We'll do it our way.* You couldn't let these informants believe that they had too much leverage. They were subject to the same rewards and punishments as anyone else. Barboni would have to understand the rules. McCain had only humored him by occasionally "buying" his information. Barboni would have to understand that sometimes "no" just doesn't work.

"What's he sayin'?" asked McCain.

"He says it ain't the Italians. He says that he hears its just one guy causin' all this trouble."

McCain crossed the open floor to Barboni, stopping within arms' reach.

"Nick tells me that you don't have much to say today, Vinnie," said McCain.

"Look, Mr. McCain," whimpered Barboni, "I've already told them everything I know. Would you please tell them to untie me?"

"Did you just say 'please', Vincent?" asked McCain. "So you want me to help *you*, but you refuse to help *me*?"

"Look, Anders, I've already told "the Fist" everything I know... honest."

McCain shook his head and moved out of the way just as Nick's fist connected with Barboni's jaw. A sickening sound reverberated through the room as knuckles connected with flesh. Barboni's lanky body surged backwards. His chair lifted onto its rear legs and slammed back down.

"That's *Mister McCain*," said Nick, annunciating the syllables. "What makes you think you've earned the right to call him by his first name? Huh? You two bit wop!" Nick spit on Barboni for good measure. "Now, remember who you're speakin' to."

McCain continued, "What are the Italians up to?"

"I swear, Mr. McCain. They're not up to anything, nothin' 'cept regular business."

"Just *regular* business, huh? So, you're tellin' me that 'regular business' doesn't involve destruction of *my* business?"

"I can't tell you for sure, but as far as I know, they don't know nothin' about it. As a matter of fact," explained Barboni, "they're as in the dark as you about the whole thing. Word has it that Joe the Boss has everybody watching their backs so that the same thing doesn't happen to them."

"Is that so?" replied McCain.

"Yes, sir."

McCain paced the floor. "What's this you're sayin' about 'one guy' who's causin' all this trouble?"

"That's just somethin' I heard," replied Vincent.

"Tell me about it."

"Some people are sayin' how one guy is after you. Some say he's a ghost."

"Come on," taunted Rocci.

"It's just what I heard…" Barboni's words were cut short as McCain slapped him across the face. A mixture of spittle and blood flew from his mouth.

"What do you take me for?" demanded McCain.

"Nothin' Mr. McCain," Barboni professed.

"Do you take me for some child who's scared of the Boogie Man? Do you think I'm stupid enough to believe that one man could have done all this? There were six people on the Jersey crew. Six. Do you really think one man could handle six armed men, three of them in hand to hand fightin'?"

"I'm only tellin' you what I heard," pleaded Barboni. "You don't think I'd lie to you, do you, Mr. McCain?"

"Of course, you'd lie to me. That's what you do for a livin'. Half of the information you give your clients is a lie.

You're a go-between, Barboni. You tell each side what they *want* to hear."

"It's not like that Mr. McCain. Honest… it ain't like that."

"The truth is," explained McCain, "one man couldn't cause this much damage. The Jews don't have the guts or organization to take me on. That leaves the Italians. Don't feed me anymore lies!"

"But, Mr.…."

"Shut up!" he said, pointing his finger at Barboni. McCain stopped questioning the man and walked over to Nick.

"Do you want me to see if I can get anything else from him?" asked Nick. "I could put on the glove."

Nick loved using his glove. The glove had a way of getting information when nothing else seemed to work.

"I don't think he knows anything else," McCain replied. "Then, again, we can't be sure. We're in too deep to let him out of here. We can't have him runnin' back to the Italians with any of the information we've been questionin' him about. Good Lord," McCain said, shaking his head in disgust, "they'd think we were weak."

McCain stuck his hand under Nick's overcoat, and produced a semi-automatic pistol. "They'd think we were afraid," he continued.

McCain walked over to Vincent Barboni whose eyes widened in horror. Without a second thought, McCain pointed the gun muzzle toward Barboni's face and pulled the trigger. The concussion knocked his chair over backwards. Barboni's body hit the floor with a resounding thud.

"And we can't let that happen."

Riding home in the back seat of his car, McCain's thoughts were taking shape. Why would the Italians want to attack him like this? There had always been rivalry between different gangs, but most of that had subsided in recent years.

Giuseppe Masseria was the problem, also known as "Joe the Boss". Joe the Boss had been an enforcer for Saietta and Ciro Terranova. He had seized his opportunity when Saietta was convicted and sent to prison. About that same time, Terranova struck it rich in the artichoke business. The loss of Saietta and Terranova left the Morello gang abandoned and without direction. Joe the Boss had seen his chance and taken control of the "leaderless" gang. If he continued at the rate he was going, within five or six years, he would control most of the racketeering in New York. Joe the Boss was ambitious. He wanted all the business, and he was determined to take control. He was already attacking all the other Italian gangs and forcing them to merge with his family. Why not the Irish and Jewish as well? The man was strong headed and ambitious. But so was McCain.

I guess that's why I hate him.

* * *

When Anders McCain walked through the front door of his Manhattan penthouse, five children surrounded him. The mob grabbed at his legs, vying for his attention.

"Hello, children," greeted McCain. "Where's your mother?"

"She has dinner ready," said Georgette, the youngest.

"Well come on then," replied McCain, "let's not keep her waiting. Let's get to the table, shall we?"

Dinner smelled wonderful. Coming home was McCain's favorite part of the day. He *needed* the distraction... the normal life. He ran a hand over the Yule post as he passed the stairs. The wood was smooth and cool. The action of touching the banister helped trigger his transformation. Placing his hands on things in his house helped him become "Father".

"Did you have a good day at work today, Father?" asked Robert, McCain's middle son.

"Yes, of course," he replied. "And how did we do at school today?"

The children volleyed to tell their father about their day as the group mingled toward the dining room.

Edwina McCain was busy setting the table when Anders and his entourage entered. She was a pretty woman, but pale. Her blonde hair was piled neatly in a bun that sat atop the crown of her head.

"Did you have a nice day at work, dear?" asked Mrs. McCain.

"I've had better," he replied.

"Well, isn't that a shame. Perhaps some nice, hot beef stew will help?"

"It couldn't hurt," he replied.

"Well, have a seat then. Children... have a seat. Let your father catch his breath."

Today had been the most stressful day he'd had in a while. This was his respite. Home was the reward for a long day... a nice, normal dinner. If only for a few hours, Anders McCain could be a normal husband and father. He could leave all the complications of his world outside in the rainy New York weather.

Mrs. McCain joined the family at the table. "Are we ready?" she asked. She looked at McCain, expectantly.

He knew what she wanted, though he had never grown comfortable with the ritual. He had never felt enough peace to perform it… *especially on a day like today*.

"Andy," said McCain, speaking to Anders junior. "Would you say grace?"

Eight

Would you like to take a walk with me this fine mornin', John?" interrupted the voice of Reverend O'Hare as John Grady was about to make a new entry into his journal.

"I would Reverend, but I was just about to begin my studies," replied John as he carefully closed the cover of the book.

"Oh, nonsense!" Studying is for scholars, and neither you nor I were called to be scholars. We were called to be pastors. And, pastors aren't much good if they're not out learning about the people that they're called to shepherd."

"I see your point, Reverend," conceded John.

"Please," replied O'Hare, "call me Tim. I know I look old to young eyes such as yours, but, I'm not a dead saint for God's sake."

In the center of Flatbush Avenue, a streetcar laden with people crawled along a recessed track. A coiled wire connected the car to a network of airborne cables, which covered the area like an intricately woven spider web. The weather this morning was particularly nice. New York had been experiencing a warm front following a short spell of cool weather. Today, the sun felt especially warm on John's face.

He had been wrong. There *were* trees in New York, depending on one's location within the city. Luckily, his part had trees planted along the street. They were nothing compared to the trees he grew up climbing, but any trees were better than none.

Automobiles puttered by on the streets interspersed by the occasional horse drawn cab. People scurried about the town like ants searching for food before the onset of winter.

A strong sense of irony followed John as he strolled through the streets of Brooklyn. In a way, finding this city had been a dream of his for a long time. *Or a burden?*

The city was larger than he'd imagined. Last week, he'd ventured into Manhattan. He'd never seen so many tall buildings in one place. Pictures couldn't portray the enormity of the fabricated landscape. Being there in person had been altogether different. He'd felt so small with those concrete behemoths towering over him. At one point, he had found himself feeling disoriented as he gazed upon the skyline. John was content that he didn't have to live in the largest part of the city. He got along just fine here in Brooklyn.

"Here we are, John," Tim's voice interrupted his thoughts for the second time today. "This is the place. Have you ever been in an apartment before?"

"I can't say that I have," he replied.

"Well, you're in for a treat."

* * *

The first thing John noticed was the sickly smell. When a small German man opened the door, the two ministers were immediately struck by an unnatural odor. John had smelled the stench before. He was reminded of the shanty of a sharecropper family he'd visited while in Louisiana. The odor was the result of too many people living in a small space. There were ten people living in this two-room apartment. Herman and Bessie Keiser rented their living room out to four other people, a family of Jews. The apartment was bigger than the log cabin John had occupied while living in Missouri, but he hadn't had nine other people living with him. The people were crammed into the place like a can of sardines. All of the residents on the seventh floor shared one privy room at the end of the hall. The room contained a washbasin, a toilet and a water closet. With four apartments on this floor, there must have been thirty people sharing the tiny privy room. And, as if the conditions couldn't get any worse, Molly, the baby, was running a high fever and showing signs of influenza.

John couldn't help but notice the large bruise on Mr. Keiser's cheek. He had his suspicions about the origins of the wound. Mr. Keiser owned a small fish market on the sidewalk outside of a store on Second Street. And unless Mr. Keiser was exempt, he was most likely paying a "protection tax" to the gangs, like most of the city's businessmen.

Every place he'd ever been, the system was the same. The majority suffered so that the few elite could prosper. *It's just the way things are.* But John couldn't accept that reality. He had never been one to merely accept things as they were. There may have been a time in his life when it was possible to allow injustice to go unnoticed, but that time had passed. He *had* to question things. Situations *could* change for the better. There had to be the hope of a better future. After all, without hope… *we have nothing.*

"Thank you so much for stopping by, Reverend," Mrs. Keiser said, shaking Tim's hand as they prepared to leave. "And, you as well, Reverend Grady."

"You're welcome, ma'am," replied John.

"We'll see you at church Sunday, Mr. And Mrs. Keiser," said Tim.

"Thank you so much for stopping by," added Mr. Keiser.

"You just make sure you keep us updated on wee Mollie," replied Tim. "We'll be prayin'."

* * *

John and Tim walked back toward the church for some time. John was quiet.

"What's wrong, John?"

His eyes traced the cracks in the sidewalk. "I don't understand how they can live like that. I feel…"

"Sorry for them?" asked Tim, finishing his sentence. "Yes, the conditions can be quite hard here. That's the reason they need us. That's why we need to remind them that God loves them. It's a hard life. People here do what they have to do in order to survive. Sometimes that means renting your living room out to four other people."

"That's not what I mean," replied John.

Tim tipped his head to a young woman who was pushing a baby carriage. "Good day, Mrs. Green."

"Good day, Reverend," she replied smiling.

"What do you mean, John?"

"What I'm trying to say is that, I feel sorry for them… because they accept their situation."

"What is their situation, John, other than the lot which they've been given in life?"

"I'm not talking about being poor, Tim. You must understand what I'm saying. You've been here too long not to notice."

"I think I know where you're going. And it's not something you want to get involved in."

"Why?" John asked. "Why is everyone so afraid?"

"The Kaisers are making it, John."

"Are they?"

"What would you have them do?" asked Tim, growing frustrated. "Would you have them rise up and fight? Would you have the peasants take up arms? Would you ask these fathers to give up their lives? Their sons?" Tim stopped and shook his head. He looked into the sky for a moment then returned his gaze to John. "Do you think you're the first man to have these thoughts? People have tried. Who do you go to… the police? They're as afraid of the mob as we are."

"I've seen war and I've seen oppression," explained John. "Those who were oppressed died long before those who went to battle. They died in *here*," John said, pointing to his heart.

"God has a plan for everything," replied Tim, "including this. Our job is to help people find that plan."

"I can't accept that," confessed John.

"You'd better learn."

Nine

The sanctuary of Mount Zion Methodist Assembly was spacious. The room was large enough to seat four hundred people if the need arose. Varnished oak beams supported the high vaulted ceiling. Smooth wooden pews were stacked in two columns that ran from the front of the church to the back, disappearing underneath a balcony accentuated with a stained glass window. The pews were set into a flawless wooden floor and separated by a strip of burgundy carpet running through their midst. More stained glass windows lined the sides of the sanctuary, lighting the room in a rainbow of surreal colors. The pipes of a gigantic organ towered behind the pulpit area just aft of the choir loft. There was no limit to the possibilities of *something* when *someone* cared enough. John was looking at someone who cared.

He hadn't paid much attention to Mary in the past weeks. John didn't think that he had done it consciously, but he had, nevertheless. He was unsure about the way she made him feel. She was a nice girl... a hard worker... strong willed... *and what else? Attractive?* No. It wasn't that she was attractive... there was a certain energy about her. *She's attractive. Why is that so hard to admit? There's nothing wrong with a man finding a woman pretty.* He knew one thing for sure — she was sassy.

John watched her as she polished the banister with an oil soaked rag. She was a studious worker and performed her job with care. Her white blouse was buttoned to the neck and tucked neatly inside a long, gray skirt. Strawberry blonde hair was drawn neatly to the back of her head and careened between her shoulders in soft curls. Blue light from one of the colored windows embossed her figure, giving the lady an angelic quality.

"Your work is... beautiful," John said, interrupting the silence.

"My work?" she replied without turning around.

"Your cleaning, I mean."

"You talk as if I were painting a picture. It's just cleanin'. But, thank you. I try to do the best I can. This is the easy part. The hard part is cleanin' up after two men," she said with a hint of sarcasm in her voice. She turned, allowing him to see her blue eyes for the first time.

"Yes... I imagine so." He turned to go, but hesitated. "Lunch was delicious. My compliments to the chef."

"Well, your welcome, Reverend Grady," she said, stooping to sit on the altar steps. John moved closer and placed his hand on the banister that ran behind the organ.

"I wouldn't..." Mary began to say, but stopped. John quickly realized what she had been attempting to tell him.

"Oh dear," she said. "Let me see if I can find a clean cloth..."

"No need to worry," John interrupted. He wiped his hand on the leg of his pants.

"Reverend Grady!"

"What?" he chuckled.

"No self respecting minister should be wipin' oil onto his preachin' clothes. Now that's a man for ya'."

"There was a problem," he explained, "and I found a solution."

"Yes... you did. Now, there's the problem of you gettin' an oil stain out of your trousers. I'll have to wash those for you."

"You don't need to worry," he replied. "I'll take care of them."

"When will you surrender and let me take care of your washin' and cleanin'?" she asked. "It's my job."

"I'm sorry. I'm just used to taking care of myself. I'm not accustomed to being waited on."

"Well it's not so bad, ya know. You could try it."

John was enjoying the conversation and that frightened him. Talking to a lady could be refreshing. But, there was more to what he was feeling, wasn't there? She reminded him of... *No. I'm not going to think about her.* Was he in danger of revealing too much? *Relax. You're talking about laundry.*

"I'm glad you're speakin' with me," she said, interrupting his thoughts. "I was beginning to think you didn't like me."

"No," he replied. "That's not it at all. It takes me a little while to get comfortable with people."

"Well… we'll have to do it again sometime, Reverend."

He chuckled.

"Is something funny?"

"I don't think I'll ever get used to being called Reverend. I'm trying… really."

"What would you like to be called? Pastor? How about *Father Grady?*" she taunted.

"Now you're teasing."

"Oh no, I'm much too respectful to tease a minister," she giggled.

"How about *John?*" he offered.

"Reverend John it is!"

"You're a handful."

"Alright… John then."

He smiled.

"Does your name sound odd to your own ears?" she asked.

John bowed his head in an attempt to hide his emotion.

"It's nice to see you smile," said Mary in a soft tone.

"I smile," he replied, slightly defensive.

"Not really…"

She *was* getting too close. Without knowing it, she had pricked something inside of him. He *knew* he shouldn't have been talking to her. The statement was ludicrous. Of course, he smiled.

"I have to go," he said hastily. "I need to prepare for Bible study tonight."

"I'm sorry," she apologized, having recognized his change in demeanor. "I've overstepped my bounds." She stood up.

"No… really," he said, attempting to soothe her. "I just have some things to do. I'll talk with you later."

"Fine," she replied.

He turned and made his way to the door that would lead him into the depths of the church, back to the safety of his room… and *deeper*. He had let her read *too* much. Who was she to tell him that he never smiled? What could she know after a month and only a few conversations? Could that be true? *It can't be.* But, it was true. And if she could see it, who else could? He would have to start smiling.

Mary watched John disappear through the door at the front of the sanctuary. He was a strange man. What had she said that touched him so deeply? She had commented on his smile. Everything was going well until that moment. *You dunce!* She hadn't meant anything by the statement. She had only mentioned it as a matter of conversation. She only wanted to lengthen their meeting, to talk a little longer.

John seemed to need *something*. Most men needed a woman. But there was more to John Grady than basic needs like that. He seemed driven by a stronger force… bound by something greater than his will. The mystery intrigued her.

"What haunts you, John Grady?"

Ten

George Burt stepped from the deep shadows of the small concrete structure and into the world of forgotten names. Leaving the interior of the mausoleum should have been comforting, but there could be no comfort in this place. A thin layer of fog drifted slowly across the ground, glowing eerily in the pale moonlight. Ominous stone markers crept across the gentle, rolling hills for miles. The headstones seemed to have no end, disappearing somewhere behind the horizon. Greenwood Cemetery was the largest graveyard in the Brooklyn area.

George Burt had no idea how many deceased were buried here, but there were more graves than he'd ever seen. The cemetery was merely a small testament to how many souls had ended their lives in this desolate city. Burt didn't plan on becoming the next.

He'd never been afraid of corpses, like many people were, especially those that were already in the ground.

Nevertheless, his idea of a relaxing evening didn't include working in a foggy cemetery. His nerves were on end and any random sound startled him. Shaky hands maneuvered their way under his coat and produced a small, silver flask. Burt took a swig of the liquid and savored the warmth as it trickled down his throat. A cold draft blew across his neck and he shivered.

Burt understood the need for discretion, due to the recent attacks, but, this seemed a bit extreme. The attacks on the Jersey and Flatbush Avenue crews had Anders McCain on high alert. He had lost an enormous amount of booze and other valuable products in both instances. George Burt had also heard rumors that people within the Irish organization were being probed for information by an outside source. Of course, no one would be foolish enough to admit to having divulged secrets, but there *were* rumors circulating. The word from McCain was for everyone to be on the lookout for the Italians. He believed that Joe the Boss was moving in on Irish territory. Burt had heard a different story.

Some men were saying that the killings were the work of one man... *That's not what they're saying.* It had been *fantasized* that this *thing* wasn't a man, but a ghost. They were saying that this *ghost* couldn't be seen, let alone killed. *They were shot. It couldn't have been a ghost. Ghosts don't use guns.* Burt knew only one thing right now. Ghosts abounded in the graveyard this night.

The small mausoleum that was being used as a makeshift warehouse was nearly full, meaning that their crew would have to find a new storage area. That was perfectly fine with Burt. He didn't have any desire to step foot into that building again. After all, until recently, the mausoleum had been the permanent resting place of Thomas Avon. The removal of Mr. Avon had been the worst part of the cleaning process. His body had been in the tomb for nearly a hundred years. Because the casket was badly rotten, its bottom had fallen out as they were moving it. Luckily, there hadn't been much left of Mr. Avon other than bones and rotted clothing. *Don't forget the hair. He still had hair.* George hadn't known that hair could survive that long, but it was still there… and long. *It had been growing.* The thought sent chills throughout his body.

The caretaker had taken the remains and stuffed them into burlap sacks. George had no idea what he did with them afterwards. He *hoped* that the caretaker had the decency to bury the bags somewhere. He *feared* that they had simply been discarded like common trash. George Burt couldn't help but think that somehow he had cursed himself. *No Georgie… you were cursed when you added three souls to this place.* The dead deserved to rest.

"Hey boss," said a young man, "can we get out of here?"

"This is probably the safest place *in* this city," replied Burt. "Anybody that could hurt you is already dead."

"Yea… that's the part I *don't* like," he replied, crossing his arms to ward off the chill of the night.

Burt looked around. He had never been in charge of so many men. Since the attacks, teams had been merged. There were fifteen men guarding the mausoleum and flatbed truck. Everyone was heavily armed. Each man carried a pistol, as well as knives and bludgeoning objects. Several men even carried sawed-off shotguns. They were a small army… and as foreman, he was in command. George Burt had become a man of importance.

If the Italians were on the move… *we're ready for them.* In a way, Burt hoped they *would* come. All of the men did.

The Irish had lost ten of their own people, and the boys had a hunger for vengeance. Besides, the sooner this situation with the Italians was handled... *the sooner we can quit comin' to this stinkin' graveyard.*

"You boys hurry up and get the rest of those boxes into the mausoleum," said Burt. "We've been here long enough already. I've got somebody to visit and then I'm gonna get drunk!"

The men laughed.

He had someone to visit, all right. *That old hag still owes me an insurance payment.* The truth is the lady had already paid the full amount that McCain demanded from the storeowners. Burt, however, had become comfortable with skimming a little extra for himself. Everyone did it. Burt respected the dead. The "living" was something entirely different, especially the weak-willed people of this city. They practically begged to be victims.

"I'm sick of sittin' around waitin' for the wops to come and get us," offered a large man with a crooked nose, "I say we stick it to 'em."

"If you want to go and start a war with Joe the Boss, be my guest," Burt scoffed.

"Yeah, go ahead, O'Malley," taunted another man. "We're right behind you."

All of the men laughed.

"You wanna say that again?" replied O'Malley, "to my face?"

"Knock it off!" interrupted Burt. "Let's get out of here."

O'Malley and another man went to work while the others stood, guarding the perimeter. Nothing stirred. The night was still... *too still.*

"We're done, boss," said O'Malley after carting the last box. O'Malley nodded to his partner, suggesting that he seal the door, then reached into his coat and produced a shiny metal box. He opened the cover and pulled out a cigarette. He offered one to Burt, who declined.

"C'mon Skip!" prodded O'Malley. "It's just a door. I've seen dead people move faster!"

Some of the men chuckled.

"Skip!" called Burt.

The two men turned and faced the door of the Mausoleum, which was still open. The interior of the structure was dark. The blackness seemed to consume any light that the moon may have offered. Skip should have been closing the two iron doors.

O'Malley approached the opening. A muffled grunt came from the tomb, followed by a shoe, scuffing on the concrete.

"Quit messin' around and get these doors shut!" demanded O'Malley. His voice quivered.

All of the men turned to face the Mausoleum and began gathering towards its front.

"Hey, maybe one of the wops got him, O'Malley," taunted one of the men.

"Yea. Here's your chance to do somethin'," said another, joining in.

O'Malley now stood at the doorway. He peered inside and whispered. "Skip?"

The last thing George Burt saw of O'Malley was his hand clawing for one of the wrought iron doors. The door slammed shut with a loud clang. O'Malley had vanished. The blackness had devoured him... sucked him in. One moment he was there… the next… A scream echoed from the tomb's interior.

"Jesus!" said one of the men.

"What the…"

"O'Malley!" yelled Burt. "O'Malley!?"

O'Malley made no reply. One of the mausoleum's doors was still ajar. George could see nothing… only disgusting darkness… darkness that should have remained undisturbed… darkness that was the abode of the dead.

Men reached into their coats and drew pistols. One produced a double-barreled shotgun. Burt fumbled for his own revolver. Silence ensued. Nothing stirred except for the quickened breathing of the men. Vapor floated from their mouths into the frosty night air.

Burt felt the slow rise of gall from his stomach and into his throat. Disturbing the dead just wasn't right. Nothing good would ever come of it. Now, more than anything, he wished he could stand in front of Anders McCain and tell him that there are some things that shouldn't be done, no matter who you are. He doubted he would ever get the chance.

George Burt's first glance of the ghost was brief. Almost seamlessly, the black of the mausoleum's interior had taken shape. A figure lunged from the door shrouded in shadow.

Burt's body could provide him with no reaction. He had heard of people being frozen with fear, but had always been disgusted with someone who would panic. Somehow, he had become one of those people. Burt couldn't move. He couldn't think. All he could do was scan the entrance of the mausoleum and hope he never saw the figure again.

The first gunshots came from *his* men. One of the double-barreled twelve gauges discharged, followed by a rapid succession of pistol shots. The sound of battle erupted into the autumn night. The bullets missed their intended target. Instead, they impacted the mausoleum, spewing a concrete powder into the air.

How'd we miss? But, there was nothing to hit. The figure that had emerged only moments earlier had completely vanished.

George's mind was a fog. His world was lost in a barrage of muzzle flashes and panicked screams. His men were yelling things at each other... things he couldn't make out. He was confused... lost. His hands were wet. *Why are my hands wet?* A cold dampness surrounded his body. It took him a moment to realize that he was lying on the ground. Cold dew soaked into his clothing. Then, he remembered. There had been two flashes of light. The ghost had fired at them. That's why Burt had hit the ground.

He pushed himself to his knees and saw the first of his wounded men. The man was young. Burt didn't even know his name. He was one of the men who had teased O'Malley. The kid was slumped face first over the bed of the truck

The second man was lying on the ground, holding his stomach. He screamed in pain and clutched his gut with blood soaked hands.

"Charlie..." the man cried. "Charlie! Help me... please. My guts are blown out..."

"Shut up, Johnny!" replied Charlie. "Just be quiet and keep your head down!"

"Don't leave me here... please. You fellas gotta help me!" he managed to say as he lifted his head up to look around.

Only three of the men remained in plain view. Everyone else had scattered during the shooting. Two men were peeking around the truck.   Some were hiding behind headstones.

Burt felt something hard and cold in his hand. It was his revolver. He had managed to hang on to it. George lay on his belly and crawled under the truck. He kept his eyes glued on the opening of the mausoleum. Nothing moved. Had the figure gone back inside after the first volley of shots?

"I think he's still inside there, fellas," whispered Burt.

No sooner had the words left his mouth that a figure emerged.   Burt unloaded his revolver toward the person. The other men fired as the man held his hands out in front of himself. He shook and convulsed as the volley of bullets struck his body, then twisted and fell on his back.

"Stop!" somebody yelled.

"We got him!" a voice echoed.

"Stop shooting!" another voice screamed.

The gunfire trickled to a stop. As the smoke began to clear from the air someone screamed, "We got Skip! Oh God... we killed skip!"

Skip lay on the ground, motionless.

Burt's eyes were fixed on the unmoving figure. How many times had he seen a man die? He shouldn't have been bothered. Yet, there was something sickening about killing one of your own. *It could have been me.*

The clink of shells being unloaded caught Burt's attention. All around him, men were frantically dumping empty casings and fumbling for fresh cartridges with trembling hands.   He realized that he had run out of bullets in his own gun and wished he had thought to keep extra shells with him. He'd never had to reload before.

The next thing George Burt saw would haunt his dreams for the rest of his life. About twenty yards behind and to the right of the mausoleum, was a statue like none he had ever seen before. It was tall, at least ten feet. Two giant stone angels stood on each side of a cross, facing each other. Their solemn, graven faces looked upon the object they were guarding with the utmost reverence. Their inside wings were lifted high and met each other in the center of the monument forming a protective arch that encircled the cross from the top and protected it from the back. There was a solitary figure standing in front of the cross.

The figure that Burt first assumed was a statue of Christ came to life. The ghost walked down a small flight of stairs and made a straight line towards the truck. One of the men had managed to reload his gun and drew to fire at him.

"There it is!" the man screamed.

The ghost threw open an outer cloak. His arms reached across each other and drew two pistols. The shots were so fast that the movement was barely perceivable. The Irish man, who had drawn the gun, was struck by both shots and bent backwards over an ancient headstone, knocking it partially out of the ground.

Some of the other men were beginning to shoot. The ghost returned their fire and struck a man who was using the front of the truck as cover. The man stumbled out and fell face first into the grass, landing just in front of Burt. Their eyes made contact.

A horrible thought crossed George Burt's mind. *I'm hiding.* But, there was nothing else that he could do. His weapon was empty. *You could take his.* He stared at the freshly killed man. *It's right in front of you.* No. As far as he could tell, the ghost had no idea he was under the truck.

I'll wait until he isn't paying_attention. Sure. That's what he would do.

Burt's men fired chaotically. Bullets struck both the ground and tombstones all around the ghost. But, he continued to walk directly toward them in a straight line. He picked his shots, hitting everyone he aimed for. In contrast, Burt's men were exposing themselves and firing wildly, hitting nothing.

The ghost dove right, rolled on the ground and sprang upward from behind a headstone. He fired two shots.

Both bullets hit the top of a tombstone one of the Irish men was hiding behind. Shards of rock ripped into the man's face. He fell to the ground screaming with his palms pressed against his eyes.

An Irishman began to run behind a row of high headstones, firing his lever-action rifle. He pumped the lever downwards and back up, over and over again, firing at the ghost. The ghost followed suit. He returned the man's gunfire while running parallel to him, behind another row of headstones. Bits and pieces of rock and marble flew everywhere. Tombstones cracked and fell as explosions of light and lead continued to leap from each man's gun. Burt had never seen anything so violent, so primal. There was a kind of poetry in the carnage.

The ghost crossed his arms under his coat and holstered his guns, produced two more and began firing again. The Irish shooter had been so intent on the gunfight that he hadn't noticed the three vacant gravesites that were about to expose his body. It took only a moment for the ghost to get a bead on him and fire twice, hitting the Irishman with both shots. He fell behind the next headstone and out of Burt's line of sight.

Bang! The sound was piercing. George Burt screamed. Two men were blown into the air as the mausoleum exploded into a million pieces, filling the air with dust and debris. The truck lurched sideways onto two wheels. Burt scurried out from beneath the vehicle and joined another man behind a large tombstone. It was O'Malley. He had a large gash on his head. O'Malley had escaped the mausoleum before it exploded. The ghost hadn't killed him. Burt looked back to see his two remaining men running for the maze of gravestones and trees deep within the cemetery.

"We've got to get out of here," Burt said to O'Malley.

"I'm with you!" he replied. "I don't know who that is, but it ain't no wop!" O'Malley peered around the grave marker and scanned the cemetery. "Get in the truck!"

O'Malley crawled to the passenger side of the truck and slipped through the open cab and into the seat, where he hunched as low as his large form would allow. Burt belly crawled to the front of the vehicle and grabbed the crank handle. Three turns and the engine sputtered to life. He duck-walked back and slid inside the cab. With a grinding of the gears, the rear wheels spun on the wet grass and they were off.

O'Malley accelerated the truck towards the maintenance road they had used to enter the cemetery. He entered the road with a fast turn and sprayed gravel as the back end slid around. O'Malley shifted gears again, pushing the flatbed truck towards its top speed.

"Don't kill us, O'Malley!"

They were only a few hundred yards from the gate now. A street lamp lit the entrance. Burt never thought he would be so happy to see the wrought iron gate of a cemetery. But, wait... The gate was closed. *How could it be closed? We left it open!*

But, the road ahead held an obstacle even worse. There, standing in the middle of the path stood the dark gunfighter, resolute and unmovable. O'Malley stomped the accelerator to the floor.

"We'll run him over!" screamed O'Malley.

The idea seemed like a good one. The truck was moving at top speed now. He would have to move or be mauled.

The ghost calmly opened the right side of his coat and tucked it behind a pistol on his belt. Burt could see another pistol lodged under his right arm. He drew one of the guns and pointed it toward the cab of the truck. One well-placed shot blasted from the revolver and struck O'Malley in the shoulder. The truck veered sharply left and ran into a section of graves, plowing over tombstones. The vehicle slammed face first into an open grave. Burt was thrown through the front window of the truck and landed head first into a pile of dirt. The smell of fresh soil was disgusting, especially knowing the purpose for which it was intended.

Burt pulled himself out of the mud and crawled to his feet. Three rows of mausoleums lay to his right. The tombs ran along the northeast fence for half a mile. Burt knew that if he could get into that forest of concrete buildings, he might have a chance to reach a gate or climb the fence. He rose to his feet and ran as fast as he could toward the mausoleums.

The short run seemed like a great distance. By the time Burt had reached the cover of the first mausoleum he was out of breath and panting heavily. *Slow your breathing, Georgie... he'll hear you.* He backed against a cold, marble wall. His hands flattened against the stone as he peered around the corner. He scanned the row of crypts... then, in the other direction. Nothing. Everything was dark and still, which should have been comforting, but wasn't. Burt was surrounded by *the dead.* They were everywhere. He was outnumbered. He could nearly smell the stench seeping from the rotting corpses that filled the tombs... the very tombs that were providing him shelter.

You've got to run, George. But, what if the ghost was already here? He could be waiting... out there in the dark. *The only chance you have is to run. Now run!*

Burt bolted for the second row of vaults. Upon reaching them, he gave a quick check and made his move toward the last row. He nearly tripped as a horrible sound erupted behind him. Somewhere, in the distance, a horse whinnied.

There shouldn't have been any horses in this area, especially at this time of night. *Relax. The caretakers use horses to hall dirt. And what else? What else do they use horses to hall in cemeteries, Georgie?*

From his hiding place, Burt could see the glow of a street lamp in the night sky. He knew the meaning of that light. The illumination marked freedom. That halo of light signaled one of the north entrances into the cemetery. *Please God... let it be open.* If it weren't, he would climb the gate.

Burt bolted from his hiding place and into the shadows of the ivy-covered fence. The gate was open. No more than fifty yards lay between life and...

George Burt stopped in his tracks. Behind him, the crackle of hooves on gravel, sent his mind reeling. A monster stormed from the shadows of the tombs and galloped towards him. Steam erupted from the nostrils of the beast as mud and pebbles flew from stomping hooves. A rider sat atop the cold steed, clothed in black. The train of his coat swarmed around him.

Burt had never cared for the Bible before. He had never liked the stories. The ancient tales seemed ridiculous. But, from all the bedtime stories his mother had ever told him… from all the times she had read from that archaic book… one story flooded his memory. *And I looked, and behold a pale horse… and his name that sat on him was Death, and Hell followed with him.*

Burt ran on legs of stone. His heart beat rapidly. Breath came in short gasps. The ground wouldn't let go of his feet. He ran as hard as he could, but the sound of hoof falls grew closer. *They won't let me run! They won't let go!* The dead would have their revenge on George Burt this night.

There was a whipping sound in the air behind him. Burt could feel the hot nastiness of the horse's breath on the back of his neck. The world around him lost all structure. Nothing existed except the path that lay before him. He ran as fast as he could toward the open gate.

The bullet wasn't as painful as he had expected. It struck him in the back of the head with a sharp crack. A second bullet seemed to hit him in the waist, stopping the forward motion of his body. He jerked into the air and sprawled flat before hitting the ground. His breath had been stolen. *I'm dying. Oh God…* Blackness began to overtake him, and then… he was being dragged. *I'm not dead.*

Burt looked up to see the rider in black, seated on a pale gray stallion. He pulled a taunt rope that was cinched around Burt's feet. Burt's mind was lost in a clutter of random thoughts. What was the rider doing? Then, he realized what had happened. *He lassoed me!* There had been no sound of gunshots. Burt had been lassoed. The rope had struck him hard and had pulled him off of his feet. He'd had his breath knocked out, but he was alive.

With a quick movement, the rider slid from the saddle and hit the ground. Boots crunched in the gravel as he stepped toward Burt. The man looked horrible. He wore the mask of an executioner.

"Don't kill me," whimpered Burt.

"I'm not going to kill you," replied the man.

"What do you want?"

The gunfighter perched above Burt, grabbed the collar of his coat and pulled him from the ground. Burt peered into the gunfighter's lifeless eyes.

"I need a name... and then I want you to give your boss a message for me. You tell him that his transgressions have been counted... "

"...and the reaper demands payment."

Eleven

Anders McCain lay staring at the ceiling, waiting for his eyes to focus. His mind was still lost in another world far away from the darkness of his bedroom. His mind struggled to gain consciousness. What had awakened him? The sound had come from something in the room, hadn't it? *Who's in here?*

The telephone rang for a second time. McCain jumped out of bed quickly, waking Edwina McCain.

"What's wrong, dear," she asked?

"There's nothing for you to worry about," replied McCain. "You just go on back to sleep."

He hated the feeling of being awakened from a deep sleep. McCain was getting older. He could remember a time when the slightest movement would have awakened him. A man needed fast reflexes to survive in his business. Heavy sleepers had a high mortality rate—a statistic to which he himself had contributed to on several occasions.

McCain picked his silver pocket watch off of his bedside table. He pushed the stem and the cover sprang open. The time was one twenty-five in the morning. He eased into his robe as the bell rang for a third time. His bare feet were nearly silent as he walked across the hardwood floor to the desk. He sat down, gripped the chrome telephone and pulled the earpiece from the receiver.

"Yes?" McCain asked into the mouthpiece of the telephone.

"Mr. McCain…" replied a timid voice. "It's Ronald Thompson…"

"Go ahead, Mr. Thompson."

"I'm sorry to wake you at such an early hour, sir."

"I'm sure it's important, Mr. Thompson."

"Yes, sir," replied Thompson. "I'm afraid I have some bad news, sir. The Brooklyn crew was supposed to report their numbers to me by eleven o'clock. They failed to do so. It's not the first time I've had problems with Mr. Burt… so I didn't think too much of it."

"I'm assuming you have a point to make, Mr. Thompson."

"Yes, sir… I received a telephone call from Captain Adams less than ten minutes ago…"

"How many are dead?" asked McCain, getting to the meat of the conversation.

Silence followed as Thompson struggled for his nerve. "Twelve."

"How many were on that crew?" asked McCain.

"There were sixteen. Two of the men escaped and ran for help. One of them is in bad condition after crashing a truck. The foreman, Mr. Burt… well, no one knows where he is."

"And the merchandise?"

"All gone," replied Thompson, gravely. "…destroyed."

Heat surged toward the surface of his face and his grip tightened around the cold body of the telephone. McCain pursed his lips and spoke. "I would very much like to speak with the two men who escaped. Arrange it for me first thing in the morning, Mr. Thompson."

"Of course."

"Mr. Thompson, do you own a gun?"

"No, Mr. McCain."

"Buy one. Do it in the morning. Thank you, Mr. Thompson."

"Mr. McCain… I'm afraid this is getting outside of my area of expertise…"

"Thank you, Mr. Thompson," finished McCain as he clicked the receiver, cutting him off.

McCain's forehead began to boil. He slammed the earpiece into the receiver. Who had the guts to do this to Anders McCain?! They had escaped clean for the third time. Why keep going? Did these fools think that they were untouchable? *They'll pay… their families, too.* He would make sure that the entire city got the message. *No one stabs Anders McCain in the back!* He contemplated ripping the telephone from the wall. *Control… Channel it… think!* He had to think. Anger would accomplish nothing. He had to figure out this situation.

Twelve men were dead. There were four survivors. Thompson had said that two of them ran away. Another was injured. Where was the fourth? *Where is George Burt?*

The crew operating the cemetery was heavily armed. It would have taken a small army to better them. Surely the Italians were behind this. No one else could consistently pull off these kinds of attacks. But why did they continue to destroy the product? Why didn't they steal the stock and redistribute it? *None of this mess makes any sense.*

He'd lost thousands of dollars worth of products in the warehouse explosions and more at the cemetery. Where was the logic in the attacks? Why would Joe the Boss carelessly toss away all of that money? If he was attempting a takeover, why not seize the product rather than have it destroyed?

There was *more* to these acts. The message they carried suggested something other than business. *It's personal.* Someone was out to destroy him. *It'll take more than a little liquor....* But there was more on the line than money. His reputation was being slandered. McCain couldn't provide safety for his own men. He was becoming the laughing stock of New York. His men were being killed left and right and he was powerless to do anything about it. *People will see it as weakness.* Perhaps the Italians were going for the jugular. They weren't trying to overrun his operation; they were trying to destroy his character. Joe the Boss would raze the Irish organization to the ground by creating a lack of faith in McCain's own men. *Men don't obey cowards.* The time for patience was at an end. If McCain acted now, he *could* salvage his reputation.

"Anders," said Edwina McCain, peeking around the doorjamb of their bedroom. "What's wrong?"

"Everything. Everything is wrong. I'm afraid I have to go to work."

She moved across the hall, her bare feet lightly padding the cool floor. Her gown flowed as she gracefully walked to McCain. She placed her hands on his shoulders and began to rub gently. "I want you to promise me one thing."

"Yes dear?" replied McCain.

"Kill the bastards."

He placed his hand on hers. "What would I do without you, darling?"

* * *

Smoke and dust still lingered in the cool September night. The man in the shadows watched as a battalion of policemen meandered through Greenwood Cemetery. The graveyard was awash with long shadows created by the numerous flares the police used to light the crime scene. There was a pile of rubble and a foundation remaining of what used to be some type of burial chamber. The man in the shadows had seen these vaults before when his trail had led him through large cities. Rich, white men preferred to be buried above ground. Perhaps it was a way of feeling superior to all of those that would lie below him. The white man's way had always been one of domination and the need to feel superior.

Strewn about the crime scene were several blanket-covered objects. The man could see the form of humans beneath them. The bodies were a good sign. *He* was close. The police were searching the area vigorously for any clue. The man in the shadows felt no need to investigate. What he saw was proof enough. The evidence was in the tombstones. The grave markers behind the ruined mausoleum were shattered. The majority of gunfire had been directed at an individual running from left to right and using the headstones as cover. Directly across from the devastated tombstones was another row of headstones that the main shooters had been using as refuge. Given the fact that those markers were in tact and the number of bodies lying around, the police were looking for an expert. Their killer had hit his intended targets with precision. The attacker was deadly.

The man knelt down on the gravel maintenance road that ran between a row of mausoleums and the ivy-covered outer fence. With a calloused finger, he traced an impression that lay next to his muddy, leather moccasin. The hoof prints had stopped and a man had dismounted. There was no mistaking the footprint he had tracked for nearly two decades. At long last, his search was drawing to a close—here nearly three thousand miles from where it had begun.

He ran a finger along the edge of the stiff piece of rawhide that covered the right side of his face. The covering that had once felt so foreign had now become a part of him. The man stood and looked toward the lights of Brooklyn.

Hello, brother. It has been a long time… but I've found you.

Twelve

John Grady struggled to the surface of his prison called "sleep".

Across the cemetery strolled an angel, parting the fog as she moved. Her hair was amber and her skin was fair. It seemed as if God himself had endowed her with a beauty that was eternal. She looked to him with yearning in her soul... a yearning to be with him. She beckoned to him with those beautiful green eyes that he had looked into so many times... the same eyes that had given him strength when he felt as though he could go no further. Now, those eyes contained a sadness that seemed to wrench the very core of his soul.

She lifted her arms... reaching for him. He longed to run to her... but he couldn't. His legs were like lead. Perhaps this time she would reach him. Your almost here! Run! Please God let her make it.

But, there was the devil, silhouetted on the top of the hill, standing amongst the tombstones. There was no mistaking him. He stood in the shadows... always. The devil was always there. And then he saw the wretched orb... the devil's white-eye shone forth from beneath the horrid leather mask. Like a thousand times before, the monster drew a shiny object from beneath his cloak.

John tried to scream but his voice had been stolen. He tried to warn her... to run for her, but the corpses wouldn't let go. There were dozens of them grabbing at his feet, holding his legs, clawing their way to his arms. They stared at him with pale, lifeless eyes. "You were supposed to be different," they moaned. "You were supposed to give life, not follow the way of the world."

The devil pointed his gun toward the angel and spoke. "This is hell. This is the lot you've chosen, Preacher."

A blinding light blazed forth from the hilltop, followed by a clap of thunder... and the angel sank.

"Annie!" screamed John Grady as he bolted awake.

Instinct told him to reach for the small golden object hanging around his neck. He felt it... and wrapped his fingers around the ring. He'd almost wished the memory hadn't been there. If only she had been a dream. If only his entire life had been nothing more than a terrible dream. But there was no waking from this nightmare.

Thunder rumbled far away in the city. *It must be raining.* Of course, there was no way to know that for sure while tucked away in this dungeon beneath the church. John understood the purpose for putting the living areas underneath the building. The basement was vast and needed to be used. But, it was tough living in an area without sunlight. One went to sleep in darkness and awoke in darkness. And, it was darkness that brought the nightmares... and morning, only remorse.

And how do you think you should feel about the life you're living?

And what kind of life was he living? Wasn't he doing God's work?

Perhaps... in some ways.

No, in all ways. God's work involved... *demanded* both mercy *and* justice.

Is that what you're doing? Is this justice?

Yes, his actions *were* justice. Not all justice functioned in the same way. Justice was an *idea*. One person's version of justice might be completely different from another's. Who determined that one person was right and the other is wrong?

That's called anarchy, John.

Was it anarchy to ensure that those who lived beyond the law... those who the law *refused* to touch were held accountable?

Dealing with outlaws is not your concern.

Then, whose job was it? If the law won't deal justice, then who will? A man had to be ready to right wrongs and to preserve life.

Do you preserve life?

Of course, he did. John was committed to making sure that those who held life in cheap regard would live to regret their transgressions. He would make sure that the man who held this city in the grip of fear would answer to someone.

But, why should he answer to you?

Because there was no one else.

There is God.

God was not concerned with justice.

Of course He is.

No, God was concerned with working in a person's life. His concern was doing whatever it required to carry out His will. *Why is that so hard for you to accept?*

Because… God's will allowed *injustice*.

Perhaps that is because God's idea of justice is different from yours.

Why did he always do this? Every morning he awoke to a battle with his conscience. The conversation always started and ended the same way. He continued along his chosen path. There *was* no other choice.

Your quest is about him… it's about vengeance.

But didn't *he* deserve to be brought to justice? Hadn't the man in the white derby caused enough pain and suffering in this world? Why was the murderer allowed to roam this earth untouched? Where was God's justice in that?

That's how God works.

John *hated* that phrase. How many times had his father uttered it? The saying had been his Pa's way of accepting things that he couldn't understand. God could never be understood. He was too large; his thoughts were too far beyond man's thoughts. When a person felt they had God figured out, he would act beyond their comprehension. His father had been able to accept that. John couldn't. The people of this city needed tangible help, and he was doing a lot of good work here.

You're also doing a lot of bad work.

Only to those who deserved it.

I thought they deserved justice.

They were getting it.

John threw the covers back and swung his legs over the side of the bed. The room was black as pitch. John didn't mind, though. Even though he enjoyed sunlight and the outdoors, darkness had never really bothered him. Darkness was a tool. He used it.

Darkness was a state of mind that could empower or defeat a person. God created both night and day. Why not reclaim both for his purposes?

John stood up and slowly inched toward the light switch. It was amazing how efficient one could become at moving around in the dark. The key was memorization. An area had to be memorized before it was entered. That was the only way darkness could be used as an advantage. To the unsuspecting victim...

You were saying?

...to the outlaw who was unaware of your presence, your quick movements could appear supernatural. The actions were simply a chess game that had been played out in advance. All of the moves had already been made. The pieces were simply unaware of their participation.

Two more steps... and then the wall. The light switch was chest high. With a click, the hanging globe buzzed to life. Electricity was an amazing commodity. John had no idea how many matches he had struck in his life. How many candles had he burned? How many times had he had to shelter a wick from the wind or adjust the flame to avoid scorching the glass of a lamp? Now, with a flick of the finger, one could get light.

John knelt beside the bed and retrieved a canvas satchel from underneath. He sat down at the desk and placed the bag in front of him, then reached inside and pulled out a leather journal.

Contained within the pages were years of hard work. The book was full of rumors and clues, names and locations. For many years the journal had remained incomplete. Now, it was a virtual book of connect-the-dots, revealing a man that, in some way or another, he had searched for his entire life.

The journal was given to you for another reason. It was meant for recording life… yet, the text within leads to certain death.

His father had given the journal to him on his eighth birthday. James Grady kept his *own* journal. As a child, John had seen his Pa write in it daily. In the mornings, before anyone else in the house was awake, his father would get up to pray. In his leather journal, James Grady kept a record of the things that he believed God was saying to him. Sometimes, John would get up after hearing his father rummaging through the house in the early hours. His father never knew, but on occasion, John would watch him. He had always wanted to be like his father and sometimes asked to see what was written within the book. So, on his eighth birthday, James Grady presented his son with his very own leather-bound journal. His father told him, "If God speaks, what he says is important enough to write down." That was the last birthday John would spend with his Pa.

John could remember a time when God spoke. Some people said God speaks in big, unmistakable ways. Others said that he spoke in whispers, like the gentle breeze. John hadn't heard God speak in a long time. He'd chosen *not* to hear. He preferred to drown God out with whatever means he could. God had nothing good to say about the things he needed to do. John wasn't bold enough to say that he knew better than God, but he didn't have to trust him either.

He had tried using the journal in the way his Pa intended. He prayed just like his mother told him, asking for things like mercy and forgiveness for the killer of his father.

Mostly though, he asked God for justice... to see the evil man punished.

In its early days, the journal was full of questions but contained few answers. His mother said that God didn't work on the same schedule that people did. She said that *time* was his tool and that he had plenty to use.

So, John began to seek the answers to his own questions. And, the pages began to fill with names, places, and times. Then one day, a trail emerged. At the time, John was working at a mine outside of Fallen Oak, California. He'd nearly given up when he'd met a man who loved to spin yarns.

Charlie was an Italian from New York City. The man was a disgusting loudmouth that loved telling stories about his time as a bootlegger, working for a big mob boss. John didn't like him and knew that most of his stories were outright lies. But, one day something caught his attention.

"Saietta," Charlie had said in one of his sentences. John had been eating what cowboys referred to as a "brown lunch", beans and jerky, when the name struck him. John had no idea why the name had made such an impact, but, after that instance, he began to pay attention to Charlie whenever he would talk of his adventures. After hearing story after story about running illegal liquor into dry counties and working as an enforcer for Saietta, John's diligence paid off.

That day, Charlie told a story of how he and a few others were made to accompany two enforcers to New Orleans. The men were to establish a distribution warehouse so that Saietta could smuggle liquor into dry counties all up and down the Mississippi. He talked of how vicious one of the enforcers had been and how on occasion he had seen the man kill people for the simplest reasons. Charlie said that the man was as bad as they came. He had a calling card... he wore a white, derby hat.

John read the date written in his journal... *June 1899.*

Though John never told his mother, Victoria Grady could sense the path that her son was moving toward. She had feared it all of his life. She had watched as his faith in God had dwindled and his understanding of himself had increased. Persuasion fell short, and eventually a mother had to let go... and she did.

It was Joe who had convinced him to follow his destiny. Joe was an Apache and had been his father figure since the loss of his Pa. Joe's life was built on tradition and honor. He was a bold and truthful man, and he was aware of the havoc an un-righted wrong could wreak in one's life. Because of this, he had encouraged John to track down and find the man who wore the white derby. Joe believed that the man's crime deserved justice. And, in order for John Grady to live again, he would have to be the person to deliver that justice.

His quest would eventually lead to a name, and later, a location. Seventeen years had passed and John found himself in this underground room beneath Mount Zion Methodist Church. He allowed his finger to trace the delicate page of the journal. All of his work... all of his questions... the journey ended with the name written on this page.

At last, the man with the white derby would understand justice.

Anders McCain would face the reaper.

Thirteen

The white orb glowed beneath a hardened piece of rawhide. Anders McCain sat behind his desk with his hands clasped in front of him. He leaned forward on his elbows and eyed the man seated across the desk.

McCain had been caught off guard. Heat surged into his face and spread throughout his extremities. These surprises were beginning to frustrate him and when he got frustrated, he got angry. Knuckles faded to white and fingers tingled from loss of circulation. How could he have allowed this to happen?

McCain's morning had begun earlier than usual. After being awakened by Ronald Thompson, he had left his family's two-story penthouse and gone downstairs to his office. Having an office system just under his living quarters was one of the benefits of owning and living in a luxury hotel. *The Rendezvous* was located in lower Manhattan. McCain's hotel was the crowning achievement of his life.

The Rendezvous was the one thing that he operated which was *almost* completely legal.

The first thing McCain had done after learning of the attack at Greenwood Cemetery was to alert Nick Rocci. Four men had survived the shootout. One was seriously injured after crashing a truck. Nick was searching for George Burt, the foreman. Burt was missing and he hadn't checked in. Either he was dead or somewhere running scared. Nick would find out.

McCain had met with the other two escapees by daybreak. The men had been through the thick of the gunfight. McCain had questioned them as to what they witnessed.

"It was just too dark, Mr. McCain," Harold Raimes had replied. "It was like we were fightin' an army or somethin'... I didn't see nothin' but shadows. There had to be at least five of them."

James Grimes had relayed a different version of the gunfight. "I'm tellin' you, Mr. McCain, there was only one. He was like a ghost or somethin'. The guy was all over the place. Our bullets just went around him."

McCain hadn't bothered to ask them why they had run. He understood how it felt to fight amidst impossible odds. McCain could remember a few times when fast feet had saved *his* life. And, there was no doubt that if the two had stayed around, they would have been killed.

The fact that professionals had raided the cemetery was undeniable. Whoever it was had been familiar with explosives. They'd managed to blow the mausoleum without causing too much damage to the surrounding crypts. Then, the culprits had proceeded to engage and defeat sixteen armed men... heavily armed. *Not heavily enough...*

It had to be the Italians. They were the only reasonable answer.

After his conversations with Harold Raimes and James Grimes, he'd met with Ronald Thompson.

"How bad is it?" McCain had asked.

"It's pretty bad, Mr. McCain," Thompson had replied. "We lost all of our Brooklyn stock in the first attack. The Flatbush Avenue fiasco was an enormous loss. That warehouse contained the majority of our stock for both Brooklyn and Manhattan. The product at Greenwood Cemetery was our attempt at a restock. All of it was destroyed. We have nothing in this area. I've figured that we've lost two hundred and thirty-three thousand dollars and six cents. That, of course, is cost. The street value is much worse."

Insurance prices have just escalated.

McCain would inform Nick. The money would have to be remade. He couldn't allow that much money to be lost. It would take time, but he would get it back. He was too easy on the businessmen of his area, anyway. What would be a few more dollars a week from each of them? With patience, the money would be made back in a couple of years. But, the Italians could no longer go unpunished. Joe the Boss would pay for this. If he wanted a war... *he'll get a war.*

"Mr. Thompson, I've spoken with a man. This man deals in certain acquisitions... *hardware*."

"Of course," Thompson had replied. "Weapons," he said in an uneasy tone.

McCain had been preparing for the inevitable retaliation that he would have to carry out against the Italians. He had already spoken to a man who could supply their needs. He

107

had located a German arms dealer several weeks earlier. The man claimed to be able to acquire a new type of gun. He termed the weapon a "sub-machine gun". The weapon was a handheld version of the larger machine guns. The Bergman MP18 was smaller than a lever-action rifle, yet delivered four hundred and fifty rounds per minute. Because the model was brand new, he would only be able to acquire fifteen of them. Along with the Bergman MP18s, the dealer could obtain two German-made, rifle grenade launchers and a Vickers's machinegun. The Vickers gun was a powerhouse used by the British military.

If Masseria were going to attack with an army, McCain would respond with one of his own.

"We've already discussed prices and the issue has been settled," said McCain. "He'll tell you what we owe."

"You trust this man, Mr. McCain?" asked Thompson.

"He knows who I am. I trust *that*. He'll stick to the discussed prices."

During the course of his conversations with Nick Rocci and Ronald Thompson, McCain had left his office several times. On the last occasion, just after sitting behind his desk, a voice echoed from the shadows of the rear office corner.

"How much is one man worth?"

McCain nearly jumped out of his chair. With a quick movement, he grabbed the short-barreled Peacemaker .45 from a desk drawer and swung it around toward the man behind his right shoulder.

"You won't need that," said the voice.

"I'll decide that," McCain replied. He strained to make out the figure standing in the dark. "I'm going to kill you. I'm going to kill you because you thought you had the right to surprise me and live. Know that."

"You should check your gun."

"Sure," McCain scoffed.

The man stuck his fist out into a swathe of sunlight that bled through the curtains. Cartridges plopped to the carpeted floor as the man's hand opened.

Without taking his eyes from the corner, McCain glanced at the rear of the revolver's cylinder. *Empty!* How long had the man been inside his office?

"All I have to do is yell and this place will be swarming with armed men!" explained McCain.

The man in the shadows spoke. "If Wounded Hawk wanted to kill you... You would be *dead*."

The man stepped forward into the sunlight. The first thing McCain noticed was the ghostly eye. His dark hair was long and braided on the left side. He wore a business suit complete with jacket, shirt, and vest. His pants were tucked into a pair of knee-high leather moccasins—the kind trappers wore. And his face... *My God.*

The right side of his face was covered in a horrible leather mask. Evidence of scars crept from beneath its edges... and the white eye shone from a cutout in the rawhide.

Moments later, the Indian was seated in front of his desk.

"You won't need all of these weapons," said the man. "You are not going to war with an army."

The man had definitely been in the office for longer than McCain had first thought.

"I don't know what you're talking about," McCain replied.

"I know what hunts you," the man said.

"Do you now? And how would you know that?" McCain reclined into his seat and released his grip. Blood began to flow back into his fingertips.

"Because, I know him," explained Wounded Hawk. "I have known him most of his life. He plans to kill you."

"You're insinuating that I'm at war with one man?" asked McCain, insulted by the idea.

"I'm not insinuating. You have a blood debt on your head."

"This is the twentieth century," replied McCain. "You want me to believe that a gunfighter is roaming the streets of New York waging a personal war against *me*?"

"You would rather believe that this 'Joe the Boss' is after you. You don't want to believe that one man could destroy you. That frightens you."

"You have no idea who I am," countered McCain... "Or *what* I am."

"If you must hate these Italians then hate them," Wounded Hawk continued. "Go to war with them if that satisfies you. This is good. It is mankind's way. But, understand that your war will solve nothing. There is a man out there that hates you in the same way you hate this other gang. He will stop at nothing to destroy all that you are."

"Then, let him come," replied McCain.

"He has been coming. And, you have been unable to stop him."

McCain jumped to his feet and slammed his fists onto the desktop. "How do you know that?"

"I know much about you. I have tracked the one who hunts you for many years. To hunt an animal, you must discover its food source. You, Anders McCain, are *his* food source."

McCain eased back into his seat and gathered himself. "Would you be willing to disclose information regarding your *prey?*"

"I cannot," Wounded Hawk replied. "But, with your help I will kill him."

"How can *I* help?"

"In the way a worm helps a fisherman."

McCain bellowed a hearty laugh. "You want me to be bait? No. I don't need your help. *I* will kill this man."

"You may try," replied Wounded Hawk. "But, you will fail." Wounded Hawk stood up. "It is my fate to kill this man. He is the reason the spirits still allow me to walk this earth. And, I will never be allowed to pass until *our* blood debt is settled." Wounded Hawk turned and walked to the door.

"Tell me," asked McCain. "What have I done to this man?"

"He believes you killed his father."

That could be true. How many fathers had McCain killed? How many orphaned sons had vowed revenge against his name? But, this one was different. This man was serious.

"I would gladly pay you for the information," offered McCain as he stood.

"I am afraid you misunderstand me," Wounded Hawk countered with disgust. "My destiny is bigger than your pocket. The preacher will die by my hand and no others'."

"Who is this man?" demanded McCain.

Wounded Hawk turned and disappeared through the office doors. McCain ran into the hallway after him.

"Who is this man!?" he screamed. But, the only answer was the echo of his voice as it reverberated through the empty hallway.

McCain uttered a few words of frustration. If this man, this *Wounded Hawk*, was telling the truth, then McCain had a blood debt on his head. It wouldn't be the first time he had to kill a man or be killed. Besides, McCain had the advantage. He had the money, the resources, and the manpower to hunt this avenger down.

He was troubled, though. This *Wounded Hawk* had entered his office unnoticed, unloaded McCain's revolver, and sat silently for hours. The man was obviously a skilled assassin, a subject with which McCain was very familiar. Wounded Hawk could most likely kill anyone he had a mind to kill. Yet, he couldn't kill *this man*.

He walked to the glass case that stood on the far wall of his office. Within it lay a belt he had worn for a large part of his life. He reached into his pocket and produced a small golden key, then slid it into the matching keyhole and turned. There was a pop, and he lifted the door of the case.

Minutes later, McCain stood in front of a mirror with the brown leather gun belt wrapped securely around his waist. The Remington Frontier .44 didn't slide from its holster as quickly or smoothly as it once had, but it felt reassuring in McCain's hand. Adrenaline crept through his body and into his limbs. It was amazing how quickly one's confidence could return. McCain would never be caught off guard again. And this *gunfighter*, if he were real, would understand the meaning of revenge.

McCain walked to his desk and retrieved a note, which had been left after the Jersey Crew was attacked. It was addressed to him, and read: See you around.

He crumpled the piece of paper tightly within his fist. "I'm counting on it."

Fourteen

ohn Grady's fingers clinched the edges of the pulpit. His knuckles turned white as the blood squeezed out of his hands. He didn't recognize the physical change that was happening to him, but he was aware of the zeal that flooded into his voice. The story of King David had always impassioned him.

Charles Kell sat in the second row with his eight girls. He stared intently at Reverend Grady, enthralled by every word that radiated from his lips.

"King David," John reiterated as he began to close his sermon "was a man after God's own heart. He was a warrior... to the core of his being. He was passionate and courageous."

The last sentence garnered some nods from the audience. Charles and several other men continued to listen. There was a new emotion in their eyes this morning, one John had never seen.

"When we think of courage," continued John, "we tend to define it as the absence of fear. That's a mistake. *Courage* and *being unafraid* are two separate things. *Courage* is acting even though you *are* afraid. *Courage* means that we step out and choose to move even when fear has us frozen in place. King David was a man of courage. He did things that scared him."

Tim O'Hare sat behind John's left shoulder, in the pastor's chair. John could see him from the corner of his eye. Tim's hand was planted on his chin in contemplation. What was he thinking? *Why does it matter?* Why was John so worried about what Tim thought? If he were honest with himself, he would have to admit that he *wanted* perhaps even *needed* Tim's approval. *Don't all boys need fathers?* But, John had a father. He'd been stolen from him. He didn't need Tim to be that for him. He didn't need any man's approval.

"Do you think that David wasn't afraid of Goliath? How could that be possible? He was a little boy facing a twelve-foot giant! The only weapon that David knew how to use was a sling. A shepherd used the sling to scare off predators, not to destroy armies. But, David trusted that God wanted to defeat the Philistines. So, as the Philistines stood on the battlefield, mocking God, David marched out to face Goliath. He walked right up to that big giant and delivered God's justice."

He stepped back from the pulpit and stepped to the side. John looked at Tim as he stepped around the pulpit and brought himself face-to-face with his listeners.

"God's will doesn't come without a price or without fear," he explained in a calm voice. "And, it's never written clearly. Sometimes, we must simply act and trust that God

115

will use us, just as he used David. David became the greatest King that Israel had ever had."

* * *

John stood in the doorway of Mount Zion Methodist Assembly shaking the hands of the parishioners as they left. How many times had he watched his father do the same thing? How many times had he stood beside James Grady and shaken the hands of the worshippers as they left for their afternoon retreats? It was in the doorway of a church that he had met Joe, his surrogate father. And, it was in a doorway of that same church that John had first seen the man in the white derby, Anders McCain.

Tim stood beside him, also performing his pastoral duties. John was growing closer to Tim. They didn't agree about everything, but such was the way with friendship. John was not naive. He knew that he had strong opinions of his own that may not have sat well with Tim. A man had to let some things pass, to be sensitive to the opinions of other people. Tim definitely had his own opinions. John had never agreed with all of Joe's philosophies, either. And, deep down inside, he craved friendship. There had been too few encounters with friendship in his life.

Charles Kell and his family neared Tim. "Well, Charles... how is that shoulder feelin' today?" asked O'Hare.

"Its doin' a lot better, Reverend," replied Charles. "And, how are you today, Reverend Grady?"

The *look* was still in Charles' eyes. John had seen it many times in his life, but never in Charles. Something had happened. *Hope* was a hard emotion to conceal. You could beat a man down, take everything he had, and leave him

116

unrecognizable, but you couldn't smother hope. It was always there, lying underneath, like an ember waiting for the faintest breeze. That ember was glowing in the eyes of Charles this morning. John had no idea what had ignited it, but he was pleased. Men needed hope.

"I'm just fine, Charles," John replied.

"That was a fine sermon, Reverend Grady," Charles said. "Fine, indeed."

"Well, thank you."

"I was wonderin' if we might talk about it a little more. I'd like to get your idea on some things, if you have the time. Perhaps, I could drop by the church this week?"

"That would be great, Charles. I look forward to seeing you."

Charles eased out of the doorway and into the street followed by his entourage of women. John didn't know whether he should be jealous or pity the man. The job of protecting nine women in this city was an overwhelming charge. How could one man do it?

* * *

Lunch was delicious as usual. Mary was quite a good cook even if the meal was as simple as soup and sandwiches. Soup had been a favorite of John's mother. He supposed it was a simple meal to make on a Sunday. His Ma could put a kettle over the open hearth in their backyard and then attend to the ritual of getting ready for church. Afterwards, the soup was always ready as soon as the Grady family made it home. Soup brought back many memories. It was a funny thing how certain smells and tastes could do that. Sometimes, John strained to remember his childhood... his Pa. He had trouble recalling the memories on command, but a taste or smell... or even a look from someone, and the images came flooding back. Mary had been the cause of recollections on more than one occasion. She reminded him of his mother... her blonde hair... her delicate skin...

"Did you have enough, Rev...," hesitated Mary, suddenly remembering his request, "... John?"

"Yes, Mary," he replied. "It was delicious as usual... just like my mother used to make."

She grinned sheepishly. "That's quite a complement. Thank you." She tucked her chin into her chest, a little embarrassed.

Tim tried to hide a smile, as Mary walked back into the kitchen.

"What?" asked John.

"Oh... nothin'," replied Tim.

"Well, it better *stay* nothin'."

Tim looked toward the kitchen. Mary's shadow cast a delicate figure along the walls as she went about her after-lunch duties.

"She's a heck of a woman," said Tim.

"She is." replied John.

"She'll make a great wife someday... to some lucky man."

"Yep."

It was no secret that Tim thought of Mary as a daughter. It was also no secret that John was an available bachelor. He knew that this moment was inevitable. He had dreaded it. There were just too many complications in his life right now. It was not the right time to talk about relationships.

"You know, she's not married," stated Tim, as if John wasn't taking his cue.

"Thank you, Tim. You know what?" asked John sarcastically, "neither am I. Hey… you don't suppose that the two of us should…" He waved his finger back and forth between himself and the kitchen.

"For God's sake, boy!" exclaimed Tim. "Do you like women?"

"What kind of question is that?"

"Then, what's your problem?" questioned Tim. "Can't you tell that she has it in for you?"

"No… I think you're wrong," replied John, wiping his mouth with a napkin. "She's polite… caring… enjoys my company. It's a good basis for friendship."

"God help us all. What's wrong with you, boy? If I was twenty-five years younger, do you think I'd be sittin' here talkin' with an old man? I'd be findin' somethin' else to do, you can bet on that. And someone else to be doin' it with!"

"Tim," chided John, looking to make sure that Mary hadn't overheard.

"Well, maybe she needs to hear."

Tim may have been right. Perhaps, Mary did need to overhear the conversation. If he were to be honest, he'd have to admit that he wanted to be around her. From the moment they'd met, her personality had grabbed him. She was fun and witty. She was a tough survivor, a trait that was necessary for the women whom John had grown up around. She was also beautiful… as beautiful as John had ever seen. Mary reminded him of a place he had not felt in many years. As much as he tried to pretend that he had no desire for her, even the slightest touch from her hand proved differently. He caught himself desiring to brush against her as they passed through the hallways. He longed to speak with her, in truth.

But, honesty was not a luxury that John could afford. And a woman was of no use at this point in his life. He had a mission. There was one purpose to his life. Bringing justice to Anders McCain was the only reason he was still alive. It was the reason for which he had suffered so much in his life. McCain was the reason God had brought so much hurt into his life. God had used his Pa, Joe, and... *Annie.* God had been shaping him all of his life to do the thing that no one else could do... *to bring down a mass murderer.*

Nothing could come between John and his destiny. His life could not afford love. Maybe, one day they would get their chance. *Perhaps never.*

"Listen, son," said Tim, breaking John's thoughts. "Whatever it is that's weighin' on your mind so hard... it's not worth it."

John looked up at Tim and peered into his prying eyes. Had the man read his mind? "I don't know what you mean," replied John.

"I'm not just talkin' about the girl, lad. I've been watchin' you. What's sittin' so heavy on you?"

John thought for a moment. He wanted to tell Tim to leave it alone. He wanted to say that it was nothing, but he didn't. "Things you wouldn't understand."

John felt comfortable with Tim. He trusted him. He wished that he could tell him everything. He needed to tell someone. The pain had become an acid that for decades had eaten his soul from the inside out.

"I understand," replied Tim. "Sometimes, a man just has to work things out for himself. Just don't let whatever it is work you out of the life that the good Lord intended for you. Most of the time, we're the destroyers of our own lives. You can't fix everything. You have to be weak so that God can use you. If you're weak, people see God doing the miracles in your life... like killing giants."

"Like David did," replied John.

"Yes," replied Tim, "like David did. You preached a great sermon this mornin', John. You forgot one thing, though. David's strength and self-reliance is what caused him to fall. If he would have stayed weak, there would have been no limit to what God could have done in his life."

If he'd have stayed weak. It was a disgusting idea at best. Weakness is strength? *Nonsense.* Weakness had caused the downfall of civilizations. And, it was weakness that allowed the mobs to rule this city. Weakness had allowed Anders McCain to destroy lives for far too long.

James Grady had believed that the weak would someday rule the strong... that people would see God through his meekness and servitude. He had bet his life on the promises of God...

And he had lost.

Fifteen

Wounded Hawk's moccasins padded gently on the Manhattan sidewalk as he slipped through the city streets. The moon shone brightly on this cold December night. The shadows created by the yellow sphere were harsh and plentiful. The large buildings and concrete streets should have amazed him. Instead, they angered him. The white man had always been adept at inventing ways to destroy the natural beauty around him. The native people of the Americas had managed to preserve their land and resources for thousands of years. And, within less than two hundred years, the white man had managed to cover, in concrete and mortar, more land than any man could use. This was only one of the reasons that the white man filled Wounded Hawk with disgust. The entire race deserved death. It seemed as if the white man yearned for extinction. He lived his life with hate and loathing for all other living creatures. Because of this, the white man was easy for Wounded Hawk to hate. He derived pleasure from killing the white man. His hatred for the race gave direction to his life.

His grandfather, Thunder Crow, had always warned him of hatred. Thunder Crow had said that the emotion was natural and could be used to great ends. But, if allowed to take control of the mind, it assured one of death and destruction.

Wounded Hawk had never agreed with his grandfather. Thunder Crow had given into the "way" of the white man. He had abandoned the ideals of the Apache warrior, and with that abandonment, had lost the respect of his offspring.

...except for the intruder...

The *Intruder* could never be true Apache. Although the intruder desired to be a part of Wounded Hawk's people, the white blood that coursed through his veins could not be changed. Wounded Hawk knew that this caused great jealousy in the heart of the intruder. Because of his jealousy, the intruder was driven to seek the affection of Thunder Crow. He succeeded. And Wounded Hawk watched the heart of his grandfather turn from the true ways of his people to the weakness and corruption of the white man.

At one time, Wounded Hawk and this preacher had been brothers. They were never true brothers, of course, but brothers bound by a blood oath.

A white gunman had killed the preacher's father when he was a child. Thunder Crow had felt pity for the boy, whose father had befriended him. He took the boy as his grandson and raised him side by side with his true grandson, Wounded Hawk. Though Wounded Hawk was several years older, the boys grew up together. They made a blood pact, a gesture binding their friendship forever. That friendship had been broken.

Thunder Crow had both boys educated at a school run by a local mission church. And, as Wounded Hawk grew in knowledge, he became angry over the manner in which the white man had treated his people. He discovered a small group of Apache who still chose to live the warrior way. The sect believed that the Apache should continue to resist the white man through force — a path that Thunder Crow, once a great warrior, had chosen to abandon.

As Wounded Hawk's hatred for the white man continued to grow, Thunder Crow had become increasingly opposed to his ideals. Eventually, Wounded Hawk joined the Apache war parties on regular attacks. He found that he enjoyed killing the white man and he found satisfaction in taking the scalps of his enemy.

But, despite all of his efforts and all of his successes, he could not win Thunder Crow's approval. Instead, his grandfather took pride in the training of Wounded Hawk's white brother — a son of the very people who sought to obliterate the Apache. Wounded Hawk's anger grew beyond his control, and in a confrontation with his grandfather, his white brother interfered and chose his fate.

Wounded Hawk touched the leather mask that covered the right side of his face. The thing felt coarse... unnatural. Yet, Wounded Hawk found that it had become a part of him. The covering gave him meaning, passion, and served as a reminder of the mark the white man left upon his people.

He wandered into the night, craning his head upwards toward the giants that loomed over for miles in every direction. Scattered windows projected yellow squares of light onto the sidewalk before him.

After walking for some time, the city opened into a large expanse of wooded area. The locals called it Central Park.

Wounded Hawk recognized it as the only reminder this city had of how the earth was intended to look. He disappeared into the darkness of the refuge.

Within minutes, a small teepee of twigs and tender sat before him. He produced a piece of flint rock and struck it several times. Sparks shot forth and landed in a small clump of dried grass. A barely noticeable plume of smoke arose before him as he sat cross-legged in the shadows of the forest.

Wounded Hawk was closing in on his prey. The preacher was within his grasp. After nearly twenty years of following a trail littered with disappointment and failure, Wounded Hawk would have another chance. He had already scouted seven Methodist churches within the Manhattan vicinity. His search area was growing smaller. Anders McCain, however, remained the key.

All of his life, his white brother had sought vengeance against the killer of his father. And, now, he was here in New York waging war against the leader of a white organization.

Wounded Hawk recognized the irony.

If he followed Anders McCain, the preacher would reveal himself. The preacher had no choice but to take his revenge. Wounded Hawk was sure of this. They had studied under the same teacher.

Wounded Hawk's breath floated before him and hung in the still, winter air. New York was a damp place. He preferred the dry air of the West. But, it was the cold moist air of New York City that his white enemy breathed. And, it was this same air that *he* would breathe until his game of fate was finished.

He wrinkled his disfigured cheek beneath the rawhide.

This battle would be *his* victory. With this last scalp…
…his destiny would be complete.

Sixteen

Sunshine poured through the kitchen window of Mount Zion. Mary Lyles busied herself in the kitchen cleaning up after the morning's breakfast. She had prepared eggs and toast for the ministers. Unfortunately, there weren't too many ingredients that she could use to create breakfast. In general, there were eggs and bread, which could sometimes be accompanied by bacon or salted meat. The pastors never complained, though. They understood that times were tough. Often times, they would go without one or more of their meals to help feed less fortunate people, though Mary was careful not to allow them to sacrifice *too* often. After all, it was her job to care for these men. *Lord knows they could never do it on their own.* She was glad that she had someone to take care of, though. She was blessed to have a job at all... *and a place to live.* So many people were suffering in this city. There were so many who were doing without the basic necessities.

At one time, Mary had been one of those *less fortunate* people. That was before Reverend O'Hare had discovered her. There were things that she had done in her life for which she would be eternally ashamed. But, she had survived the only way that she could. Didn't God understand that? There were days when she was able to forget about her sins. And, there were days when it seemed as if her past were fast on her heels. She often felt that way when John was around.

Why did she desire to be with him so badly? She couldn't understand how she might ever deserve a man like John Grady, a man of faith. Her life had been so dark and full of mistakes. Often, she found herself dreaming of a future with him, and then she would come to her senses. *Why would he want a woman like me? How could he ever forgive me?* But, John wasn't the root of her self-doubt. She doubted the possibility of *any* man coming into her life. How could a husband ever forgive her for the things she'd done? *But, I had to… to survive.* She'd had to care for her siblings after her parents had died. What else could a teenage girl do to earn money?

Mary dipped her hands into the hot soapy water and produced a clean plate. She reached for the red and white checkered dishtowel, but it was not on the counter. Instead, it was in the hands of John Grady.

"John," she said, slightly startled. She was glad that he couldn't read minds.

"Can I help?" he replied.

"Oh… You don't need to bother with this."

"It wouldn't be any bother," he replied. "Actually, I *wanted* to help you finish."

He dried the plate and placed it into the open cupboard. Mary quickly washed the next one and handed it to him.

"Would you like to take a walk?" he asked.

"Yes," she managed to reply, though taken off guard by the invitation. "With you?"

"Yes. With me... and Mattie's children. Mattie found some housework for the day and I've been promising the children that I'd take them for a walk if it warmed up."

She gazed upward into his eyes. Could he see the way she felt? She hoped that he couldn't. But, another part of her wanted to tell. She felt safe, but uncomfortable. When he was around, her thoughts were a big jumble of nonsense.

"It's a beautiful day," he said. "I don't think we'll get another one like this for some time. Would you like to go?"

* * *

In between gusts of cool wind, the sun had almost enough time to warm John's cheeks. He was reminded of the mild winters back in California and of a childhood spent roaming about the wilderness. But, then a winter draft would strike his face with a sharp tinge of pain and awaken him to the reality of Brooklyn.

It *was* a beautiful day. And this walk had been a good idea. Bringing Mary hadn't been his idea, but he was glad to have her alongside. Tim had suggested that he take her. John got the feeling that Tim was enjoying the game of matchmaking and couldn't imagine him giving up any time soon. Tim had recommended that a walk would be a casual setting for the two of them to talk. The children would keep the conversation from getting too serious. *Why are you so afraid of having a real conversation with a woman?*

Mattie's children ran ahead of them, darted past the Lunch Room Restaurant and leapt over a waste pail outside of the American Express Company. They jumped and skipped and managed to include any child they met into their playtime. Children amazed John... the way they instinctively accepted others. People had to be taught to hate. John didn't figure that they had any concept of the "mess" that surrounded their lives. They were loved and had a place to live. *Ignorance is bliss.*

Mary strolled alongside him. She looked radiant this morning. Her golden hair hung loosely about her shoulders while blue eyes reflected the beautiful, sunny sky. Her skin... her lips... the curve of her waist beneath the gray wool coat... There was nothing about her that John disliked. If only he had met her at some other time... in some other place. But the *here and now* is what they had been given. John knew there were no perfect circumstances for love, but they could be better.

"Thank you for invitin' me, John," she said, breaking the silence.

"You're welcome," replied John. He nodded ahead toward the children who were busy jumping cracks in the sidewalk. "Sometimes I envy them... their innocence."

"Yes," she replied, "but then you would *want* to know. That's the trouble with bein' a child. You always want to grow up... to know what the adults know."

"I suppose you're right," he replied.

"I'd give anythin' to be a child again," she said, "...to go back and have another try at the world."

"I wouldn't," he replied. "Because of that one moment, the moment when you realize *what* the world really is... that's when life comes crashing down on you."

"You're a mysterious man, John Grady."

"Reverend Grady," interrupted little Jake Hammond, "could we go to the park?"

"I don't see why not," replied John. "How does the park sound, Mary?"

* * *

Prospect Park was very much alive on this nice autumn day. Squirrels scurried about on the leaf-covered ground, trying to find the occasional overlooked acorn. Birds chirped in the treetops, filling the air with a melodious sound that seemed out of place in the cold city. Children ran and played through the woods on the edge of Long Meadow. Mattie's children wasted no time joining in on a game of chase that was already in progress.

Prospect Park was a large recreational area in the middle of Brooklyn. It was composed of over five hundred acres of forest, meadows, lakes, and waterways. John often went to Prospect Park to seek solace. The park was usually crowded, but there were places where one could be alone. John especially liked the creek beds that he found in the forested ravines. He had sought the solace on numerous occasions.

John and Mary watched the children play from a small park bench

"Do you want children?" she asked.

"Now?" he asked sarcastically.

"Someday," she giggled. "Why aren't you married, John?"

John was stunned. "Why aren't you?" he replied, dumbfounded.

"I hadn't met the right man, I suppose. Now… back to *my* question."

He hadn't spoken of marriage in years. He'd decided to leave the past buried… Some would say that his way of coping was unhealthy. He didn't care about other peoples' opinions, though. As long as the pain stayed away, he was doing something right.

But now, he found himself *wanting* to talk. He *wanted* Mary to know things about himself. What was he doing? Why was she making him feel this way? She had no right to know.

"I *was* married once," he said. His tongue had betrayed him.

"Oh…" replied Mary with a tinge of hurt in her voice. "I'm sorry. It was none of my business…"

"No," he replied, "I want to tell you." In front of them, children dance and played, an old dream long since surrendered. "I was young… *we* were young. Anne and I…

"Anne?" interrupted Mary.

"We met when I was assigned to a pastorate in Seminary, Missouri. Seminary was a little town with some big problems. I'd hoped that I could make a difference there. Anne was the church's schoolteacher. We were both young. We fell in love and before long were married. Four months later… she was gone."

"What happened to her?" probed Mary.

"She was killed," he replied without emotion. "She was killed because there are bad men in this world and not enough good men to stop them. She was murdered because I took a stand against the outlaws that were tearing Seminary apart."

"I'm sorry, John."

"It was a long time ago."

Mary sat in silence.

"Mary," he continued, "you're an incredible woman."

Her cheeks flooded with a rosy hue.

"This isn't easy for me," he hesitated, searching for words. "There is something that I have to do…"

She placed her hand on top of his and squeezed reassuringly.

"It's all right. Don't say anything else." Mary squeezed his hand one last time, rose to her feet, and joined the children at play. John enjoyed the feminine outline of her body as she danced and chased after the children. He subdued the warm goose pimples that wanted to take over his body.

Tell her more. But there was too much at stake. Too many lives hung in the balance. Mary was a distraction. Perhaps there would be a time in his life for happiness… *perhaps not.* Maybe his only remaining purpose was doing what no one else would do.

For everyday that Anders McCain walked this earth, an innocent person paid the price for his procrastination.

Seventeen

fter walking Mary and the Hammond children back to Mount Zion, John was greeted by an unexpected visitor. Minutes later he and Charles Kell sat staring across a small table in the pastor's study. John remembered that last Sunday, Charles had asked if he could stop by the church and visit. Now, Charles was here, and he was clearly nervous about what he had to say.

"Reverend," started Charles. "I don't know how to approach this subject, so I'll just say what's on my mind."

"Alright," replied John.

"What you talked about this past Sunday… about justice and how God expects us to do something…"

John gave an encouraging nod.

"Well," continued Charles, "I've been thinking a lot about that."

Charles released a frustrated sigh and resigned himself to say what was on his mind.

"It's no secret what's been going on in this town. The gangs are breaking us. And, they do it because we make it easy for them. They come every week to pick up their money and we just give it to them. Every once in a while, we say something they don't like or can't give them enough and we get a busted lip or a black eye. That's the extent of taking up for ourselves."

John could see that Charles was getting angry.

"Do you have any idea what it feels like to have your manhood trampled on every week? Someone comes into your business, that you've poured sweat and tears into, and slaps you around. Then, they take your money and say that they're protecting you from the Italian gangs. Well, I've never had any problem with the *Italians*."

"You have every right to be angry," John interjected.

"I *want* to do something about it. You don't know how many times I've had to fight the urge to drive a butcher's knife right through some kid's skull. Cause that's who they use to do their dirty work... young men. Boys."

"Those men still make their own choices, Charles."

"And, then there's this "ghost" that's giving Anders McCain so much hell. Some people are angry. The Irish are taking more money from us to make up for their losses because of this ghost. But I say he's a hero. I'd love to be standing right there beside him the next time he hammers McCain. Then I think, 'Why don't you just do something yourself?' And I start to... and then I think of my girls. What would they do if something happened to me? There's just too much to lose."

Frustrated, Charles shook his head. "Am I making any sense?"

"Yes," John replied. "It's all right to feel the way you do. A man *always* has something to lose. That's why men like Anders McCain can take what they want. They use the fear of your loss. It's easy to give your life for a cause that *you* believe in. But are you willing to give the life of someone you love? Those who have little to risk, gain little. Those who have much to risk, gain much."

In front of John sat a man who was changing. Charles Kell was tired of being in bondage. And, John was sure that Charles wasn't the only one. John needed someone like Charles to help him in the fight. No one man ever won a war, but many.

"Are you saying that I should do somethin'?" asked Charles.

"Yes," John replied. "But, not alone. I know that there are others like you... others who are sick of pretending that this city isn't being terrorized. Surely this is heavy on the mind of others.

"There are others," affirmed Charles.

"Get those people together. One person won't scare Anders McCain. But, a neighborhood united, will. Take a stand."

"Is this right, Reverend? The Bible says to love your enemies, to turn the other cheek."

"I think you've run out of cheeks."

Charles pushed away from the table and stood. He looked as resolute as any man John had ever seen. He thrust his hand outward as a gesture of thanks. John took Charles' slender, clammy hand in his own and gave it a confident shake.

"Thank you, Reverend Grady."

"No. Thank you, Charles."

He watched Charles leave. John was alone. And in the solace, his misplaced focus became evident. He'd been right. Mary was a distraction. As of late, her friendship had begun to change him. He enjoyed the change… liked who he was around her. But, it was an illusion. He needed to get busy. He'd allowed McCain to experience some respite over the last few weeks. The recess was over. The murderer's moment of justice had come. John had all the information that he needed to get Anders McCain.

It was time to meet the man in the white derby.

Eighteen

Rain poured from the night sky, drowning any hope that the uncharacteristically sunny day had entertained. Lightning filled the air with flashes of violet interspersed with claps of booming thunder. The temperature had dropped from the low sixties to the high thirties within hours. Only two years earlier a winter storm had battered New Jersey's coastline, wreaking havoc and destruction. The city had been forced to build a sea wall with excavations from the Lincoln and Holland Tunnels. The winter of 1914 had begun just like this one.

Davey Roberts watched the rain drops streak down the windows of *The Rendezvous* lobby. Less than an hour ago, he had been outside in the freezing downpour working on a new shipment. The Irish organization had ceased storing any of their inventories in the Brooklyn area. McCain had lost too much money during the attacks, and neither he nor the police had managed anything concrete from their few leads. So, every evening the men were forced to transport the goods from the protected warehouses in Manhattan directly to the Brooklyn pubs and juke joints. On this night, Roberts had been chilled to the bone.

He'd never planned on working for someone like Anders McCain. But, very seldom did a young man's plans come to fruition in this hard world. McCain offered Roberts a chance to get out of this place... a chance to be something in this world. He didn't agree with the extortion practices, but it was part of the job. Roberts surmised that there were only two options: be the *extorter* or the *extorted*. He'd had enough of the latter in his lifetime.

"C'mon, Davey boy," taunted Joe Rawlins who was seated across the poker table. "We ain't got all night."

Davey Roberts looked at his hand again. He had a pair of nines and a pair of fours. It wasn't the strongest hand, but two pairs could be used to bluff.

"I'm in," Roberts replied.

The time was a quarter till two o'clock in the morning. Poker nights were a part of the ritual for "grunts" like Roberts. Every evening, eight men spent the night in the lobby of *The Rendezvous*. They were the first line of defense against anyone who wanted to reach Anders McCain's penthouse. If anyone managed to make it through the lobby, they would encounter guards stationed between the elevator and stairwells of every floor. The floor guards were a recent addition due to the sporadic attacks. Roberts didn't imagine that the Italians would just barge in and start a gunfight in the middle of downtown Manhattan.

What the... A shadow passed by the window on the street outside. *Just someone walking by.* He couldn't imagine who would be out on a night like this at this late hour, but he was sure he'd seen someone.

"I'm callin' you," said Joe Rawlins, a graying man with a leathery face. "Lay em' down, gentlemen."

A couple of expletives filled the room as the other four men laid their cards on the table.

Roberts reclined back in his chair. There were worse places that a man could be than in the lobby of a luxury hotel on Broadway. He looked around the dimly lit space. The room was large and divided into two areas by an uncarpeted walkway that ran from the front entrance to the elevators, and then to the stairwell at the rear. Four tall, marble columns supported the ceiling on each side of the aisle. The left side of the room contained a registration desk and groupings of chairs, sofas, and coffee tables for guests to converse and relax. On the furniture nearest the entrance, two guards sat trying to fight off the sleep that would eventually overtake them.

The right side of the room contained a long cocktail bar made of cherry wood and seven oak dinner tables. Four of the dinner tables ran along the length of the bar. The remaining three tables, where the other five guards were playing poker, were grouped together in the front left corner of the room. One additional guard was seated in a chair beside the elevators with his head tucked into his chest. One of the two guards on the other side of the lobby nodded off.

Roberts wasn't far from falling asleep himself. The heavy blanket of cigarette smoke in the air wasn't helping matters.

"Whose deal is it?" asked one of the enforcers seated at the table.

"You gonna deal, Davey?" grunted another man.

Davey Roberts took the cards and began to shuffle. He noticed Tom Rawlins rubbing his knuckles.

"You smack somebody around today, or somethin'?" asked Roberts.

"What day don't I?" replied Rawlins.

The men broke into laughter as Roberts began to deal.

"Some little book worm thought he could get smart with me," explained Rawlins. "Sometimes I wish some of these gutless nobodies would at least put up some kind of fight. You know? You wouldn't feel so bad."

The men laughed again.

"Hey," piped up another man, "anybody seen all the broads workin' in that butcher's shop over on Union?"

"Yea," replied another. "They're all over the place... couple of real lookers too... gotta be sixteen or seventeen years old!"

"I've been thinkin' about takin' a taste of that," replied the first man. "I'm just waitin' for the right time."

"They'd melt like butter," lamented the other.

"Are you fellas gonna pay up?" asked Roberts, breaking the conversation.

This was the part he hated about the job. The men could be so animalistic. Once a conversation moved in a direction, it would snowball until the men worked themselves into frenzy. Davey Roberts didn't want this conversation to head in the direction of harming one of those young girls. He was no saint, but he knew right from wrong. And rape was one sin that he didn't figure God was too willing to forgive.

These men could be vicious. Had they always been like that? Perhaps, they had been like him once, but one compromise after another had led them to a place where they no longer recognized the morals that were once so clear. But he was sure that some of them were just plain evil. They *enjoyed* watching people suffer. They *enjoyed* seeing the fear in the eyes of their victims as they bowed to the power of the *enforcers*.

The Irish organization had begun as a noble cause. Immigrants who couldn't find work banded together to form a society within a society. The organization did business within their "families". Eventually, the organization branched out to protect businesses from rival gangs. At first, the protection was necessary. But, eventually as the organization began excelling in illegal ventures, the *protectors* became the *robbers*.

Roberts feared that if he continued down this road, he would become like them. Someone wanting to move up in the organization had no choice but to become an enforcer. Enforcers were allowed to take whatever they could above Mr. McCain's share. Because of this freedom, they even convinced themselves that it was their right to take money from the people in their territories. Often times, they would beat and rob the merchants until they couldn't even afford to keep their utilities paid.

Lightning flashed, followed by booming thunder. Davey Roberts saw the figure illuminated outside of the front window. Tom Rawlins must have seen the startled look on his face.

"What's wrong with you, boy?" asked Rawlins.

Roberts shook his head. "I thought I saw somethin'."

"Out there?" asked another man. "They'd have to be crazy."

"Those ghost stories have you all shook up, boy," said Rawlins. "They got you seein' things. All that talk is a load of junk."

"That ain't what I heard," replied another. "I talked to George Burt yesterday. He said the guy in the cemetery was a gunfighter… said bullets didn't hurt him."

"George Burt is a coward tryin' to save his own neck," replied Rawlins. "The ghost is a wop assassin, that's it. He ain't invincible. But it's hard to shoot somebody when you're runnin' the other way like Burt did. If Mr. McCain had any sense," he said in a lowered voice, "we'd all be out there huntin' the killer down."

"So why don't we do it," argued another. "Why don't we go out there and find some skinny wop and make him talk. We'd be McCain's right hand guys instead of sittin' in his lobby like paper weights."

A bolt of lightning struck across the street, rattling the lobby windows. The lights flickered and went dark.

Jing-a-ling.

The front entrance opened. Amidst the roaring deluge outside, Roberts heard two hard footsteps on the marble floor, and then the door closed. Davey Roberts felt lost in the shadows of *The Rendezvous*.

The lights buzzed to life, blinding everyone. Roberts scanned the entrance through squinted eyes.

Standing in front of the door was a tall man dressed in black from head to toe. Roberts' eyes followed the water as it streamed down his coat and landed in small puddles at his feet. The man wore black cowboy boots underneath black pinstriped pants. His body was covered in a duster-style coat like the men wore out west. Protruding from underneath the lapel of the duster was a white halo, which resembled the collar a preacher might wear. His face was covered in a hood. Two eyes gleamed from beneath cutouts on each side of his nose.

"Holy…" muttered Tom Rawlins.

Davey Roberts tried to breath, but couldn't. The only thing he could think to do was to push away from the table and reach for his revolver.

Nineteen

John Grady had stood outside of *The Rendezvous* lobby for several minutes. His concentration had been so intense that he had barely noticed the soaking rain as it pelted his body. What was happening to him? One moment he had been determined to enter the lobby and engage McCain's enforcers and the next moment he'd frozen in his tracks. *Why?* This was *it*! This was the moment he'd waited for all of his life. Anders McCain was about to receive payback. He would be punished for his crimes. At last, someone would make McCain understand that he was mortal.

But, John had stopped. He couldn't make himself enter the hotel. After all of these years... the sweat and tears... the miles he'd traveled... the love he'd lost. What had stopped him? What had changed?

Then he'd recognized *who* had caused the hesitation.

Mary.

She was changing him. She was bringing something into his life that he'd not felt in years. Call it what you may... hope... conscience... love... John wanted to be free.

Lightning had flashed, revealing John's reflection in the window of the Rendezvous. He'd seen himself clothed in black like a demon from the pit of hell. What had he become? Was he using evil to fight evil? In the window he'd recognized the white of the clergy collar that he'd chosen to wear on these missions.

Lightning flashed again. He had nearly turned and walked away when he heard the voice of his father's reasoning. *That's right John. Show mercy.*

John's nose wrinkled as a puff of hot breath left his nostrils. He knew this would happen. He knew that if he let her get too close he would lose heart. Of course. God had brought her into his life so that he could trick John into doing it *his* way. But, he was doing it God's way. Anders McCain was an outlaw. He'd hurt and killed many people in his lifetime without any punishment. He deserved to die. *Don't we all? Doesn't death await all of us?*

God was tricking him. He'd almost quit. He'd almost turned around... but he wouldn't. He would go forward.

"If this is the way you want to play it, then you can have her," John muttered into the freezing night. *I don't want her and I don't need you! I've never needed you! I've seen what happens when you have things your way. So, I'll do it my way. I won't be like my father!*

With complete resolve, he had stepped into the street and walked across to *The Rendezvous*.

John knew the lobby like the back of his hand. His informant had given him detailed descriptions of the hotel's physical characteristics and schedules of the employees and guards. There were eight workers inside the lobby at this moment. John had watched them from the darkness across the street. Five were playing poker, two were nodding off on the sofa, and one was asleep at the rear near the elevators.

With each step he took, his anger grew. He could see the men playing poker in their safe haven. He could only imagine the conversations that they were having. What unfortunate person's money were they playing cards with? Who had they robbed or hurt for it? Now, the killers were just throwing it away.

By the time he'd reached the doorway of *The Rendezvous*, burning venom had overtaken his body. He recognized the danger in losing control of his emotions, but he no longer cared.

Then the lightning struck. The bolt hit somewhere across the street and temporarily knocked the power out. Just as he pushed the lobby door open, everything went black.

John was blind. His eyes had been adjusted to the lighted interior of *The Rendezvous*. He froze. Then the lights flickered back to life.

John found himself standing in the foyer of *The Rendezvous* with all eyes upon him. He'd always made it his practice to let his enemy draw first. Shooting out of self-defense seemed to soothe his conscience. This time, however, he found himself standing in the middle of crossfire without any close cover.

He was about to draw when he saw the kid push away from the table and reach for his jacket pocket. People had developed many theories about western gunfighters and how they selected their shooting order in a gunfight; the ridiculous ideas of fat book worms that made their living with pencils. Joe had always taught him to shoot the man who was the biggest threat. So, as the boy fumbled chaotically for his pistol, John calmly drew from under his left arm and shot. Davey Roberts stumbled backward, slumped over the bar then, slipped to the ground.

The enforcers, who weren't stunned, began drawing their own weapons. A few smart ones ran for cover. By now, two other men had their pistols nearly drawn. Adrenaline surged through John's body as he slammed his open palm onto the hammer three times. Two bullets struck Tom Rawlins, dropping him like a statue. He fell onto the edge of the table and flipped it upward. Poker cards and money flew into the air before the table toppled onto its side.

The second man was struck in the forehead, spraying a red mist across the window of *The Rendezvous*. A fourth man dove over the bar, while his comrade leveled a double-barreled shotgun at John. Metal clicked behind him. One of the men from the leisure area cocked the hammer of his weapon. John dropped onto his back just as the man in front of him squeezed off his shotgun. The concussion rumbled past John's face as buck shot flew over him and into the man with the pistol. The enforcer stumbled backwards, toppling an "easy" chair as he landed in it. John drew a second pistol from under his right arm and fired two rounds into the shot gunner before he could cock the second hammer. He quickly popped back onto his feet and hid behind the nearest support column. Bullets sent marble debris scattering into the air.

Five down. Three left.

Two of those had taken cover behind the bar and registration counter. The third man had just fired several shots. One bullet had blown through the collar of John's coat.

John was in a situation that could end in disaster. Two of his opponents were behind cover and another was at least a hundred feet away. He was stuck in the middle of the lobby. With every gunshot, splinters of stone exploded from his narrow hiding place. Whatever his next move was, he had to act before the barrage of lead found its intended target.

John lurched to his right and left the sanctity of his diminishing refuge. He rolled behind the front angle of the bar and into the area where the men had been playing poker, then stepped over the body of Tom Rawlins before slumping against the bar. The hard wood of the bar felt reassuring against his back, and gave him a small measure of safety. He now had cover between himself and the remaining three enforcers. One of them was directly behind him, inside the bar.

John holstered the two short-barreled peacemakers under his arms and drew the two standard pistols from his hips. One of his guns had been empty, while the other was down to half a cylinder. With three men zeroed in on him, a complete twelve rounds would be wise. Half empty pistols had cost many lives.

Time was running out. McCain, snuggled eight stories above in his penthouse, may not have heard the shootout. But, the guests on the floor above had most likely heard it. Before long, the hallways would be flooding with curious people. Flushing out the remaining enforcers, would take too long. John would have to try something else.

From his crunched position in front of the bar, he spoke. "I'm about to stand up and walk to the stairway. Anybody who doesn't want to be killed better get on out of here."

Intimidation could work. Given the opportunity to escape a life and death situation, most men would gladly choose life. A series of quick footsteps echoed from the back of the lobby as somebody fled up the stairway. The shooter at the rear had decided to live. Of course, John knew that he was running to warn someone.

"You, behind me," continued John. "Put your iron on top of the bar and slide it away from you."

Following his voice was the metallic thump of a pistol being laid on the countertop. The weapon slid down the length of the bar and was followed by a shaky voice.

"Please, don't kill me…"

"That's up to you," John replied. "You, across the way! I'm getting up now. If I see you, I'm going to blow your head off. You understand?"

John peeked around the corner and saw two eyes behind the registration desk.

"Yea," replied the man. "I get you."

John knew that what he was about to do was very foolish. He stood to his feet, brandished both pistols in front of him, and started his journey toward the elevators. Neither man made any move as his boots clopped on the stone floor. Two elevators and the stairwell door stood in front of him. Only eight floors away awaited the man he'd wanted to stand before for most of his life. The hotel would now be on high alert.

Getting to Anders McCain would be hard, but not impossible. With fate driving him forward, John Grady stepped into the shadow of the stairwell.

Twenty

Because McCain's Penthouse was on the eighth floor, John Grady felt sure that *he* hadn't heard the shootout. Most likely, the second floor, possibly, the third, would know that something had happened. John wasn't concerned with the levels that housed guests, but with the seventh floor.

Besides containing McCain's business offices, the seventh floor was also the living space for at least twenty of his enforcers. McCain kept the best of his thugs closest to him. John would have to leave the stairwell and navigate through the seventh floor to a separate guarded stairway, which led to McCain's penthouse. He would have to do this without using his pistols. A shot in the stairwell or on the seventh floor would alert McCain and his men for certain.

John had another problem; the rear gunman had run up the stairway ahead of him. He would most likely be running to warn the others. He would have to act quickly, lest his plan be ruined.

Upon rounding the corner of the first floor landing, John felt a sharp pain sting his hip. He reached underneath his coat and shifted the bulky object into a more comfortable position. The grappling hook had always been a cumbersome object to carry. Even though the points weren't that sharp, careless handling of the device would send it digging into your skin.

His surrogate father had given him a grappling hook when he was a boy. Joe, who made his living as a trapper, often went into San Francisco to trade his animal pelts to the wealthy merchants. Upon returning from one trip, he had given the boys, John and his grandson, Wounded Hawk, a grappling hook. Joe had informed them that in past wars sailing ships would use grappling hooks to board the ships of their enemies. The boys became adept at using the hooks to throw rope swings into trees so that they could fly out over their favorite swimming holes. A good grappling hook could also be used for climbing mountains *or scaling high buildings.*

John passed the second floor landing. So far, he hadn't experienced any resistance on the stairs. What had happened to the rear gunner? Had he gotten help?

His original plan had been to take out all of the men in the lobby. But these kinds of things rarely went according to plan. The power outage had changed everything. He'd been caught in crossfire and had to improvise.

John was an excellent gunfighter, but to charge a man over a hundred feet away with no cover was suicide, not to mention the other armed men. *Crazy* didn't win wars.

Joe had always taught him that to win a fight, one had to win the battle of the mind. You had to defeat your opponent before you ever faced him, *in his mind.* That was impossible if you were wounded or killed. But, if you could convince your adversary that you were impossible to defeat, even supernatural, he would already believe he'd been conquered.

In order to do that, John had learned to fight from behind cover, moving from object to object as quickly as possible. Movement gave the warrior a sense of speed and cool headiness. Nothing could be more nerve rattling than fighting someone without fear.

Upon passing the fourth floor, John heard panicky voices in the hallway. There was only one logical reason for guests being awake at this time in the morning; the gunshots had been louder than he'd thought. He would have to expect the worse; McCain may know that he was here. With guests ringing phone lines all over the hotel, navigating the seventh floor would not be easy.

The absence of any sound on the fifth and sixth floors gave John a tinge of hope. He'd been wrong about how far sound would carry in this structure, but only by two floors. *But what about the rear gunner?* The gunner had only been two minutes ahead of him.

As he neared the seventh floor, John reached into his coat and retrieved his bone handle-hunting knife from its stiff leather scabbard. Joe had presented him with the knife after John had killed his first deer. He had made the handle of the knife from the animal's thighbone. John used it often, especially when hand-to-hand combat was necessary.

With his left hand, he produced a tomahawk with an ornate brass blade. The rear of the weapon was composed of a hammer-like bludgeoning tool that slowly tapered into a wide cutting blade at the front. In the body of the blade rested the cutout shape of a bear's paw. Ornate red beads wrapped the shaft downward for the first several inches, eventually giving way to a tanned, leather wrap. He had made the tomahawk himself. The weapon was beautiful *and* deadly.

John froze. *...voices in the hallway...* The men were awake. Light spilled beneath the crack in the doorway. The voices grew closer. John had to act quickly.

If he ran through the door, he would have to make a choice. The hallway ran in both directions. McCain's office and the stairway to the penthouse were to the right. He wasn't sure from which direction the men were coming. The last thing he wanted was to enter the hallway facing the wrong direction and get shot in the back.

They were right on him. It was now or never.

With all of his might, John laid his shoulder into the free-swinging door. The enforcer received a heavy blow to the face as the door flew open. He stumbled across the hallway, crashed into the wall, and rolled to the ground with his face in his hands. Blood already started to flow from his newly broken nose.

John pivoted right to find two more enforcers running toward him. He ducked and spun himself around the first enforcer just as a heavy wooden object whizzed over his head. In a fluid spin, John's knife sliced into the first man's neck and the tomahawk slammed into the second man's head. The second man dropped to the ground before he could fire the sawed-off shotgun. John stepped over the carnage and continued toward his objective at the end of the hallway.

A fourth and fifth enforcer were coming from the direction of McCain's office. One of them produced a large Bowie knife. In the hands of a good fighter, the Bowie knife could be deadly. John was an expert knife fighter.

As he readied himself to face the knifeman, the man with the broken nose grabbed him from behind in a bear hug. Instinctively, John slammed his head back into the man's face, causing him to release his grip and fall to the ground in agony.

The enforcer took his first slash with the knife, missing John completely. His second attempt was a jab. John moved to the side and with a back fisted strike, stabbed the man in his chest.

The sixth enforcer turned and ran towards the end of the hall. John broke into a run after him.

By the time John reached the stairway that led to McCain's penthouse, the enforcer had already made it to the landing and was running for McCain's door. John flung the tomahawk up the stairway. It struck the enforcer in the middle of his back and caused his muscles to tighten. The man fell against the wall and tumbled backward down the stairs. He ceased rolling at John Grady's feet.

Only one more… Just one more life and it'll all be over. I promise.

And, he meant it. John *hated* the killing. Even now his body shivered at the acts he had just committed along the hallway. But, that was the way of justice. The wicked *had* to pay. Those who lived by the gun would die by the gun. These men hadn't been good people. They were the worst of the worst. The men in this hotel were the ones who did the *dirty* jobs. They were murderers.

John looked to the top of the stairs. *Only one flight left. One set of stairs and all of this will end.*

He stepped onto the first stair… then the second. With each step the guilt melted into the recesses of his mind. The foyer grew near. He could see the door and a frosted window that was set into its upper half. A crystal chandelier hung from the ceiling and cast a pale glow about the small room.

John stepped onto the landing and moved toward the door.

Had McCain been warned? Where would he be? John didn't want to shoot the man in his bed. He wanted to *face* McCain. He wanted to look the man in the eyes and tell him who it was that delivered justice.

John grasped the door handle and depressed the thumb lever. It was locked. He'd have to kick it in. At least the noise would get McCain out of bed.

A gunshot rang from behind him and shattered the window of McCain's door. John wheeled around to find the gunner who had run up the stairway. He dropped his cutting weapons and fell to his knees, drawing a pistol. He slammed the hammer of the gun once and struck the enforcer just as he fired a second shot. The man wobbled and fell to the floor.

The element of surprise was gone. McCain would be awake for sure now and probably running for a weapon. *Good... no guilt.*

John prepped, took a step and kicked the door in.

McCain was running down the stairway when the man dressed in black burst into his home. The crash had caught McCain off guard and caused him to stumble down the stairs. His Remington .44 pistol, which had been clutched loosely in his hand, tumbled away from him as he fell face first to the bottom of the stairs. The pistol clopped onto the wooden floor and slid into the foyer of the penthouse. McCain scurried along the floor after his weapon until a sharp boot thrust into his ribs and sent him scrambling back against the banister.

The humility of the moment enraged him nearly as much as the intruder stepping through his doorway. He knew that he would eventually meet his enemy face-to-face, but he had no idea it would be in his own home. What kind of man was this that could get to him in his own hotel?

The dark man pointed a peacemaker at McCain and cocked the hammer. *So... this is how it ends?*

John Grady had kicked McCain so hard, that he'd hurt his ankle. But, he relished in the fact that McCain's pain must have been much worse. The man had cowered against the stairway railing like a boy afraid of the dark. John hoped he would have the guts to make another move for the gun.

After all this time, Anders McCain was sitting in front of him. All John had to do was pull the trigger. One more shot and it was all over. He could go back to Mary and tell her the truth. He could dedicate his life to making a difference. He could face God. *Just one shot will change everything.*

John spoke. "Get your gun."

"You want me to *what*?" replied McCain, enraged.

"I said 'get your gun'," John replied.

"Why? Why don't you just shoot me unarmed, like the coward you are?"

John couldn't believe it. The man had the audacity to call *him* a coward? After all this time and all the suffering, John Grady was the villain?

His free hand groped for the mask and ripped it from his head. Enraged eyes glared at McCain.

"Do you remember me?" asked John.

McCain shook his head with a grimace. "No."

"Too bad," John replied.

The trigger moved beneath his finger. Just as John expected to hear the explosion of a gunshot, a scream erupted from the stairway.

"Don't hurt my daddy!" yelled a small boy as he raced down the stairway.

The child rounded the corner and threw himself onto McCain. Tears streamed down the boy's cheeks. "Please, don't hurt my daddy," sobbed the child as he buried his head into McCain's chest.

A searing pain shot through John's being. He was stricken to the core. *He's a father? He's a father!* McCain had a family? A wife and several other children had gathered at the top of the stairway and were watching in horror.

Emotion bombarded his mind from every conceivable direction—hate, anger, sympathy… all smothering his capacity for logical thought. He could take the shot. He could rip the child away from McCain and finish it. If he didn't, how many people would suffer? How many people would die before anyone else would ever have this opportunity?

The trigger wouldn't move. John fought the urge to scream aloud. Memories of his Pa and his screaming mother flooded his mind. He saw himself clutching his father's lifeless body. How many nights had he spent crying and asking God why he'd taken his Pa? How long had he searched the face of the earth looking for the vengeance that would fill the void in his soul?

The wide eyes of McCain's son reflected the image of a tall dark figure. From within the silhouette, near the neck line, a white halo glowed.   With one shot… just one pull of the trigger…

…and this little boy would become like *him*.

John stumbled backwards and out of the penthouse.

Twenty-one

Wobbly legs carried John Grady as he retrieved his weapons from the landing. A huge part of him felt as if it would rip away from his body and return to the penthouse to finish McCain. What would be left for him? Could he carry on with life? Would he be able to let go? He didn't believe that he possessed the strength to do so. But, John wouldn't knowingly create an orphan. *It wouldn't be the first orphan you've created.*

He rounded the bottom of the stairwell on the seventh floor and stepped over the two wounded enforcers. One still moaned from the tomahawk injury to his back. John turned right and headed for McCain's office.

Raised voices came from behind doorways in the hall. McCain's men were awake now and were beginning to come out of their rooms. John would have to switch to his less preferred escape plan.

He hooked a left down a large hallway that contained offices on both sides. At the end of the corridor were a receptionist's desk and two large wooden doors leading to McCain's office.

McCain's office would offer the best route of escape for the plan that John had in mind. The men would be heading for McCain's penthouse. After realizing that John wasn't there, they would have to perform a search, which would buy him precious minutes.

He pulled apart the hefty oak doors and entered the darkened office. While crossing the room toward the large bay windows, John reached into the inner pocket of his coat and produced a small package. In his hand lay two sticks of dynamite topped with a rudimentary timing device of John's design. He placed the explosives on a ledge midway up a wall that separated two of the large windows. He estimated a fairly safe fuse time and twisted the spring-loaded dial. In about sixty seconds, the slow rotating dial would strike a piece of flint and ignite a one second fuse that ran directly into the dynamite. John had toyed with the idea while working in the mines, but hadn't developed it until it was needed for a *different* line of work.

He ran back to the office doors, preparing to use them as a shield during the eminent explosion.

Upon opening the doors, John was hit with the hardest punch he'd ever taken. Before the impact, he managed to catch a glimpse of an iron-covered fist as it flew toward his face. The hit knocked him senseless. John stumbled backward into the office, dazed and wobbling. A thought immediately crossed his mind. *How much time?*

Nick "The Fist" Rocci charged in as John attempted to throw a punch of his own. The swing went wild; Rocci ducked and smote John in the ribs with his gloved hand. Bones cracked. John bowled over in pain. Nick Rocci followed with a punch to John's face. His jaw went numb and blackness began to overtake him.

John pulled his knife and slashed at the Italian, slicing a gash across Rocci's thigh. He knew that time was running out. He had less than thirty seconds until the explosion.

Nick came at John again. The man wasn't afraid of John's blade. This wasn't the first knife fight the muscular Italian had ever been in. John wasn't accustomed to fighting opponents who were without fear.

He attempted to square off with Rocci, but in his dazed state, he was no match for the two fast jabs that weakened his knees. As John reached for his tomahawk, the final punch caught him in the gut and sent him to the floor. Nick grabbed John and flung him across the room into a large writing table, which toppled over.

John fought the urge to lie down and succumb to the darkness that was overtaking his mind. Speckles of a hundred colors danced in the air around him. *How much time?* John propped himself onto his elbow and looked over the toppled table before him.

Nick grinned at the prospect of what he would do to the man who was clad in dark clothing. But underneath his mask, John had a smile of his own. He ducked behind the table and braced himself just as the bomb exploded. Nick Rocci was blown backward as the room swarmed with wood, brick, and glass. Rocci hit the carpet face first and slid toward the front of the office.

When John lifted his head, the room was a foggy mess. The scent of smoke and dust hung in the air. A large hole appeared in the back of McCain's office. His desk and furniture had been blown into other parts of the room.

John's escape route had been created; seven stories lay between the office and freedom.

Though the pain was excruciating, John used the table to drag himself onto his feet. Bones ground in his rib cage.

Nick Rocci was a bloody mess that lay on the floor. His clothing had been torn away from his back, revealing huge lacerations. He moaned as blood dripped from his mouth and seeped into the dust-covered carpet.

John stepped over him and stumbled toward his newly formed exit. His short respite was interrupted by the sound of excited voices approaching from the hall. McCain's men were coming. There was no hiding the assault now. The whole city would know that Anders McCain had been attacked. Many would rejoice, but some would be angry. John knew that McCain would strike back.

In his weakened state, John had to be careful as he leaned through the open wall. The rain had ceased and Broadway lay shimmering in the night nearly a hundred feet below— ninety-two feet to be more precise.

John hadn't settled upon his next idea without tedious study. After receiving details about *The Rendezvous* from his informant, he'd come to Manhattan himself and walked the street. He'd calculated the heights of the hotel and its surrounding buildings.

Above the twenty-foot high lobby, *The Rendezvous'* floors were twelve feet tall. The building next to McCain's hotel was two stories higher than the floor where he was currently trapped. On the other side of that building, was his escape route. The smaller structure was two stories shorter than the floor from which John would swing. So, if he estimated the length of the rope correctly, he could swing out from *The Rendezvous,* around the taller building, and after losing momentum, end up ten feet or so above the rooftop of the shorter building.

John had made swings of that distance before when he swam in rock quarries as a boy. Of course, the quarries were filled with water and he was purposefully jumping into them. No matter, the dynamics of this swing would be the same.

John pulled the rope and the three-pronged grappling hook from the leather strap on his belt. He leaned over the edge and took aim midway down the neighboring building's rooftop. The hook started twirling in the air as John executed his lassoing technique. He'd used the skill many times to catch cattle and had adapted it to use with the grappling hook.

But, the hook missed its intended target and clanked against the edge of the building before swinging back toward John. He quickly pulled the rope in and coiled it into a circle for another chance. He would have to get it right this time, because the men were about to reach the office.

Whoop... whoop... whoop... The hook zipped by his ear. He released and the projectile flew through the sky, this time flying over the edge of the recessed rooftop.

The enforcers were nearing the door; they would break through at any moment. John reached into his coat and produced another bomb. He twisted the timer for what he thought would be twenty seconds and tossed it toward the center of the room.

This was the tricky part. He had to make the hook catch onto the roof's ledge or it was useless. His heart beat almost painfully. *Easy... easy...*

The rope became tight as the hook caught something solid. He tugged twice to test its perch. The doors burst open. John jumped, leaving solid ground and swinging into the night air. Wind rushed by his face as all else faded away.

Inside *The Rendezvous*, the men opened fire with their Bergman submachine guns. John arced away from the hotel and swung over Broadway. A deadly barrage of bullets whizzed by him, and struck the buildings across the street. The weapons fired at blinding speeds.

As his swing reached its greatest distance from the building, John felt centrifugal force ripping at his limbs. His hands began to slip down the rope and a sharp pain blew through his thigh. He hadn't recognized what caused the pain at first. The bullet's impact felt like a punch from the stocky man's iron glove. The agony only made him hold on tighter.

As John neared the shorter building, his position changed so that it paralleled the position of his shooters. Bullets ricocheted off of the building his rope was attached to and blew bits of stone and glass into the cold air. Fire blazed forth from the barrels of the small guns as they released their onslaught of lead.

Orange light illuminated *The Rendezvous*. The interior of McCain's office exploded in a swathe of smoke. Chunks of mortar fell toward the street below. The timer had struck its flint. The last thing John saw as he swung around the taller building were two bodies falling to the pavement below the hotel.

Now that John was over the shorter building's rooftop, he needed to let go of the rope. But, he couldn't. It was caught in an iron grip. The rope hit the corner of the taller building, which shortened its length drastically. For the last second of his swing, John's speed increased. He slammed into the side of the taller building with a bone-crushing thud and fell ten feet to the rooftop below.

As he lay in the pea gravel, rain started to fall again. He hurt in so many places that he could no longer distinguish which parts were causing the pain. A numbing sensation spread its way along his body and crept into his head. Water poured from the sky, creating a channel of blood that ran towards the rooftop gutters. John watched the crimson stream, but couldn't comprehend that it was his own. Nothing mattered in this moment. McCain's home was in ruins. Many of his men were dead or out of commission. It would take weeks before he regrouped enough to seek retaliation. For now, John was safe.

And with that thought, he closed his eyes and allowed sweet darkness to overtake him.

Twenty-two

Tim O'Hare fumbled in the dark for the light switch. With a click, the hallway was bathed in a quaint amber glow. Outside the church, the rain continued to fall. Even from the living quarters down in the basement, Tim had been able to hear the pounding thunder. The storm had raged all night long, drowning the city with its ice cold water. Despite being a quarter past six in the morning, darkness still clung to the sky just beyond the back door's window. Tim couldn't imagine who would be knocking so fervently at this time of the morning.

He'd awoken at six o'clock, as was his usual custom. His mornings began with prayer and meditation. Within a few minutes, the knocking had broken the silence. He had returned to his praying, trying to ignore it. *What if someone needs help? What if a poor soul has been stuck outside in that freezing rain?*

If there was one thing that Tim had learned about God, it was that if you wanted to speak with him, you'd better listen when he spoke back. *Yes, Lord,* he'd conceded.

Tim had risen from his knees and shuffled toward the rear of the church. As he'd passed by the kitchen, he'd noticed that Mary was already awake and busy making breakfast.

"Good mornin', sweetheart," greeted Tim.

"Mornin', Reverend," she'd smiled back. "Sounds like this is goin' to be a busy day, already. Should I make some extra breakfast?"

"You might as well, just to be safe," he'd replied.

Moments later, he stood before the door peeping through a small viewing window. In the alleyway, sputtered a black car covered in minute bursts of falling raindrops. A man clothed in a heavy gray coat and wide brimmed hat stood under the covered door stoop only a few feet away.

"How can I help you?" Tim asked through the closed door.

The man addressed Tim through the window. "My name is Father Whittier. I have someone in my car. He asked me to bring him *here*."

Tim cracked the door to better hear the man. He looked to be in his forties and was a man of small stature.

"I tried to take him to a hospital," Father Whittier continued, "but he was adamant that I bring him to you. Please, hurry. He's hurt badly... could be dying."

Tim followed the man as he stepped into the street towards his car. Freezing droplets of ice water ran down his neck and under his shirt, causing him to gasp. Father Whittier opened the car's rear door to reveal a dark shape lying across the seat. The *thing* seemed without form. As Tim leaned into the cabin, he recognized the pungent odor of gunpowder. He placed his hand on the seat and tried to get a better look at the man. Upon feeling a sticky substance, he raised his hand into the twilight. A grim realization dawned upon Tim. *Blood...*

Then, the man moaned Tim's name.

"Mary!" screamed Tim.

Tim and Father Whittier dragged the heavy man through the corridor and into the kitchen where Mary awaited. "We need sterile water and bandages."

Mary gasped. "John."

"Mary," repeated Tim. "Get busy, girl!"

The two men laid John onto the long dining table. His face had been mauled. Blood leaked from his nose and his mouth. One of his eyes had swollen shut while the other had been split along the eyebrow. Shivering convulsions racked his body and caused blood to trickle from a hole in his pants.

Tim stood aghast. "Good, Lord."

"He wandered into my church about an hour ago," said Father Whittier. "I have no idea what he was doing in downtown Manhattan at this time of morning."

"We have to get these wet clothes off of him," whispered Tim. "Help me take his coat off, Father."

"I thought he'd been shot and robbed," continued Father Whittier. "But, then I found these." He strained to pull a heavy knapsack from his shoulder and handed it to Tim. Tim opened the cover to find a wad of gun belts and revolvers. There was also a bone handled knife and an exquisite tomahawk. Both were stained with blood.

Father Whittier continued the removal of John's clothing. Underneath the black shirt, lay a body covered in scars. Ancient bullet wounds and gashes riddled the man's torso.

"I don't know what all of this means," Father Whittier whispered, perplexed at what he saw. "Is he a pastor here?"

Tim put the satchel onto the ground and resumed his work. "Yes. He's my assistant. And, I have no idea what he was doing in Manhattan or why he has these... weapons."

But, deep down, Tim did know the reason. Hadn't he feared this? He'd recognized the signs that John had been exhibiting. He'd known the possibilities when he'd requested that John join his ministry. Tim had thought that he could keep an eye on John if he were closer to him... that he could guide the young pastor in the right direction. He'd been wrong.

Mary returned with a pot of hot water and an arm full of dishtowels. She placed the container on the table and began shredding the rags into smaller pieces. The men had taken John's shirt off and were working on the buttons of his trousers.

"Mary, you'll have to leave," said Tim.

"You of all people know he wouldn't be the first naked man I've ever seen, Reverend," she replied, resolutely. Father Whittier blushed.

"Do what you must," replied Tim. "Once you've cut those bandages, go to my room and fetch the leather bag from under my bed."

By the time Mary returned with the bag, John lay naked on the table. A large bruise spread across the ribs of his muscular torso. And, on his right thigh, a small gunshot wound oozed blood.

"Give me the bag, lass," commanded Tim.

"He needs a doctor," replied Mary.

"I said give me the bag, Mary!"

She handed him the bag, which he sat on the table next to John. After opening it, he produced a surgical scalpel and a pair of scissor retractors. He placed the blade of the scalpel just above the gunshot wound.

"What are you doing?" asked Mary with concern.

"Don't worry. This isn't the first bullet I've had to remove."

The scalpel sank into John's flesh.

Twenty-three

Flooded roads and gray skies remained in the wake of the winter rain storm. Wounded Hawk watched the police and medical workers pour into and out of *The Rendezvous* from the alleyway across the street. Onlookers lined the sidewalk, gawking at the large hole in the building. The covered gangway had been torn to the ground by falling debris. Two blanketed corpses lay amidst the rubble at the base of the hotel. Several other uncovered bodies were visible through the windows. In the lobby, Wounded Hawk could see three dead men lying in front of the bar. Tables and chairs had been overturned and a marble column had been shot to pieces. The preacher had struck McCain. And though he had failed at killing the man himself, it had been a mighty blow.

Wounded Hawk watched McCain talk to a policeman as he paced through the lobby. He knew that McCain would want revenge and assumed he would attempt it in a clumsy fashion. But, Wounded Hawk also understood that the preacher wasn't finished with McCain. Wounded Hawk, more than anyone, understood the consequences of a blood debt. The preacher would make another attempt on McCain's life. And, Wounded Hawk would be there *with* or *without* McCain's approval.

Inside *The Rendezvous*, McCain looked around at the disheveled lobby. Bullet holes splintered the bar. Two bay windows would have to be replaced. The marble column alone would cost thousands to repair. The damage in the lobby, however, was minor compared to that of the seventh floor. The explosion had compromised the structural integrity of the floors above and below. McCain didn't care to guess the cost of those repairs.

Upon finishing his conversation with one of his officers, Captain Douglas Adams approached McCain. "We haven't found any eyewitnesses yet, Mr. McCain., though many people *heard* the shootout."

"No," replied McCain. "I didn't suppose there would be many at two-thirty in the morning." McCain kicked a chunk of marble down the aisle of the lobby. "I want him found, Douglas."

"I know you do. People in the neighborhood claim to have heard rapid gunfire. The witnesses' descriptions made it sound like the shooters used automatic rifles... *military weapons*. Those kinds of guns would be illegal, considering they would have to be bought from foreign sources and snuck through customs. This could be a tricky investigation."

"How's that?"

"The real question is this—how *deep* do you want us to look?" Adams surveyed the front of the lobby. "Henderson," called Adams, addressing the officer whom he had spoken with, "take a break."

"I'm fine, captain," replied Officer Henderson.

"Grab some coffee, will you," commanded Adams.

"Right away, sir," said Henderson as he made his way outside toward the caravan of vehicles.

"Mr. McCain," started Adams, "there's no hidin' what happened here. A bomb exploded in mid-Manhattan. There are dead men all over your hotel. In the past, I've managed to keep things pretty quiet for you. But, this…" he said, swinging his hand over the lobby. "Men higher up than I am are goin' to look into what happened here. My hands will be tied… I'm not the Pope. If the Italians hit you…"

"This had nothing to do with Masseria," interrupted McCain. "This is the work of one man."

"One man… You really believe all this nonsense on the street? You mean the ghost?"

"He's no ghost. He's flesh and blood… and we hurt him. My man, Nick, roughed him up pretty good."

"Perhaps, he's a hired assassin who's working for the Italians," Adams countered. "It would make sense. Everyone knows that Joe the Boss has it in for you."

"No. It's personal."

"How can you be sure?"

McCain turned to look Adams in the eyes. "Because he walked into my home. He could have tried to kill me anywhere. The man wanted to see the fear in my eyes! He wanted me to know that *he* was in control… that he'd plotted every move… that he'd won the game." *He did exactly what*

I would have done. "Then he took off his mask and asked if I remembered him."

"Did you?"

"No. There are many men who would like to kill me." McCain struggled with his next sentence. He trusted no one in this world other than Nick and himself. But, if Captain Adams were going to be of any help, he'd have to be forthright with the man. Besides, Adams knew that McCain wasn't a saint. "I *may* have killed his father."

"How could you know that?"

"A man visited me… an Indian. His name was Wounded… *something*. He said that I had a blood debt on my head. He was crazy, but I think he was telling the truth. Anyway, I didn't believe him… then, this *assassin* shows up in my home."

"What did the assassin look like?"

"Tall… thin… dark hair…" recalled McCain. "He was in shadow, silhouetted from the light in the hallway. His eyes seemed… transparent."

"That's not much for me to go on," replied Adams.

"What can you do?"

"I could start a personal investigation and do the work myself."

"A lot of good that's done so far. Why can't you do more?" asked McCain. "Can a man walk into another man's home in this city, destroy it, kill his employees and not be investigated?"

"I thought that's the reason you liked living in this city, Mr. McCain."

McCain took a step towards Adams and looked him square in the eye. "Listen, you little piss ant… I may be caught in a delicate situation here, but don't forget *who* I am.

175

I know that people think I've grown weak, but they're mistaken. Nothing has changed." He stepped away from Captain Adams for a moment and bit his lip.

"Is your wife still enjoying your new apartment, Douglas?"

"Yes," replied Captain Adams. "We're very grateful."

"Good. Don't forget who pays the bills. Without me, you'd live like a *cop.*"

"All I'm trying to say," Adams continued carefully, "is that an investigation into your hotel could open up doors that you don't want opened. And, I would be powerless to do anything."

"What's your suggestion?"

"We come up with a simple story... one with an *explanation*. Then, the police wouldn't have to dig up any old skeletons. Perhaps, a disgruntled employee shot up his coworkers and tried to kill his boss. He blew up your office and in the process was killed himself."

"Yes," said McCain, starting to think. "He's lying out there in the street right now. The poor fellow was blown out of the building."

Adams escorted McCain past the dead men in the poker area and outside to a covered body.

"Is this him? Is this the man who tried to kill you, Mr. McCain?" asked Adams, as he pulled the blanket from the man's face.

"Yes," replied McCain. Every bone in his body shuddered at the thought of hiding his "would be" assassin's crime. He would make the ghost pay. "That's the man who tried to kill me."

"Well then, this *will* be a simple investigation, after all. I'll look more closely into the other matter, myself."

176

McCain turned and walked toward the elevators. Edwina and the children were understandably upset. He would have to find another home immediately. The location would have to be safe... a place that he could keep heavily armed... a place where questions wouldn't be asked.

"Mr. McCain," called James Adams.

"Yes?" he replied turning around.

"This *man*... he knew your hotel *too* well. You may have a traitor in your midst."

"Yes," McCain said, affirming Adams' suggestion. "I've considered that." And he had a good idea *who* the traitor was.

"Happy hunting, Mr. McCain."

Twenty-four

John Grady soared through the dark Manhattan sky. Stinging wind pummeled him from every direction. His arc seemed to slow at its pinnacle, and suspend hundreds of feet above the hungry concrete of Broadway. His body weight had grown to that of a freight train and caused his fingers to slip down the rope. As he finally rounded the apex of his swing, the grappling hook popped loose from the edge of the rooftop. John flailed into space and grasped furiously for some handhold but found none. His body spiraled downward, out of control. The hundred-foot fall stretched into thousands of feet. Eventually, his hurting body and the hard pavement of Broadway met in a deadly embrace. Blackness consumed his vision and he waited to meet God. What would he say to him? How would he explain his destructive quest of righteous vengeance?

But, nothing happened. Is this it? Is this all there is?

Then, the laughing began. It echoed through the canyon of buildings and reverberated down the alleyways. Victory was his! Anders McCain had won... again. John attempted to raise his broken body from the sidewalk but found it impossible. Struggling against some invisible force, he turned his head and looked upward to the hole on the seventh floor of The Rendezvous. From the depths of the hotel stood a man with a pistol tied to his thigh. His mocking laughter shook the very foundation of the earth. Upon his head rested the cursed white derby.

Then, from the corner of his eye, the gleaming barrel of a pistol moved toward his temple. Straining, he forced his eye to adjust focus and follow the arm. Upon the man's shoulder rested a wretched face. A pearlescent eye bore through him from behind a hardened leather mask. The gunshot resounded, forcing John toward semi-consciousness.

Heavy eyelids struggled to open, leaving him unable to distinguish dream from reality. One moment he believed himself to be awake, the next he would slip back into a state of confusing images. An immeasurable weight pressed down upon him. During a brief surfacing from his groggy prison, John had seen an angel at the foot of his bed. She had been clothed in a flowing white robe. Golden hair careened down her shoulders and spread onto her chest. She'd spoken words so soft that John had not understood them, though the timbre of her voice had lulled him back to sleep. The vision had been the most glorious thing he'd ever seen. He tossed and turned, struggling to stay awake. How long had he been like this?

After uncountable cycles of agonizing repetition, he finally awoke, tired and confused. Lava boiled to the surface of his thigh, ready to erupt at any moment. The throbbing was ceaseless, and locked his muscle in place, making his leg immovable. His jaw was swollen and clicked when he tried to open his mouth. Dried blood caked the inside of his nostrils and forced him to breathe through his lips.

He took a deep breath and nearly gasped as a piercing ache shot through his chest. Ribs ground as he slowly relaxed his muscles and allowed the air to leave his lungs. What in God's name had he done to himself?

The blur around him began to resemble the image of his living quarters. A kerosene lamp lit the room, providing a comforting measure of light. Only a narrow slit was manageable between the lids of his right eye. He slowly reached a weak hand to his face and felt the monstrosity. *My God.* Stitches dotted his eyebrow where they closed a large gash that had been opened by the stocky man's glove. *The iron fist...* Memories of the fight began to come back.

He'd escaped *The Rendezvous*. McCain's organization had been hit hard, but John had let McCain live. A low groan left his lips, accompanied by flying beads of saliva. McCain had a son. He hadn't been able to kill him in front of his son.

"John," whispered a soft voice.

The voice was familiar, but he couldn't quite place it. *The angel.* But it wasn't an angel at all; the voice belonged to Mary.

"You're awake," she said while moving to his bedside. "Thank God."

John attempted to speak, but only managed a syllable ridden mumble.

"Don't try and talk. Your jaw is swollen badly." She placed her hand on his and gave it a delicate squeeze. "Are you thirsty?"

He squeezed her hand in response.

On the bedside table was a pitcher of water and a metal tube about six inches in length. She dipped the tube into the container and placed her finger over the opening. She placed the open end of the pipe into the corner of John's mouth and released her finger. Cool, refreshing water spread onto his parched tongue. The liquid tasted like relief from the heavens.

She repeated the process several times. "I've been givin' you water like this for three days."

Three days.

"You've been runnin' a high fever for the last couple of days. The wound on your thigh got infected. Reverend O'Hare removed the bullet and stitched you up, but we finally had to call a doctor. We told him that you'd been beaten and robbed. He gave you penicillin just yesterday evenin'. We were very worried for a time... thought you might die."

John felt like he had died. Even now, he could barely stay awake.

"You need more rest," she continued. "Tomorrow mornin', I'll make some chicken broth for you. Before you know it, you'll be back on your feet."

John gave her hand a gentle squeeze. Like a child, he fought sleep for fear that he would miss something important... afraid Mary wouldn't be there when he awoke.

"Don't worry, John," she soothed as if reading his mind. "I'll be right here. I've been sleepin' on a cot just beside your bed. Rest."

And with her reassurance, he relaxed and let sleep enfold his battered body.

Twenty-five

Ronald Thompson stood on the sidewalk in front of First National Bank after making his daily deposit. Steam drifted from under the curbside. Manhattan was bustling with activity on this cold, gloomy morning. The wide street was packed with automobiles puttering their ways north and south along the boulevard. A horse drawn wagon crossed the intersection headed to a construction sight somewhere in the distance. Throngs of people moved along the edges of the street, creating a crowded river of living bodies. One who was careless could find himself swept away in the current of American dreamers as they stopped at shops to gaze through the windows or at a restaurant to have a cup of coffee.

"Extra, extra…" called a boy who sat on top of a three foot tall stack of newspapers. "Explosion in Manhattan found to be result of embittered employee. Read about it, now!"

Thompson didn't know how McCain had pulled it off. The man was in control even when things were out of control. He'd managed to create a "dummy" trail in order to keep authorities from looking too closely at his business ventures. Of course, authorities were already onto him. But with some well-conceived paper trails, *provided by yours truly*, McCain would be safe for a while longer. It didn't hurt that half the police force was on the organization's payroll, including the "higher ups". Thompson tilted his head backward and breathed in the frigid air of winter. He nearly gagged as the cold draft struck the back of his throat, and he released a disgusting cough in response to the irritation.

All along the length of this bustling avenue known as Broadway, massive buildings scraped the sky. New York was the center of the American industrial revolution. Civilization was changing. Technology was making the world a better place, in which an enterprising man could make a fortune. The old world of sweat and tears was rapidly being replaced by a world of speed and opportunity. *Except for him...*

The man in black, the ghost, didn't belong. In the midst of this fresh world entered a man who refused to relinquish the principles of an extinct era. He brandished a style of frontier justice, and a black and white ideal of right and wrong. Ronald Thompson had grown up reading the picture books about Billy the Kid and Wyatt Earp, but who could have imagined... gunfighter... The concept belonged in a dime novel. Ridiculous or not, Thompson was caught in the middle of a strange and dangerous fairy tale.

McCain's organization had been hit hard in recent months and cash flow was at a minimum. Thompson didn't know how to tell him, but something drastic would have to happen. Thompson was not naive. He realized what that *something* would be. McCain had his ways of making money. Among his trades were supplying booze to independent distributors and clubs, cornering fruit markets, and smuggling illegal goods. He also had his hands in gambling in other parts of the country, and, of course, there was his neighborhood "insurance policy." His insurance racket had grown to cover the majority of Brooklyn and parts of Queens. Ronald Thompson had been paying policemen to overlook the "questionable" business.

McCain's reach, however, stretched much farther than the confines of New York City. He controlled a large chunk of the liquor distribution all over America, especially into the west. New Orleans was the distribution center for many of his products, legal and illegal. From there, his gunboats could run products to any port on the Mississippi River. And if there were a dry county anywhere close, McCain was bootlegging liquor there.

Despite his many sources of income, the insurance scam was the starting point of McCain's recovery plan. He needed capital *now*.

In recent weeks, enforcers had been reporting a surge in the number of businessmen who offered resistance during collection visits. And in the three days since the attack at *The Rendezvous*, people had become very brave. Perhaps, they believed that McCain's power was dwindling. The people were finding hope in the midst of the ghost's attacks. But, before long, McCain would ensure that their hope was crushed.

In a way, Thompson hoped that McCain's power *was* diminishing. Ronald Thompson didn't consider himself a "bad" man. *Though, I may work for one.* Terrorizing innocent people didn't make him feel good about himself, *but the money isn't bad.* And, that's what life came down to. In the end, it was survival.

Thompson had spent his entire life trying to live the "American dream". That's why he went to college. That's the reason he'd studied so hard. But, somewhere along the way, he'd gotten lost. He'd developed a conscience. So, he decided to work for the city government, thinking that he could make a difference. One day, he realized he couldn't.

He had been researching *strange* transactions that continually led back to city officials. When he'd brought the problem to his superiors, he was told to leave it alone. Weeks later, he was even demoted. After that instance, he decided to stop fighting the system and to make it work for him as well. But, when the "little fish" gets caught, it always gets thrown back into the water. So, Thompson was fired.

Boohoo... He'd never had it so good. Now, he was wealthier than any of the men he'd ever worked for. *And, I'd love to rub it in their faces.*

So, what did it matter *who* got hurt? As long as he didn't know, there was no reason to fret.

Ronald was about to cross the street when a royal blue Cadillac pulled up in front of him. His stomach dropped when he recognized the white-walled tires. Anders McCain was seated in the back.

"Mr. Thompson," greeted McCain.

"Mr. McCain," replied Thompson, taken off guard. "To what do I owe this unexpected pleasure?"

"Oh, I was in the neighborhood and thought maybe I could give you a lift back to the hotel."

"Thank you. But, I... had a few more errands to run."

"I'm sure they can wait. Besides, I think it's going to snow," said McCain as he pointed to the dark gray sky above.

"I suppose a ride would be all right."

"Of course it would. This would be the perfect opportunity for you to inform me about our financial situation."

McCain opened the back door and slid across to the opposite side. Thompson climbed inside and sat his briefcase on the floorboard as the Cadillac pulled away from the curb.

"So... Mr. Thompson. How are things? How bad off are we?"

"Well... as far as physical cash flow... we're low," he replied. "The organization *can* recover... within a 'thin' year or two."

"We'll do what we must," McCain replied. "Do you think the two incidents were related?"

"I'm sorry?"

"What happened in New Orleans with the river boats?"

"I'm afraid I wouldn't know that."

"Mmm... I thought you might. We've always attributed it to pirates. Pirates sink ships all the time... rival operations... I don't know. Now I question everything... *everyone...*"

Thompson didn't like the direction the conversation was headed. A wave of heat flushed into his cheeks. He stuck a finger in his collar and pulled it away from his neck. The draft felt good on his chest.

"Are you all right, Mr. Thompson?"

"Of course. It's just a little stuffy in here."

McCain spun the crank-handle, cracking his window about an inch. "Better?" he asked.

"Thank you," replied Thompson.

McCain turned and placed his fist under his chin as if he was pondering some great mystery. Thompson had heard that he had once been an enforcer out west. Apparently, he'd worked for Ignacio Saietta as an enforcer at the front of his bootlegging operations. Rumor had it that McCain had been one of the deadliest operators Saietta had working for him. McCain had supposedly become an accomplished gunfighter.

Looking at McCain now, the stories were hard to believe. He was a graying, middle-aged man. Deep folds ran from his nose to the corners of his mouth. Heavy eyelids sagged low, nearly obscuring his deep blue eyes.

Thompson turned and gazed out of his own window. The mammoth buildings of Broadway began to morph into the more delicate shapes of houses and neighborhoods. He'd been so preoccupied with McCain that Thompson hadn't noticed the change in locations. Where were they? How many turns had they taken? The surroundings looked familiar, but Thompson couldn't quite place them.

"I need your help with something," said McCain, breaking his thoughts.

"Of course," Thompson replied.

"We have a traitor in our midst."

"Why would you say *that?*"

"This... ghost... he knows too much. He's been on our heels every step of the way. He knew the layout of *The Rendezvous*. We have to find this *worm.*"

"Yes, of course we do." A bead of sweat trickled down Ronald Thompson's cheek. He hoped that McCain hadn't noticed.

Ronald looked out of the window again, searching for any excuse to escape McCain's gaze. A realization dawned on him. Now, he knew why his surroundings looked so familiar. They were driving in *his* neighborhood. The car turned onto a side street that was bordered by rows of connected townhouses. McCain was taking Thompson home. *But, why?*

The Cadillac pulled to a stop in front of a burgundy-bricked house with a red door. Black, wrought iron banisters extended the length of the short stairway up to the landing. A brass doorknocker adorned the entrance to the narrow, three-story home.

"I'm confused," said Thompson. "What are we doing here?"

McCain leaned over Thompson and opened his door.

"We're here to catch a traitor," McCain replied, motioning for Thompson to exit the vehicle. "After you."

A red oriental rug welcomed the men as they entered the house. Honey colored wood paneling covered the floor from the foyer into the living room. A banister of the same tint ran up the staircase in the back of the house.

"Mr. McCain. I'm afraid I don't know anymore about this traitor business," stammered Thompson. "But I'll do anything I can to help you find more information…"

Thompson turned the corner into his living room and suddenly lost his train of thought. Seated, in his smoking chair, was Nick Rocci. The man looked horrible. His face was stitched all over and he was forced to sit upright in the chair. Thompson had heard that the man's back looked like it had been carved in a butcher's shop.

As Thompson rounded the high-backed sofa, he was overcome with nausea. There, seated side by side, was his wife, son, and daughter. A sickening hollowness radiated from the pit of his stomach.

"Mr. Rocci," stuttered Thompson. "It's good to see that you're in such health. I thought it would take longer to recover since the accident happened only three days ago."

"Aren't you interested in your family, Mr. Thompson?" asked McCain. "Why don't you say 'hello' to them?"

Thompson's breath was coming in short, shallow gasps. A hot stream of urine began to spread down the length of his pants leg until it trickled from the bottom and onto the designer carpet. Disgusted, Nick Rocci slowly shook his head.

"Ronald," whimpered Mrs. Thompson. Her face was red and swollen from crying. His son and daughter sat farther back into the sofa as if they were trying to blend themselves into the fabric and disappear.

"Mr. Rocci," said McCain, motioning his head toward Mrs. Thompson.

The muscular Italian stood to his feet, fighting a noticeable grimace then walked over to Mrs. Thompson and took her hand.

"Stand up dear," reassured McCain. "It's all right. Go ahead and stand up."

When Mrs. Thompson stood up, Nick swung her around by the arm and flung her into the wall. Before she could fall, he grabbed her by the nape of her neck and pushed her back into the sofa where her children screamed. Dazed, she began to sob.

Ronald Thompson lunged for her, but was stopped by a punch to the gut. Nick followed through with a backhanded slap that drove Thompson to the ground.

"Be careful with his face," said McCain, reacting. McCain squatted down until he was eye level with Thompson. "Mr. Thompson," he chided, "haven't I been fair to you? I've been honest every step of the way. I told you what you were getting into and you still *chose* to work for me. I trusted you… and you've broken that trust."

"But, Mr. McCain," whimpered Thompson. "I haven't done anything…"

His words were cut off by a humiliating slap across his face. The coppery taste of blood seeped from his fleshy cheek and onto his tongue. McCain grabbed Thompson by the collar and pulled his face close to his own.

"I *trusted* you," spat McCain, hammering every word. "Don't play stupid with me." He looked at Nick and made another motion toward Mrs. Thompson. Nick backhanded her so hard that spittle flew from her mouth. Thompson made a move only to be stopped by McCain's elbow as it jammed into his back. McCain sat on Thompson, placed both hands under his chin, and pulled his head toward his back.

"I should kill you right now," grunted McCain. "But unfortunately, I need you."

Thompson's head thumped on the floor as McCain released his grip. He leaned over and spoke into Thompson's ear. "Do you understand why it's so hard for me to trust anyone? Why did you betray me?"

"I didn't," cried Thompson. "You have to believe me!"

This time Nick slapped Mrs. Thompson with an open hand that knocked the woman off of the sofa and onto the floor. Her children screamed. Thompson's daughter pulled her knees into a fetal position. Mrs. Thompson stood and tried to run away, but was too dazed. She stumbled over the coffee table and fell face first onto the rug. Nick picked her up by her gown and carried her back to the sofa. Ronald Thompson cried.

"I don't think you understand," explained McCain. "I'm not asking you *if* you betrayed me. I already know that you *did*. So, let's cut the bull and you can save your wife's face! I want to know *why* you did it!"

"I hope you're not surprised," McCain exclaimed. "The man in black asked George Burt for your name and George gave it to him. You do remember George Burt don't you? He was the foreman that survived the cemetery shootout. Well, he ratted you out just before I blew his head off!"

Ronald Thompson managed to speak between fits of sobbing. "I'm sorry Mr. McCain... He came to my house in the night... he threatened to kill me if I didn't give him information."

"What kind of information?" probed McCain.

"Things like... the kind of businesses you ran... where they were located... He had a lot of questions about our operations out West. He wanted to know the layout of the Rendezvous...

"Who is this man?"

"I don't know... You have to believe me! He always wears a mask and the collar of a preacher."

"A preacher?" pondered McCain. McCain had killed many men in his lifetime. Separating the faces would prove impossible, but a preacher would stand out. And, he remembered the man. He'd been working for Ignacio Saietta out west. Some peon had found religion and spilled

191

his guts about *private* matters. McCain and his mentor had been sent to some small town to deal with the situation. They'd been forced to kill the snitch *and* the preacher to whom he'd confessed his sins. McCain had bragged about the shooting many times. That particular killing had made his reputation grow unimaginably. Anders McCain was the "preacher killer". He feared no one, not even God.

A picture began to develop from the hazy images of time. *The preacher had a son. He'd witnessed the killing. The Indian said that I killed his father!*

"I had no other choice," exclaimed Thompson, breaking McCain's thoughts. "He would have killed me! You've seen what he's willing to do."

McCain stood up. "No... It's my fault... and I'm sorry. I've never shown you what *I'm* capable of... or you would have known that death by *him* was a better choice than betrayal of *me*. But, now you'll understand."

McCain retrieved the Remington .44 from underneath his overcoat and placed it to the temple of Thompson's son. "Do you believe I'll do it?"

"Yes," Thompson cried, while pounding his fists on the floor. "Yes, yes, yes..."

"Good," replied McCain. "Your family's lives depend on it." He lowered the gun and used his free hand to retrieve a piece of paper from his pocket. "When this preacher contacts you again, you're to give him this information. If you do, your family's lives will be spared, but not yours. You'll die for your betrayal, regardless. If you try and run, I'll find you. There is nowhere on this earth that you can hide from me. Do you understand?"

Exhausted, Thompson's crying had ceased. "Yes," he whispered, his spirit beaten.

McCain placed the note on the coffee table. "Until he contacts you, you will continue to report to work as usual. Once there, you will be placed in a room with guards so that you can be watched all day long. Should you decide not to grace us with your presence one day, we will hunt you down and kill you... *painfully*."

"Mr. Thompson," McCain continued, "you are proof that I've been too soft on the people of my area. Perhaps, they believe that I've grown old and sentimental. I can assure you that nothing is farther from the truth. To ensure that people get the point, yourself included, you can tell them that *I'm* responsible for *this*. Nick... the glove."

Nick pulled a terrible looking object from underneath his coat. It looked to be a tattered leather glove covered in heavy iron plates. One large plate was stitched onto the back of the glove and one on each knuckle. The fingers of the glove were also covered in iron. The weight of the device was apparent as Nick pulled it onto his right hand and tightened the strap around his wrist. Leather popped and cracked as he rolled his fingers into a fist.

McCain bent down and placed his knee into the small of Thompson's back.

"I can't hurt you or else the preacher would know I've gotten to you. But I'll make sure you understand how far I'm willing to go to protect the things I hold dear."

With that, Nick slammed his gloved fist into the face of Mrs. Thompson. Her nose burst, spraying blood onto the children and the sofa. She collapsed and slid off the couch and onto the ground. Thompson screamed, squirmed from under McCain's knee, and scurried to his wife. Ronald and the children cradled her in their arms. She moaned through two missing teeth and a mouth full of blood.

"Make sure people understand that Anders McCain is as determined as ever. And as for your wife, remember…"

"Beauty is in the eye of the beholder."

Twenty-six

Nearly two weeks had passed since the episode at *The Rendezvous*. John had recovered enough to sit up in bed and feed himself. His ribs were visibly bruised and caused him tremendous pain between movements. Several of them had been broken. Mary had wrapped strips of cloth around his mid-region to provide support. The bandages seemed to lessen the pain and allowed him more mobility. The swelling in his eye had gone down, allowing his vision to become normal. He'd been running a mild fever, which was a sign that his body was still fighting the infection from the bullet wound in his thigh. Stiffness still enveloped his leg, but he was now able to flex his knee in small increments. His jaw muscle had relaxed enough to allow a spoon into his mouth. Chewing was not yet possible, but it was encouraging to be able to feed soup to himself. Despite the ability to eat on his own, Mary still enjoyed spoon-feeding him. He didn't see any reason to stop her.

The wild dreams continued. As of recent years, bad dreams were standard. John could count the number of truly restful nights he'd had since the death of Anne.

For a while, he had forgotten about the man in the white derby. Seminary, Missouri had been a respite in the midst of a life of conflict. It had been his island. Her love fulfilled him in such a way that every yearning was satisfied. The happiness her touch brought was more powerful than the anger and frustration that had fueled his life. It seemed as if the skies had opened and the very face of God had smiled down upon him. Then disaster struck. And she was taken. It was as if all of the hope he had was taken with her. She left him with a burning hole in his gut and the hate and anger rushed back, all too ready to fill the void. There could be no happiness in this life. It was all fleeting. More important issues were at hand... justice... righting wrongs... *burying the pain*. So, his dreams continued, urging him forward... refusing to let him rest until the evil men faced justice.

Tim O'Hare entered the room. John had seen him a few times, but not since he was well enough to talk. Thus far, Tim had been very reassuring, even nurturing. He hadn't been looking forward to *this* conversation. Tim could be a bit naive, but he wasn't stupid.

By now, everyone would know about the shootout at *The Rendezvous*. Many people would be celebrating, finding hope and courage in the attacks on the Irish organization. But, there were those who chose antiviolence no matter what the circumstances. Tim was one of those people. The pacifist attitude just didn't seem to fit him, though. John could sense the anger buried deep beneath his external layers, and John was a compass for anger. In several conversations, Tim had become very passionate about the subject of the gangs, even confrontational, but only with John. Ma had taught him that, often, people allowed their innermost demons to surface in front of those they loved. This human characteristic irritated him, and he felt that it was cowardly. Why couldn't Tim release his frustrations onto the ones who caused them?

"Mornin'," greeted Tim. The minister sat down in the wooden chair at John's bedside and leaned backward.

"Good morning to you," replied John, attempting to grin through a sore mouth.

"You're looking much better. I'd thought I'd lost you."

"Maybe you wish you had," John replied.

"Why would you go and say a thing like that, John?"

"There would be a lot less grief on your part, wouldn't it?"

"My boy, I don't think I'm the one with the grief. John," he said, leaning forward with his elbows on his knees, "what would cause you to go and do such a thing? All those men… dead."

"Not all of them…"

"Enough of them," Tim replied. "Why?"

"You really have to ask that? Take a look around, Tim. Can't you see what he's done to these people… *your* people? He's robbing them, killing them… taking every drop of hope he can squeeze from them."

"What's happenin' in this city is horrible. But, if you think the Irish mob is the sole source of this city's problems, you're gravely mistaken. What about the Italians or the Jews? What about them? You're not killing off those men. Why the Irish? Why Anders McCain?"

"You wouldn't understand."

"Why wouldn't I?"

"Because, you're not like me."

"I know what you think. You believe me to be weak or maybe a coward. Such is the way of God. Jesus said that men would think that of us. Which is harder John—to seek vengeance against your enemies or to offer forgiveness?"

"Forgiveness is great if you're the only one who pays the price. But, when it costs other people, the price is *too* high. Anders McCain is as evil as men come. He's raped, stolen, and murdered for far too long. No, he's not the only one, but he's a start."

"Why him?" Tim probed.

"Because he murdered my father!"

The two men stared at each other in silence. Understanding crept into Tim's eyes.

"I've followed the man in the white derby for many years. His hand has been around my throat for most of my life… taking… destroying in one way or another."

"White Derby?" clarified Tim.

"I promised that he would pay for his crimes," John explained.

"You mean that you would *murder* him," replied Tim, softly.

"No, I mean *justice!*"

Tim stood up and walked to a bookshelf. He looked at the titles for a moment, while pondering some deep thought. "John, the path you're on will only lead to destruction. I know… I've been there."

"How?" asked John.

Tim didn't want to delve any deeper. His history was something that he had buried a long time ago. God had forgiven him and he didn't see any reason in digging up the past. But, if there was one thing Christianity had taught him, it was that God could use your downfalls to help others overcome their own. John was on a path that would end in certain destruction, just as Tim had been once in his life. God's mercy brought an angel into Tim's life and he'd deserted that road a long time ago. Still, he didn't want anyone to know about it, especially John. John Grady seemed to think so highly of the aging minister. *Would he ever be able to look at me the same?* Tim *had* to tell him. What if *he* were John's only chance at redemption? So, before guilt overclouded his judgment, Tim spoke.

"I haven't always been a minister. Once I was young and full of bad decisions." He turned to face John. "You have to understand; this is my *past*. I only tell you because I care for you and I don't want you to live with the guilt that I face everyday."

John watched, Tim pace the floor.

"I wasn't always the man you see standin' before you today." Tim looked visibly ashamed. "In my twenties and thirties, *I* worked for a gang boss. I was one of these men you despise so much. I started working for him in my late teens."

"My family left Ireland during the Great Potato Famine and moved to New York. I grew up in Hell's Kitchen, poor and destitute. Finding work in New York was tough at best, but nearly impossible for an immigrant like me. So I sought the acceptance that the gangs offered. These gangs started as bands of immigrants who joined together for the common good of each other. They offered people like me, even your people, John, a chance at a better life. We didn't know what the gangs would become... what *we* would become."

"The bosses began to realize that the most profitable businesses were the ones that were illegal. People have always loved sin and are willing to pay dearly for its temporary pleasures. But, one sin always leads to another. Before I knew it, I'd moved from being a simple worker to a killer."

John's eyes narrowed as he focused on Tim's words.

"I became an enforcer, John. I killed many men... even women and children. God forgive me for talking about it," he said looking upward. "At first, it was for money... then for reputation. Eventually, I killed because it became *who* I was." He stared at John intently. "Would you have killed me, John?"

"Yes," he replied without hesitation.

"And, I would have deserved it. But, God had another plan for me. His plan was that I would deliver life to people instead of death. He had a purpose for me that didn't include the detestable things that had held me in bondage for so long."

"He sent me an angel named Rosalyn. She worked at a laundry operation that ironed my suits. It was love at first sight. Little did I know the plans God had in store for me. For the first time in my life, I saw the character of God in a person. He wasn't the horrible, demeaning... scary God that I'd always believed Him to be. She taught me that he was a God of love and of hope... and peace, one whose forgiveness outweighs his judgment. He blessed me with two daughters, somethin' I thought I could never be worthy of. My angel stayed with me for twenty-three years before God took her home. And now, here I sit, hoping that God will use me as he used her."

"We all deserve death, John," concluded Tim.

"I'm not like you, Tim. You were a murderer. You killed innocent people."

"What is innocence?" asked Tim.

"Don't plague me with these questions of philosophy. If you're so righteous, why didn't you turn yourself in for all of the crimes you've committed? You say that God has forgiven you, and you may be right, but the law hasn't. You haven't faced penance for the things you've done. Your guilt does not wipe your crimes away, nor does your philosophy on forgiveness."

The statement cut Tim to the bone. He lowered his head.

"Tim, you've been nothing but kind to me. You've given me guidance and been patient, and for that I thank you. But, on this subject I will never agree with you."

Tim walked shakily to the door and paused.

"I hope you don't think ill of me," Tim stammered. "I only want to help you. More than *anything*, I want to help you." He stepped out of his door and said a silent prayer for the man. But, Tim knew in his heart…

John Grady had already chosen his path.

Twenty-seven

he dark-haired angel strolled through the moonlight. Fog obscured her feet and swirled in her wake. Anne reached out for him with ivory arms and called his name in a lullaby. But, on the hilltop was the devil, again. He was always there, watching through his translucent eye. John knew what would happen next, so, he ran towards her. Angry hands emerged from the ground and grabbed his legs. He couldn't move. "You were supposed to bring life, not death," they moaned in empty voices. A shot echoed from the hilltop and John screamed for her.

"Annie!" he yelled, sitting upright in his bed. Shaken and disoriented, he fumbled for the leather string that hung around his neck. At the end of the cord, a golden ring lay upon his chest.

"John, are you all right?" asked Mary as she entered through his bedroom door. A kerosene lamp hung from her fingers.

"Yes," he replied, suddenly aware of the object clenched in his hand. "I had a nightmare."

"You were yelling."

"I'm sorry I woke you."

"Was it about *her*?" she asked, motioning with her head toward the ring he clutched.

"It was nothing, really. You should go back to sleep."

"Are you sure? I could stay on the cot."

"You can't do that forever, Mary," he replied, although he wouldn't mind if she did. "Could you turn the light on?"

She flipped the wall switch and the globe flared to life.

"Really, I'm all right," he reassured her. "I'm sorry for waking you. I'll talk to you in the morning."

"All right," she replied. "Good night."

John could see the hurt in her eyes as she left his room. Why did he still wear Anne's ring? Hadn't he let go of her? She had been dead for over ten years. Her death had been so fast... so unexpected. Why did he keep her ring? And why, in his dreams, was Wounded Hawk always killing her? Her death had nothing to do with *him*. Wounded Hawk had been dead for years. *What about her grave, John? Who dug up her grave?* The question had always perplexed him. Anne's grave had been robbed several years after her death. John had been angry, but there was no reason to believe it was anything other than grave robbers. *But why does Wounded Hawk haunt my dreams?* John had killed him many years ago. Their brotherhood had reached a bloody climax and with great tribulation, John had survived.

He held the ring in front of his face. Its gold gleamed in the soft light. He traced it with his fingers. *Till' death do us part...* He'd buried Anne long ago, and his vows had been fulfilled. It was time to put the past behind him.

Determined fingers pulled the leather string over his head. He balled the cord into the palm of his hand and placed the memory into the drawer of his bedside table. Mary would not have to see it again.

* * *

John's condition improved daily, and, before long, he was able to leave his room. With the help of some worn crutches, John hobbled about the church, finding things to keep himself occupied.

The winter snows began to fall in late December and left the city covered in a blanket of white powder. John loved the snow; for some reason, it had always excited him. Perhaps it was the boy that still resided deep within himself. Much of his boyhood had been taken from him; robbing many of the simple things a child finds pleasure in, such as snow.

Mary continued to care for him, and despite his hang-ups, their relationship had grown. John's doubts about his intentions for her were being replaced by a flame that was growing between them. Daily, he faced guilt about Anne. He had loved her and had given himself to her whole-heartedly. But, she was gone. He had told Mary all about their relationship and that she died as a result of his idealism. She was the biggest regret of this personal war he'd waged for justice. Anne was also the reason that he could ask others to fight for themselves. John understood loss. Humans lived in a world dominated by unfairness. Doing the right thing never promised safety, just as doing the wrong thing never guaranteed justice. One had to be willing to risk everything in order to make his world a better place. He had talked his ideas over with Mary and she had agreed.

Mary understood sacrifice, and she hoped that no one would have to make the choices she'd made. John told her all about his past, including his childhood. He spoke of Joe, Wounded Hawk, and McCain. She had listened intently without passing judgment on him. Instead, she offered sympathy and understanding.

One sunny day, in mid January, she and John sat outside in the church's tiny courtyard. The temperature in the city had been above freezing for a week and the snow had melted. John had needed some fresh air and asked Mary to join him. She had been acting strange toward him as of late. He didn't understand what was happening but wanted to talk to her about the change. He'd never been good at listening to a woman. Learning to listen had been a quick lesson in his short marriage to Anne. But, he cared for Mary and he needed to make sure that she understood that. Daily, he fought the temptation to dismiss the feelings he had for her. He still had things to accomplish. Or did he?

Lately, John had found himself questioning his lifelong quest for restitution. Mary had shown him so much about kindness, gentleness, and self-control. *What about love?* Something had happened during the time that Mary nursed John back to health. He couldn't explain it any more than a man could explain God. One had to experience it. All that he knew was that his aspirations were changing from thoughts of vengeance to a life of possibilities. And, all of that promise revolved around Mary.

The courtyard was located between the main church building and the dining area. A small hallway connected the buildings on each end, creating a narrow, rectangular void. John and Mary sat on a short stone bench in the center of the small court. A bare tree stood in the middle of a brown grassy island, a stark reminder of the New York winter.

"I haven't thanked you for nursing me," said John. "You didn't have to do that."

"Well, who else would've?"

"I know what you must think of me," he confessed.

She leaned toward him and placed her delicate hands around his.

"I think you're the bravest man I've ever met," she said, her eyes aglow. "*Stupid*, but courageous. Something needed to be done. But, I don't want you to be the one to do it next time."

John wrestled with the feelings as they struggled toward his tongue. The true measure of a man's bravery was shown when trying to tell a woman about the way he felt. And John believed that it was a man's job to lay the cards out on the table.

"Mary…"

"Yes?"

Her facial expression urged him forward like a mother encouraging her child. He fumbled for the right words until he finally blurted them out in uncouth fashion.

"I think I have feelings for you."

"You think?" she replied.

"I'm sorry. I didn't mean to say it like that. I'm just not very good at these things." He squeezed her hands. "Yes, I do."

"I don't know what to say," said Mary.

"I don't understand," John replied. "You feel the same."

"Oh? And how would you know that," she said with a sassy intonation.

"Because of the way you're looking at me now."

"You don't know me, John."

"I want to," he replied.

"You don't understand," she said, pulling her hand away from his. She stood up and turned her back to him. "There are things about me that you don't know."

"Can you tell me?"

She sighed and fidgeted with her hands. "Yes." She shook her head in frustration. "I knew this would happen. It would have been too easy."

He stood up and placed his hands on her shoulders, then leaned and whispered into her ear. "It's alright."

Her heart was breaking. Butterflies danced in her stomach and her palms became clammy. She would *have* to tell him. But, what if he walked away? She couldn't blame him if he did. She knew that her heart would break, but it was broken already. She *needed* to tell him her secret. She needed to let someone into that hidden part of her past. With her back toward him, she spoke.

"After my family emigrated from Ireland, we began to scratch a livin' in the city. My parents moved from different industries whenever a better job would open. It looked as if things were going to get better for us when a flu outbreak hit the city. Both of my parents died."

"I'm sorry."

"I was sixteen. They left me with two brothers and two sisters. I had no way to make money. I began workin' as a seamstress, but the job didn't pay enough. The other children were too young to work. One day a man saw me at the market with my siblin's. He asked me where my parents were and after hearin' my story he offered me a job." She stopped talking and tried to gather her nerve.

"It's alright," John soothed. "You don't have to go any farther."

"Please, let me finish. The man introduced me to a lady who ran a brothel. I promised myself that I would only work long enough to catch up on the bills, but the bills never got caught up. It paid more than any other job I could find at my age, so I kept doin' it. Four years ago, I started attendin' Mount Zion. Tim O'Hare listened to my story and offered me the position I have now. He really is a good man, John."

"I know he is."

She had been through this confession too many times. She had nearly buried the emotions. Now, he forced them to the surface. Strength surged through her body.

"Do you see?" she asked turning to face him. "I don't deserve *any* man."

"Yes, you do. Mary, I don't deserve you. My past is darker than any moment in yours."

"Do you hear what you're sayin'? Do you want to love a whore, then?"

"You're not a whore. You did what you had to do to survive... to provide for your family. I've killed people, Mary. And, if you can forgive me for something like that, then I can forgive you, too."

"But I can't forgive myself," she said. She ran into the church, brushing past him.

After finally allowing someone into *his* past, he'd fallen in love with a woman who couldn't face her *own*. Life had an extreme sense of irony. Perhaps he had been too rash. His feelings for her had grown so strong as a result of her caring for his injuries. She needed time and he had plenty to give to her. In a way, he felt ridiculous for having approached the subject. Rejection played a terrible game with the ego.

But, she hadn't rejected him; she'd rejected herself. That pained him more than anything else. She was hurting and he couldn't fix it. John wanted to help her like she had helped him. He wanted to do something, to help her find forgiveness for herself. Only time could do that. He would have to let her cry.

John looked into the sunny sky. For the first time in years, his life was feeling *right*. Anders McCain even left his mind for moments. Could it be possible to put everything behind him... to let go?

He'd been talking to some of the merchants. Their mindsets were changing. Resistance was welling up within the people themselves. Eventually, they would take matters into their own hands and resist. John had started a good work. He had been the catalyst. Maybe his part was over. Maybe he could find release. But, inside, John knew the truth.

McCain would seek vengeance.

Twenty-eight

The day was growing late as Charles Kell neared the end of his closing routine. Golden light crept through the front windows of his store as the sun set behind the buildings of Brooklyn. Snow flurries meandered through the crisp winter air. Spring was approaching, leaving the mild winter behind. Charles knew that the worst weather was coming, though. Late winter was when the storms rolled in.

Four of his daughters assisted Charles in his evening duties. Marilyn was the eldest at seventeen. She was a sassy brunette, petite in size, but large in personality. Her sister, Carmine, was a year and a half younger. She was blonde with fair skin and a slender build. Entering their teen years were the twins, Heather and April. All of the girls were quite lovely. They swept, mopped, cleaned and dried the shop. Heather washed the windows while April wrapped some leftover ham.

Charles worked on the long, wooden cutting table. Using a stained rag, he raked the bits of scrap meat into the palm of his hand and tossed them into a waste bucket. The butchering business was a messy job, but could be profitable if you were able to keep the money you made. It took a strong stomach to gut an animal. Charles thought he would never get used to the smell of entrails and rotting meat, but now he barely noticed the stench.

"Papa, we're all finished," said Heather.

"Not quite," he replied. "Who wants to empty the gut bucket?"

Heather made a gagging noise with her mouth and shook her head as if she'd fallen into the pail.

"Not me," whimpered Marilyn.

April ran from the shop and up the stairs to their apartment. Charles looked at Carmine.

"Last chance…"

Carmine made no reply.

"Well, I guess I'll be having all the fun tonight." He grabbed the bucket by its handle, whistled as he left the storefront and walked to the back of the shop. Once there, he opened the hatch on a black iron incinerator and scraped the contents into the burning compartment.

Ring-a-ling-a-ling.

Someone had entered the store.

"Tell them that all the meat is put up," yelled Charles. "They'll have to come back in the morning."

He turned the lever on the gas line and heard a soft hiss. Charles pulled a long match from the box and struck it on the concrete floor. After lighting the pilot, he adjusted the dial and the burner flamed to life. The heat felt good in the

211

cold back room. Charles closed the door and returned to the front of the shop.

He was stunned to see a man flirting with Marilyn. His elbow was propped on top of the meat counter and Charles could see the "sweet talkin'" grin on his face.

"Didn't they tell you we were closed?" he asked.

"Yea... they did," he replied. "So?" he asked with arrogance unbecoming of his age. "I'm just talkin' to your daughters here, old man."

"You watch who you're callin' 'old man', boy," Charles replied, steam flooding into his veins. "You work for McCain?"

"Yea, I do," he replied with a swollen chest.

"Well, that's got nothin' to do with my daughter, now does it?"

Hey, take it easy," mocked the man as he backed off, holding his hands in the air. "I'm not tryin' to do anything."

Charles' heart beat hard in his chest. "Girls, go on upstairs."

"Yes sir," they replied and ran off as if they were waiting for their cue to exit.

Since the ghost had killed so many of McCain's enforcers, he'd had to hire a new crop and fast. He'd cajoled mostly young, inexperienced teenagers to do his dirty work. This kid couldn't have been more than nineteen but had already adopted the prideful swagger common to boys who thought themselves more than they were. His acne-ridden face bore the proof of his adolescence. Charles had no mercy for him, though. He was scum, just like the rest of them. Nothing was more humiliating than being bullied by boys. And, Charles Kell had had enough.

"Mr. McCain sent me to collect on his insurance. He heard you ran off Johnnie Roper the other day. From what I hear, it ain't the first time you've done it, either." The kid opened his coat to reveal a large knife sheathed on his belt. "He sent me to tell you that you got a free one the last time. But, he don't take that. All you piss ants think you can just forget everything Mr. McCain's done for you. This ghost ain't gonna protect you. We do that... don't forget it."

"You've never protected anything, son. Now go on and get out of here."

"I don't think you heard me right, Mister," the man said as he moved toward Charles in a threatening manner.

Charles reached underneath the counter and retrieved an enormous meat tenderizer. The thick shaft of the tool was two feet long and connected to a hefty wooden mallet whose surface was covered with sharp points. The tool was used for pounding large cuts of beef.

Charles rolled the shaft in his fingers as he approached the man.

"What do you think you're gonna to do with that?" asked the man.

"Why don't you pull that knife and find out," replied Charles. He couldn't believe the words that left his mouth. Charles was tired of feeling weak... sick of being a coward. He had stood up to several of these "green" enforcers over the last couple of months, but they were becoming too persistent. Charles could live with paying the weekly tax, but they had started coming twice a week.

"I've had about enough of you, Mister," stammered the kid. "Now pay up and there won't be any trouble."

"I don't think I'll be payin' today. You can tell your boss that if he needs money so bad, he should sell his stinkin' hotel."

The boy's hand reached for his knife but stopped.

"You draw that thing and I'm going to bash your head in," threatened Charles.

The young man was shivering almost as badly as Charles. He closed his coat and backed toward the door, hanging his head in shame.

"You're gonna be in big trouble after Mr. McCain hears about this. I hope you're ready cause somebody else is gonna be lookin' after your sweet girls."

Something inside of Charles Kell snapped. As the man stepped through the door, Charles rushed at him and swung the meat tenderizer into a high arch. The mallet smashed into the back of the man's head and sent him flailing to the ground. There was no scream or any blood that Charles could see, the man just got up and staggered off without talking. Several times he fell or stumbled against a wall as he walked down the sidewalk.

Charles ducked back into the shop and, with shaking hands, bolted the door. McCain wouldn't stand for one of his men to be attacked. He would seek revenge. *What have I done?* He had stood up for himself. He had *protected* his family. He had acted like all the men who had ever fought for something important. Charles was experiencing something he had never felt before. A sense of pride and dignity began to overcome the fear. He searched for a word to describe it. How could a man who had just crossed a major gang boss be feeling the way he was?

Charles took a deep breath and sighed. For the first time in a long while...

Charles Kell was a man.

Twenty-nine

nders McCain worked the top button of his brown, full- length coat. Wind whistled through the alleyways off Forty Seventh Street. Deserted was the dimly lit avenue at eleven o'clock at night. McCain and his entourage walked back to *The Rendezvous* after having had drinks at Smiley's Pub.

Only an hour earlier, McCain had been sipping strong bourbon. His Friday night ritual had been interrupted when one of the new guys entered the bar and approached McCain with his head bowed. Nick Rocci had stood and drawn his pistol, which caused the other bodyguards to follow suit. Billy Woods removed his hat and held it in both hands.

"Mr. McCain," he'd said, carefully. "I'm sorry to barge in on your evenin', sir."

"Do I know you?" asked McCain.

Nick relaxed his weapon. "He's the new foreman for the lower Brooklyn area, Mr. McCain."

"Oh... yes," said McCain, not really recognizing the man. After all, he'd been the third foreman of that crew in the last five months.

Billy Woods sat in silence. McCain liked that.

"Well?" prompted McCain.

"A man's been killed... Joey Long. He died about an hour ago."

McCain had sat back down onto the wooden chair, leaned backwards, crossed his arms and braced himself for the answer to his next question.

"The ghost?" he'd asked.

"No, sir," replied Billy Woods, feeling some relief. "It wasn't the ghost at all. A butcher killed him."

"A butcher?" replied McCain, clearly disgusted.

"Yes sir, a butcher. Right before Joey died, he told us that he'd gone to a butcher's shop over on Seventh Street. Everybody knows the man, on the count of he's got some real pretty daughters," he explained, stifling a chuckle. "That butcher ran Johnnie Roper off earlier this week. He said that he wasn't goin' to double up on payments. Anyway, he scared Johnnie off. Joey volunteered to go, on account of hearin' about them pretty girls. Joey was tough, or at least *he* thought he was. So, I let him go. Joey and the butcher had words, but the butcher wouldn't pay up. Joey said the butcher pulled some kind of mallet and whopped him upside the head. At about nine o'clock, some of our other boys found him wanderin' the streets. Joey told them what I just told you before he passed out... only he wasn't passed out; he was dead."

The only thing Anders McCain had ever feared was happening. The people were losing respect for him. This butcher was not the first person to take a stand; several merchants had in recent weeks. But, he was the first person to resort to violence. And, if something didn't happen quickly, other people would take it as a sign that they could get away with opposing him. Things were not as they should be.

McCain and his men had left Smiley's for an emergency meeting at *The Rendezvous*. He had called in all of the foremen and his high level enforcers, many of which were young and inexperienced. Some of his best men had been killed at *The Rendezvous* shootout, but others had taken their place. Ambitious men were always ready to move toward the top.

"Do you want me to call Captain Adams?" asked Nick, as he walked alongside McCain. The man's face was healing, but bore new scars on top of the acne pits that had been acquired during puberty.

"No," replied McCain. "Nick, we have to make a statement; a *blatant* one. It'll be better if Captain Adams doesn't know. I don't think he would be able to let us slide on this one. We're going to draw some attention to ourselves."

"I like it," replied Nick.

So did McCain. *Control* relied upon a frequent show of power. People had to be kept under control and *know* that they were under control. Humans had to fear their leaders. Without that fear, human beings would slowly become extinct. They would be relegated to savages all seeking to rule the tribe. But, there could be only one leader... only one alpha male. And, the alpha male always took his position with a show of strength. McCain had been docile for too long.

"We'll hit the people hard. We need to gather all of our enforcers and sweep through the city. We'll begin with all of our Brooklyn businesses. They don't believe that they need protection anymore? We'll show them what its like to fend for themselves. Let's give them a taste of how the Italians operate."

"What do you propose to do?" replied Nick.

McCain pondered for a moment. "We'll visit all of them Sunday evening; start with the ones who've given us resistance. We'll teach all of them a lesson. Just the sight of this butcher will remind people what happens when someone crosses us."

McCain walked in silence for a moment, hearing the clop of his shoes on the wet pavement. Drops of water flung from the tips of his shoes with each step.

"As for the rest of them," he continued, "empty their cash drawers. Take everything they have. I never want them to forget this night. From now on, when one of these "do-gooders" wants to cause difficulty, the merchants will lynch him themselves and save me the trouble."

"What about the butcher?" asked Nick.

"Tell our men to do whatever they want to him... and his family."

"Even the girls?" clarified Nick.

"*Especially* the girls," McCain replied with a pleasured cruelty.

"They'll like that," Nick replied. "This is gonna be fun."

"Not for you, Nick. You'll stay with me."

"Are you worried about the ghost, boss?"

"He's no ghost," replied McCain. "He's a man all right. I think he's a preacher." The words sounded ridiculous rolling from his tongue. *All evil has a little good in it... all good has a little evil.* But, which one of them was evil and which one was good? McCain had never seen things in black and white. To him it seemed that most things fell into a gray area, depending on the beliefs of the person. Many countries flourished under the rule of a dictator, but America had chosen a different route. McCain didn't agree, therefore, he would not be bound to that way of thought. Did that make him evil? What about a killer who was sworn to the ways of God? Was the preacher not evil?

"A preacher?" responded Nick, obviously confused.

"I was visited by a man who referred to him as 'the preacher'," he replied. "I noticed that he wore a white collar when he broke into my penthouse."

"That's right," affirmed Nick. "He *was* wearing a white collar. Why would he do that?"

"I don't know."

"Doesn't make sense," Nick added.

"The man who visited me told me that I'd killed this preacher's father," explained McCain.

"How would *he* know that?"

"I don't know that, either. But, we did kill a preacher once, a long time ago. His son was there."

McCain needed to get the townspeople under control, but more importantly, he needed to get rid of the preacher. How could he kill two birds with one stone?

"We need to lure this preacher out of hiding," said McCain. "I don't think it'll take much. We'll *make* him come for me."

"How?" asked Nick.

McCain stopped walking and faced Nick. "We let people know about our plans for Sunday evening."

"Let people know?" responded Nick, even more confused. "Why would we do that?"

"He'd *have* to do something. Chances are that he would come for me. Only this time, we'll be expecting him." His eyes narrowed as he thought. "We need a wide open area where he can't hide and remote enough for a lot of gunfire."

"Just get him there, and I'll finish him off," said Nick, passionately.

"No, Nick. You got lucky this last time because of the close quarters. In an open area, he'd pick you off before you could even think about drawing your gun."

"So what do we do?"

"We need firepower. Gather our weapons and tell Ronald Thompson..." McCain suddenly stopped, squinting to better see beyond Nick's shoulder.

A figure in the alleyway caught McCain's attention. He stared past Nick, trying to discern the shape in the darkness. More movement caught his eye and a wild looking man stepped from the shadows. His leather moccasins made no discernable sound on the pavement.

"How do we know that this preacher is still alive?" asked Nick.

"Because," McCain motioned to the man in the alley, "*he's* still here."

Upon seeing Wounded Hawk, Nick reached into his overcoat for his gun. The other men followed his lead. McCain lashed out and stayed Nick's hand.

"No," exclaimed McCain. "If he had wanted to kill us, we'd already be dead."

"Mr. McCain," said Wounded Hawk, in his thick Native American dialect.

"Mister... *Hawk*, is it?" replied McCain.

221

"Have you given anymore thought to my offer?" asked the Indian.

Then, it became clear. Pride was an odd fixation. The very thing one prized dearly could become the destroyer of his life. Independence was McCain's treasure. He'd always solved his own problems no matter what the cost. But, this particular problem seemed beyond his ability to handle alone. Sometimes a man had to accept help, *even if only for a moment*."

"Yes," he replied. "I have thought about it… and I'm interested."

Thirty

tuffy air filled the inside of Mount Zion Methodist Assembly on this Sunday morning in January. John Grady could sense that the weather was about to take a turn for the worst. A warm front had moved in and now the winter air was full of thick moisture. John knew that the effect of such a change in weather would eventually bring about a winter storm, for which the coast of New York had become infamous. He'd heard legends about the storms of previous years and hoped the city wasn't due for a repeat of those. Normally, sixty-degree temperatures would seem cool. But, after the chill of winter, the warm temperature fooled one's body into believing it was hot. So, to satisfy the Sunday morning congregation, who was never comfortable no matter what the temperature, the ministers had left the front doors ajar. John had seen Ronald Thompson pass through the open doors sometime during the middle of the service.

The short, weasel-like man had entered silently and with purpose. Thompson had removed his hat and had taken a seat on the end of the rear pew. John knew the motive for the man's visit and it wasn't to find God. Ronald Thompson was not a parishioner at Mount Zion, so there could be only one reason why he was here this morning. Something *big* was happening within the Irish organization.

John had contacted Ronald Thompson shortly after the fight at McCain's warehouse on Flatbush Avenue. During John McGregor's final moments, he'd given John Grady the location of the Irish organization's new storage place at Greenwood Cemetery. After the Jersey attack, they'd picked an inconspicuous location to store their "products". Then, John had caught George Burt. Burt didn't have the courage of McGregor, and quickly rambled off a lot of babble and one important name: *Ronald Thompson.* He'd explained that Thompson was McCain's new accountant. Deducing the facts of that revelation was simple enough. McCain's accountant would know everything, including the ins and outs of his business, inventory locations, information on his top employees, and a layout of the hotel. It was a shame that McGregor was mortally wounded in the attack. He could have been a good man. John hated to see good men go bad.

After seeing Thompson for the first time, John felt that the man would be an easy grab. Thompson wasn't physical in nature, and lacked just enough self-respect to make any kind of stand for himself. He'd almost felt ashamed for cajoling Thompson, but realized that he, just like McCain, had made his moral choice. John understood that because he had forced Thompson to betray McCain, the accountant's life would become worthless. Most likely, death awaited him. *Such is the way of the gun.*

John turned from the front pew, where he sat, and saw Thompson looking about the sanctuary. Thompson had no idea for whom he was searching. He'd only been given instructions on how to get word to John in case of an emergency. John would visit *him* anytime he needed information. Thompson was to never attempt to contact him unless it was a desperate situation. In case of a crisis, he was to write the information onto a folded piece of paper and place it into the offering plate at Mount Zion. Thompson was no idiot, and John realized that he probably could deduce enough clues to connect the ghost with Mount Zion. But, whom would he rat to? If he were to tell Anders McCain, he would be killed for his betrayal. So it really didn't matter *what* Thompson knew, so long as he followed John's instructions. And, if that were the case, John had good reason for the uneasiness he now felt from Thompson's presence.

Tim O'Hare continued to speak from the pulpit. John had no idea what the older man's sermon was about. As of late, he'd been unable to pay attention to Tim when he preached. The man had lost esteem in John's eyes, but not because of the things he'd done in his past. John had plenty of his own sins to worry about. He'd lost respect for Tim because he allowed his past to affect the lives of others in what John felt was a negative way. Tim had restricted John from the pulpit area; he now sat in the front row. He supposed that it was Tim's way of punishing him. He refused to let John speak because he feared that he would preach a message opposing Tim's teachings. He was right, of course.

"We'll now sing a praise of offering as the plates are passed," said Tim, bringing the service to a close.

A wooden table of dark color stood at the front of the sanctuary. Four brass offering plates sat on top of the stand, waiting for the four men who sauntered towards them. After retrieving the plates, the men walked down the aisles, one on each side of the two columns of pews. Each man passed the plate along a pew and received the one his partner had passed down the next one. The jingle of coins joined with the melodious chorus of the pipe organ. John watched Ronald Thompson from the corner of his eye as the plate reached his row. Without looking up, Thompson dropped a piece of paper into the dish. John wanted to read it immediately. What could McCain be up to? What was important enough to make Thompson carry out his second instruction?

John had a sense that deep down, Thompson really wanted to do something good. Didn't all men have that desire? Many men that worked for people like McCain did so because all the other options in life had evaded them. When faced with the prospect of failure, it was only natural to run towards one's last resort. But, there were other options in life, and disappointment did not justify wrongdoing. He had to remind himself of that when dealing with people like Thompson. Too much pity fueled a world of evil men like McCain.

The service ended and Thompson slipped out quietly and with haste. John didn't take his usual place at the door. He didn't feel like it. He'd become sick of playing minister. He'd grown tired of pretending to be perfect while his life was as dark and confusing as anyone else's. People would excuse him, though. They knew that he'd been hurt. The story was that Reverend Grady had been beaten and robbed while stopping to help someone less fortunate. The lie made

John want to vomit, but it had not been his idea. Tim had fabricated it to protect the integrity of the church. John wrenched at the irony of telling a lie to shield integrity.

While the parishioners ogled for Tim's attention, John slipped toward the front and to the four offering plates. He spotted the folded piece of brown paper in the second plate from the left. After glancing around to make sure no one would accuse him of stealing, he picked the paper up and slipped it into his pant's pocket. He eased out of the sanctuary and into the kitchen. Once there, he pulled the note from his pocket and opened it.

> *Dear Sir,*
> *Mr. McCain and family have been staying*
> *at the Steeplechase Hotel on Coney Island.*
> *Something big is happening. This*
> *information should assist you. I can say no*
> *more as I am under close scrutiny.*
> *Yours truly,*
> *R.T.*

Steeplechase? McCain's staying at Coney Island? The idea made sense. Coney Island was completely deserted at this time of year. John had come across rumors claiming that McCain had partial ownership of a park on the island, but he'd never pursued the lead. McCain had basically vanished since *The Rendezvous* attack. John hadn't been able to get any information out of anyone, not even Thompson. But, *why* did Thompson know now? How had he found out? McCain *would* have a hideaway like that. All outlaws did. Some used caves and some used cabins, but all were secluded and kept secret.

But, why was Thompson giving this information *now*? Had he just found out himself? And what was the "big" thing that McCain was planning? Was it bad enough that Thompson had suddenly developed a conscience? If McCain was planning something bad, he needed to be stopped. But, John had no idea when, where, or what he was planning.

Besides the unknown details, John hadn't completely recovered from his injuries. His ribs were tender and he still walked with a slight limp. But, there was another reason. He was beginning to let the man in the white derby drift from his mind. His feelings for Mary were slowly drowning out his desire for a reckoning with McCain. Some wars weren't worth fighting. And some debts... needed to be forgotten.

John headed down the stairs and into the basement hallway toward his room. His footsteps echoed through the empty corridor. Mary would miss him at lunch, but his appetite had been snuffed out due to the mysterious letter. John entered his room and closed the door behind him. He lay onto the bed and held the creased paper in front of his face.

Thompson was being watched. What did that make his note? Was he telling John that the note was not real? *Or* was he *really* saying that he could give no more details? There was no reason for Thompson to be honest with him, anyway. After all, John was putting him and his family in harm's way. Perhaps, McCain had stumbled onto Thompson's betrayal and was threatening him. In a situation like that, Thompson may have given McCain's whereabouts in hopes that John would kill him.

Was he reading *too* deeply? The note had given him McCain, period. If he chose to go after him again, he would know where to find him.

John rubbed his eyes and relaxed as the pressure of his headache began to diminish. One thing was certain, there was nothing he could do right now. He had no idea what was going to happen or the strength to do anything about it.

As John closed his eyes, his thoughts became a jumbled mix of sentence fragments and images. The note fell from his hand and landed silently on the rug. The onset of sleep was tempting and he could find no reason to fight it.

Thirty-one

As the afternoon dwindled on, a strong breeze began to move the humid air. A line of dark clouds crossed the Atlantic Ocean to the south as Charles Kell strolled down the sidewalk towards his butcher shop.

Sunday afternoon had been gorgeous and families had thoroughly enjoyed the day. Charles' errands had taken him past Prospect Park where he'd been convinced to bring his own family back to enjoy the sunshine. The time was a quarter till two, and there was plenty of daylight left to let the girls have some fun at the park. Charles had been so busy at the shop as of late, trying to catch up from his cash shortage due to the insurance ring. As a result, his family had suffered. *Not anymore.* Things were changing. People were taking a stand for themselves and Charles had been a major factor in their new found courage. Freedom was comforting, though Charles understood it didn't come without cost. Reverend Grady had taught him that.

Wind whistled around Charles' ears and tugged at his hair. The smell of smoked pork drifted from a cookery just down the street. But, the line of clouds grew more pronounced as they drifted toward the Lower Bay. People, who had been lazily strolling along the sidewalk, stepped up the pace toward their final destinations. *The park may have to wait.* The gale was moving too fast. Far away, a bolt of lighting streaked toward the ground. Charles hoped that the storm would be mild, but he had seen many start like this one and most had taken a turn for the worst.

Pulling his key ring, Charles stepped to the door of his store. He was about to insert the key when he noticed that the barrel was already turned. The door was unlocked. *Perhaps the girls have been playing on the sidewalk.* Possibly, but Marilyn would have called them inside with this approaching storm. Charles pushed the door inward, causing a jingle of bells to reverberate through the empty room. *No one around. One of the girls must have left the door unlocked.* He would have to chide them for that. They couldn't forget to lock the store. Carelessness was the easiest way to be robbed or worse.

"Marilyn," called Charles.

There was no answer.

Those darn women!

He slid a key into the lock and turned. The bolt clicked into place.

Charles walked toward the stairway that led to the Kell's apartment above the store.

"Marilyn! Somebody forgot to lock the bloomin' door again!"

Chill bumps prickled along his arms. It was unlike his girls to stay quiet when their "Pop" came home, especially the younger ones. On most occasions, they would run down the stairs and meet him at the door. But, now, only silence greeted him.

"Girls! Are you home?" he asked, feeling a tinge of panic. "I haven't forgotten my birthday have I?" he joked as he reached his family room at the top of the stairs.

In an instant, the room burst into a myriad of lights. Charles' thoughts dispersed as quickly. He spun on his feet and caught a glimpse of a man before his head thumped onto the hard floor. He shook his head, trying to clear the cobwebs. Somewhere, in a far away place, he could hear the echoes of his girls as they screamed his name. He tried to get up but couldn't. Something hard pressed down on his chest... *a boot*. He followed the leg to a man who bent over and looked him in the eye. The man's hand gripped a long wooden bat. He examined Charles in the manner of a curious dog.

"Is this the guy that scared you off, Johnnie?" asked the man in a foggy voice.

"Yea, Mick... That's him all right," replied another voice.

"And, this is the same fella that killed Joey?" asked Mickey Henderson.

"Yea... the butcher," replied Johnnie Roper. "Watch out, he's tougher than he looks."

"Well, he don't look it."

Across the room, the Kell girls cried. Charles craned his head backward and was disoriented by an upside-down view of his family. The girls were under the guard of several armed men. Mick leaned closer to Charles' face.

"You got somethin' comin', butcher," explained Mick Henderson. "What in the world got into you? Are you crazy or somethin'? We're *your kind*! We're *brothers*. Now why would you want to go and start a war with your own brothers? Don't you know that brothers fight harder than anybody?"

"What are we gonna' do to him, Mickey?" asked someone in the room.

"Mr. McCain said we could do whatever we want," Mick replied. "I guess we *could* kill him. But, I had somethin' else in min—somethin' we've all been wantin' to do for a long time."

He applied more pressure to Charles' chest. "You got too many pretty girls to be actin' as foolish as you have, Mr. Butcher. I have to wonder if you really thought it through."

Mick took his foot off Charles' chest and stepped back.

"Johnnie," he said, "roll him onto his stomach and tie his hands behind his back."

Charles' newfound manhood groaned to act, but he was still too dazed. He was passing in and out of consciousness and wasn't sure if he was witnessing reality or struggling out of a morbid dream.

"Lock the little ones into one of the back bedrooms," ordered Mick. "Keep the two oldest out here."

The men shuffled six crying girls toward the rear of the apartment, but left Marilyn and Carmine in the living room."

"Daddy," whimpered Carmine.

"It'll be all right, sweetheart," replied Charles, struggling under the weight of Johnnie Roper.

"Help Johnnie hold him down," said Mick, motioning to the men who were returning from securing the other girls. One of them sat on Charles' back and jammed his knees onto his shoulders. The pain caused Charles to lose his breath.

Another man knelt down and grabbed his left arm and a handful of his hair.

"Hold the blonde," commanded Mick.

A man grabbed Carmine from the back and held her in a bear hug.

"What about us?" asked Johnnie.

"You'll get your turn," replied Mick. "All of you can have all the turns you want."

Mickey Henderson grabbed Marilyn by the wrist. The girl spun and slapped him with her free hand. Enraged, Mick grabbed her with both arms as she tried to run. She kicked at his shins and clawed at his face.

"Leave her alone," screamed Charles in a voice consumed by the dawning of a terrible truth. "Leave her alone!"

Marilyn continued to struggle, forcing her attacker to throw her onto the sofa. When she rose, he slapped her senseless. Mick took Marilyn and viciously bent her face first over the arm of the sofa. Her younger sister, Carmine, wailed. Mick fumbled for his belt.

"Make sure he watches," scowled Mick through gritted teeth. "Have your fun with the blonde!"

Charles struggled underneath the weight of the three men but couldn't budge. Tears streamed down his face as the men tore at his babies' clothing. Suddenly, the price of freedom became evident and it was a cost far too dear to pay. What had he done?

Knowing nothing else to do, Charles screamed with all the breath he had and promised himself that if he lived…

These men would pay with their lives.

Thirty-two

John's door opened slowly, creaking on its hinges. From the shadows of the hall stepped a figure that bore the resemblance of a person. He couldn't tell who it was that was entering his room, but the silhouette made no sound.

"What do you want?" John tried to ask, but the words exited his mouth in a jumble of syllables. "What do you want?" he asked again, forcing the question to leave his tongue. The figure made no response, but inched closer, taking on the form of a man whom was familiar to John. An ashen eye emerged from the darkness of the shadowed figure. John tried to raise himself from the bed but couldn't. Some unseen force anchored him to the mattress, though he struggled with all his strength. He had to fight. He had to face the man once and for all.

"What do you want?" he screamed at the shape.

"I want your blood, brother," replied the form. "And I will have it this night!"

Wounded Hawk sprung from the foot of John's bed and whipped a gleaming blade from his belt. John managed to push through the invisible force just in time to stop Wounded Hawk's hand in mid-swing. With his free hand, John grasped the man's neck and swung his feet onto the floor. He stared deeply into Wounded Hawk's eyes and growled through clinched teeth.

"Why won't you die?" asked John.

"John," the Indian responded, "stop… please."

He could end the blood debt now, once and for all. He could nearly taste the life as it drained from the devil's body.

"John… wake up. Wake up!"

Through his begging, the Indian's face began to morph and blend in and out with that of a gentler one. Suddenly, the room, which had been dark, was bathed in light. Delicate white skin writhed beneath his straining fingers. Blue eyes looked deeply into his as the confusion began to clear.

"John…" Mary begged in a strained whisper. "You're killing me."

His fingers loosened and John stumbled back in horror. The bitter taste of disgust filled his mouth. John recoiled and hid his face in his hands.

Mary collapsed onto her knees and rested against the side of his bed, her chest heaving up and down.

"I'm sorry, Mary," he apologized in a tiny voice. "I'm sorry. I thought you were…" He stopped.

She remained at the end of his bed, too afraid to touch him.

"Are you hurt?" he asked.

"I don't think so," she replied. "I heard you screaming," she explained. "When I came in you were sitting up in bed. What's happening to you?"

236

"I don't know."

He stood up and paced, stretching his arms behind his head. *But, you do know, don't you?*

"Was it Wounded Hawk again?" she asked, as if reading his mind.

"The devil…" he sighed, "he haunts my dreams." He turned to face Mary. The color was returning to her cheeks. "Yes, it was Wounded Hawk." He paused for a moment, not sure if he should continue… not even sure if *he* believed what he was about to say. "He's here."

"Here?" asked Mary, bewildered. "But, I thought you said he was dead."

"I know. It sounds ridiculous, but… he's alive."

"John, I know these dreams are disturbin', but people don't come back from the dead."

"What if he never died?"

"But, you said that you killed him. You *saw* him die."

"No." He sat back onto the bed beside her. "I saw him in an explosion… and I've never seen him since."

What about the grave, John? What about Anne's grave? What happened to her hair?

"There was something I didn't tell you," he hesitated.

"What is it?"

"When Anne's grave was robbed… The caretaker told me that someone had cut the hair from her head."

"That's horrible," she said, visibly repulsed. "Why would someone do that?"

"Most grave robbers wouldn't," he replied. "They're after valuables. Cutting hair… that's personal. Apache warriors take the scalps of their enemies," he said in a calm voice, not wanting to frighten her. "But, sometimes an enemy dies before a blood debt is settled. In a case like that, they've been known to cut the hair from their enemy's corpse."

"But, Anne wasn't his enemy," she said.

"Yes, she was. Because *I* loved her, he would have hated her. Her death would have been a victory for him... a blow against me."

"John," she said, grabbing his hands. "It's alright. We all have bad dreams. There's nothing wrong with being afraid of something."

"It just doesn't feel right," he replied.

"What doesn't?"

"Nothing. Nothing feels right at this moment. Something's wrong. I can feel it, Mary." His body stiffened as he grasped her small hands in his. "I've put you in danger... all of you. I have to go."

"John, they're just dreams."

"It's not just Wounded Hawk. McCain's hunting me. By this time, he'll be consumed with rage. I'll stake *my life* on it, but not yours. I have to leave."

"I don't understand," she said, stopping in mid sentence. Panicked voices reverberated in the rooms upstairs. Someone was screaming... a woman. Tim O'Hare's raised voice attempted to calm her, but to no avail.

"Something's wrong," commented Mary.

"Let's go see," replied John.

As the two drew close to the first floor of the church, the woman's voice was joined by the panicked voices of several other girls. Upon rounding the corner into the dining room, John and Mary were met by a horrible sight. Huddled in the corner, was a group of girls who were shaken and crying. In their midst, a blonde headed girl tended a cut on the face of a brunette. John immediately recognized that they were

Charles Kell's daughters. There was no mistaking that harem, especially the beauty of the older ones. Tim O'Hare entered from the kitchen with a pot of steaming water. Mary ran over to the girls and knelt onto the floor beside them.

"What's happened?" she demanded.

"I don't know," replied Tim as he placed the dish onto the dining table. "I can't get anythin' out of them. They ran in here panicked with the two older ones bleedin'."

"Where's Charles?" asked John.

"Girls," said Mary in a soothing voice. "It'll be alright. Marilyn, what's happened? Where's your father?" Mary held the two youngest girls in her arms. Marilyn tried to speak but was overcome with wrenching sobs.

"Th... They had their way with us!" screamed the younger, Carmine.

"My God," responded Tim. "Who?"

"The Irishmen," she managed, before catching her breath. "They beat papa and Marilyn!"

Tim dipped a washcloth into the steaming water and gave it to Mary. She dabbed it onto the cut on Marilyn's cheek. Blood soaked into the wet fabric, creating an ugly crimson stain. John stood motionless, unsure of what to do. He'd never been good at comforting women.

"What Irishmen?" asked Tim.

"Th... The ones who collect the insurance," replied Carmine.

"McCain's men?" asked John, feeling an ember flare as if hit by a gust of wind.

Carmine gave no audible answer, but nodded her head.

Why would McCain do such a thing? *Don't you know?* He could gain nothing by authorizing the rape of young girls. The citizens would be outraged. Perhaps, McCain thought that such an act would frighten them back into submission, but surely the people would retaliate.

"You're sure that it was the insurance men?" clarified Tim.

"Yes," replied Carmine while trying to comfort her older sister.

Tim turned to face John. "Are you satisfied? Is this what you were after?" He stood up and stepped toward John, stopping only inches from his face. "Because if so… you got it!"

"Take a good look at this scene, John! This is the kind of thing that happens when people go to war with someone like McCain. They get hurt! They get hurt in bad ways, boy! Do you finally understand?"

John made no reply, but stared helplessly as Mary tended to the girls.

"Where's your father, girls?" asked Tim.

"He told us to come here," replied Marilyn. "Then he went to warn everyone else on account of the shakedown."

"What do you mean?" asked John.

"The men…" Marilyn faltered. "They said we all had it comin'. They were goin' to teach everyone a lesson this evenin'. They said that it would be somethin' we'd never forget."

"Who?" asked John. "*Who* is going to teach the lesson?"

"All of them," she replied. "All of the enforcers! Tonight!"

Was McCain carrying out a citywide shakedown? If he were to set loose all of his men in Brooklyn, John would be powerless to do anything about it. He could engage a dozen or so men, but not hundreds.

"Do we call the police?" asked Mary.

"McCain owns the police," replied Tim.

"He does," granted John. "But, there's no way they could allow McCain go get away with a crime of that magnitude."

"They could delay their response, though," added Tim.

"Yes," he agreed. "They could."

"Many more people will be hurt," added Mary. "What can we do?"

"Nothing," replied Tim. "We pray and get ready for those who may be wounded."

"No," said John, his voice resolute. He stormed toward the basement.

Coney Island. That's what Ronald Thompson's note was about! Thompson was giving him McCain's location so that he could stop the shakedown. But, if that were the case, why didn't he just tell him about the proposed crime? Perhaps, Thompson didn't know what the "big thing" was. Was McCain getting wise about Thompson? Was he keeping him out of the loop? If that were the case, then the Coney Island lead could be a trap. Then again, there was a strong chance that it wasn't. John was sure that Thompson had a conscience. If John could get to McCain's hotel at Coney Island and kill him, he may be able to stop the shakedown. Killing McCain would also get Thompson clear of any hot water that he may have been in. Either way, there were risks. His decision would come down to one question: *Can I trust Ronald Thompson?*

John entered his room and opened the door to his wardrobe. He removed a heavy knapsack from the top shelf and emptied its contents onto the bed. Six revolvers and a leather harness system containing rows of bullets lay before him. Mary had hidden his weapons from Tim for fear that the man would dispose of them. She'd only recently brought the satchel out of hiding and returned it to him.

He slipped the harness over his shoulders and buckled the custom-made, black gun belt around his waist. The belt held four revolvers—one on each hip, and one gun on each thigh. The harness held two shorter pistols under each arm. The device allowed him thirty-six shots before reloading.

He cinched the second holster to his thigh, and turned to look into a full-length mirror. With uncanny speed, he drew a pistol from under his arm and the opposite hip then, holstered them just as quickly. He repeated the process with different guns, using different patterns until his rhythm smoothed. Memories of Joe trickled through his head. The man had spent countless hours training him how to fight with the weapons. He'd conditioned John's reflexes to the point that the revolvers had become an extension of his body—nothing more than extra fingers. After a minute of drawing and flinging pistols about, John was satisfied. He holstered his final draw. His ribs still ached, but the pain was manageable.

One piece was still missing. The white collar felt rigid in his hands. Mary had starched it heavily. He sometimes wondered why he wore the thing. It had begun as a reminder… a way to stop himself from giving over to his innermost demons—the desires that would make him like those he hunted. But, the collar had a different effect. It frightened his enemies. Perhaps when they saw the collar, they realized that God had recognized their evil deeds. He was reminded of a prayer he'd heard Joe recite on numerous occasions.

Oh Great White Spirit whose voice I hear in the winds, whose breath gives life to the world, hear me… I come to you as one of your children. I am small and weak. I need your strength and your wisdom. Not to be superior to my brothers, but to fight my greatest enemy... Myself.

He wrapped the collar around his neck and buttoned it into place.

"Is it not enough to commit such acts," asked the voice of Tim O'Hare, "you must make a mockery of God as well?"

"You know this has to happen," replied John, solemnly.

"Do I?"

"Are you still pretending that if you just ignore this mess, it'll go away?" asked John.

Tim stepped closer to John and looked him in his cold, gray eyes. "Are you still pretending that this is God's will?"

The man was incorrigible. John didn't see any need in continuing a theological debate with Tim. It was apparent that neither person would concede. So, he brushed by him and retrieved a long coat from the wardrobe.

"John, please stop. Think about what you're doing. I know how you feel. I've been down the same road. The *hate*... the lust for vengeance... it can stop. God can give you the freedom that you're searching for. You won't find it where you're looking."

Mary stepped into the doorway. The sight of her brought forth mixed emotions. One part of him wanted to take her and run far away. But, the other part wanted to ensure that she would never have to face the wrath of Anders McCain.

"It isn't about vengeance this time," explained John. "You have to believe me, Tim."

"Then what is it about, son?"

"*Justice*... It's about making sure that McCain never hurts another person. He's gone too far."

"Vengeance is mine, thus saith the Lord. God will repay those who sin against him. *He* will answer the people's cries for justice!"

"He has answered."

John slid his arms into the sleeves of his coat and shrugged it onto his shoulders. The silk mask lay bunched in his pocket. Before long it would cover his face, hopefully, for the last time.

Mary moved from the doorway as he approached.

"I have to go, Mary."

"I know," she replied.

It was nearly three-thirty in the afternoon when John Grady stepped from the front doors of Mount Zion Methodist Assembly. The sky was an ominous black of swirling clouds. Driving wind ripped through his hair and caused his coat to fly about him. Bolts of violet lighting danced across the dark canvas. The storm had arrived and from the looks of it, it would be a tempest to remember.

John could catch the four o'clock train to Sheepshead Bay and be at Coney Island before dusk. McCain was at the Steeplechase Hotel. No doubt, he would be heavily guarded as a result of *The Rendezvous* incident. At *The Rendezvous*, John had been attacked with submachine guns. Long-range combat was not an option; he'd be ripped to shreds. McCain would have to be engaged at close range. John saw no other options. He doubted McCain's death would stop the shakedown, but it might curtail it. With McCain dead, the payroll would stop and the enforcers would find themselves alienated.

As he stepped from the curb a soft voice called from behind. "John…"

He turned to find that Mary had followed him from the basement.

She spoke, a quiet strength in her voice. "Finish it."

"Thank you," he replied, through a throat choked with emotion.

He turned and walked toward the train station. McCain had to be stopped, regardless of children, loved ones, or any other reason. This quest was no longer about him, but about the welfare of a city. For the first time in his long search for the man in the white derby, he found himself *dreading* this confrontation. He'd have preferred to walk back into Mount Zion and into the warm arms of the woman who waited for him. *That's why you're finally ready.*

This time, he would finish it, for everyone.

Thirty-three

Brakes squealed as the train stopped at a lonely depot located just off Surf Avenue. John Grady had taken the Culver Line south through Brooklyn, crossed Sheepshead Bay, and veered east to the Coney Island Station. The train ride had been somewhat different from the one that had brought him to New York City. This time, the boarding docks were void of all life. John had been the sole traveler on his car this Sunday afternoon. No sane person would travel today.

The wind roared beneath the dock's awnings as John stepped from the lonely car. No rain had fallen as of yet, but the smell saturated the air. Discarded train schedules floated on the currents like leaves falling from autumn trees. A bolt of lighting struck somewhere toward the ocean, followed by a booming clap of thunder. John buttoned his jacket, lest a gust of wind reveal the armament he wore beneath. He made his way through the near empty station passing a clerk clothed in the standard, white button-down shirt with black armbands.

"Excuse me," said John, stopping the man.

"May I help you, sir?" replied the clerk.

"What time does your next train leave for upper Brooklyn?"

"I'm afraid there won't be anymore trains running this evening, sir… on account of the weather."

"None?"

"Well… no passenger trains. We do have an empty freight train that will be heading north to pick up supplies at around six-thirty, but that will do you no good."

"Thank you," said John as he hurried toward Surf Avenue.

John reached into his pocket and produced a tarnished silver watch. The timepiece had belonged to his father. James Grady had been wearing it the day he was gunned down by Anders McCain. John had always wondered if the blemishes might have been bloodstains.

Four fifty-three. There was time. He had over an hour and a half to walk the few hundred yards to Steeplechase Park, enter the hotel, and stop the shakedown. Even if he did manage to find McCain, he would have to return to upper Brooklyn and do what he could to help the businessmen. John hung a right onto Surf Avenue and trotted down the desolate sidewalk.

Coney Island was empty. Even the security guards who watched over the parks during the off-season were nowhere in sight. Anyone with any sense had taken cover in a strong building. The gale was reaching destructive proportions, with wind speeds reaching the strength of tornadoes John had survived back in Missouri. The current of air blew eastward along the coast, striking him directly in his face. Sand drifted across the street, lifted from the sidewalk and pelted his cheeks like dozens of stinging insects. The entrance to Steeplechase Park lay ahead. Great concrete arches towered above Surf Avenue, welcoming the summer multitude of guests to Steeplechase Park, but not this day. The large iron gates were locked shut. *Good. McCain isn't expecting me.*

Directly to his left, a bulky three-story hotel loomed against the darkened sky. An American flag whipped about, atop its red-shingled roof. The white behemoth seemed lonely on this bleak winter's day. Throngs of people should have been streaming in and out, but none except John Grady dared to walk its pathways.

John knew that inside the building a terrible life form existed—one that felt no pity or was capable of anything good. Somewhere, deep within his ivory fortress, Anders McCain rested, trusting in the safety of this solitary stronghold. John reached into his pocket and produced the black hood. He pulled the covering on, tied the string behind his head, and tucked it into his collar.

Obviously, he couldn't just stroll in through the front door, so he stepped onto the two-foot high, stone wall that surrounded the park. He grasped the six-foot wrought iron bars and pulled himself upward. After placing a foot on the horizontal bar at the top of the fence, he leapt over and hit the ground rolling. The impact wrenched his side. He'd have to remember that his ribs hadn't completely healed or he would be disabled before he even entered the hotel.

He moved quickly, but cautiously across the brown grass. Even in its dead state, John could tell that the lawn had been manicured with detailed precision. He slipped past the front yard and around the left corner of the hotel into a narrow alleyway. With the hotel behind him, John stared straight ahead at several smaller buildings, which lined the eastern side of the park. Because he had never been to Steeplechase Park or Coney Island for that matter, he would have to pay close attention to his surroundings. The buildings were tight on this side of the park and would provide the cover he needed should he come into contact with those handheld machineguns again. From his position, looking toward the rear of the hotel, the rest of the park seemed more open and contained odd shaped buildings and rides. His best escape route would most likely be on the east side of the park, from where he had entered.

John shouldered past several windows in the alley and made his way toward an inconspicuous side door, most likely a service entrance. He checked the door handle. *Locked... Good.* The gates to the park were locked as well. If it were a trick, McCain definitely wasn't rolling out the red carpet. But, where were the guards? Where were McCain's men? It was hard to believe that McCain would let his guard down after *The Rendezvous* incident. Then again, the weather was horrible and if the men weren't blown away, they would likely be struck by lighting. *Then, they're in the hotel.*

He unbuttoned his coat and retrieved the tomahawk from his belt. The blade slid into the crevice between the door and doorjamb until it met the resistance of the bolt. With force, he twisted the tomahawk to the side and pried the door away from its frame. Then, while holding the weapon in its position, he waited for a burst of lightning. Within moments, the flash occurred. He lunged into the door with his shoulder just as the thunder boomed. In a burst of splinters, the door popped open, splitting the doorjamb from top to bottom. John was inside the boiler room of the Steeplechase Hotel.

The dim room received only a small amount of light from the open door and several windows, which had been painted white. Four large black cylinders lined the far wall. The large boilers were used for heating the expansive hotel in the cooler seasons. He grabbed the open door and swung it back into place. It wouldn't latch, but hopefully it would fool the roaming eye of a bored guard. He turned left and walked through another doorway that led into a series of halls. Because John had no idea where he was going, he would have to search the building. McCain liked being in an elevated location. Perhaps the trait mirrored his outlook on life. Because McCain always wanted to be on top, he chose to live in high places. *Is that why you live in a basement?*

He picked a hallway whose destination was bathed in the glow of blue sunlight. The sound of his boots on the tile floor echoed through the hall. He attempted to walk more with more stealth. Upon reaching the end of the corridor, he stopped and scanned the area.

Before him was one of the most beautiful rooms he had ever seen. The floor was made of cut marble that swirled with dozens of light colors, ranging from stark white to ashen gray. The walls were painted white and lined along the top and bottom with ornately carved, gold trim. Large mirrors lined the front of the dining hall from the floor to the ceiling and reflected the seemingly infinite extent of Steeplechase Park and the ocean beyond. Dining tables, hidden under white sheets, were scattered throughout the room. Their chairs were turned upside down and placed on top of the tables. John was strangely reminded of an Indian village full of tepees. An odd sensation entered John's mind, like the dawning of something known, yet unrecognized.

He stepped into the vast room and maneuvered between the tables. His boots clicked sharply on the polished stone. The bay windows were massive and hid no details of the park beyond. The ocean looked to be about a quarter of a mile away. Its angry waves white capped across its expanse and exploded upon the large wooden pier that lay at the end of Steeplechase's boardwalk. Directly behind the hotel, the tracks of a wooden roller coaster slithered around the eastern half of the park. In its center was a high water tower built upon a circular ring of several wooden stilts. The tower was at least seven stories high. On the west side of the park, he could see a large Ferris wheel with cabins capable of holding several people and a gigantic seesaw-like ride with two mini Ferris wheels on each end. In front of that was a four-story bell tower that stood in the center of the park adjacent to the boardwalk. The boardwalk ran through the middle of the park from the entrance gates at the front and ended in the pier at the back.

John returned his gaze to the front wall and absorbed the expanse of the park. The mirrors gave the impression of being on an island surrounded by the sea. The Ferris wheel spun slowly in its socket as the wind tugged at its large passenger cabins. And, of course, there was the storm that blanketed the sky as far as the eye could see. The sight was beautiful and ominous at the same time. John lowered his head in thought.

This hotel *seemed* empty, just as vacant as the park it overlooked. This dining room hadn't been touched. Could McCain be living here, but choose not to enjoy his kingly right of dining in such a fabulous hall? No, the room hadn't been used since the hotel staff prepared it for winter. *The feeling... what have I missed?* The epiphany hit him like a blow to the head. *The boilers! They weren't lit!* The boiler room had been chilly. He'd been in boiler rooms before. The heat should have been intense, to the point of generating a literal "wall of heat". But, they hadn't been burning. This hotel had no heat or hot water. There was no one living here. It was a trap. Ronald Thompson had betrayed him. Was the shakedown happening at all? Or had it all been a ploy to get him to the killing ground? McCain could use any weapon at his disposal in this vacated park within this raging storm. No witnesses would see or hear anything.

Stupid, John! He wanted to fling a chair through the bay windows, but right now, he needed to control his anger and think. He had to get out of here. Perhaps he could turn around and return to the boiler room. How many men were here? And where were they? Why hadn't they already attacked him?

A tingling sensation ran the length of his spine. John shuddered and took a deep breath. One-by-one, the hair on the back of his neck stood erect. His first impression was to look into the mirror, to prove he was wrong. The presence he now felt was familiar. He had sensed it many times in his life and encountered it nightly in his dreams. With a sheer act of willpower, he raised his head just enough to look into the mirror. Behind him, on the dead lawn, stood the ghost he had had left more than twenty years earlier. His brown leather duster flowed around him in the currents of speeding air. Gray suit pants ended in knee-high moccasins. The pearl-like eye beamed from beneath the soiled rawhide mask that covered one side of his face. The man smiled.

Muscles locked, gripping John like a giant's vice. Instinct told him to move, but reason assured him that to act would mean certain death. For a man, like none he had ever faced, stalked his trail this day. All of his fear, his past, the things he'd escaped, the things he still ran from—all came swelling back in one terrible realization. *Wounded Hawk! He is alive!*

John slowly turned his eyes back to the floor. *Impossible!* Or was it? Was it *really* impossible? *It's a dream!* He'd never woken up. He was still in his bed, in the basement of Mount Zion, fast asleep. Mary would be just across the hall in her room. The note from Ronald Thompson... the Kell girls... was all just a part of another whacked nightmare. But, dreams didn't feel this *real*. A stale odor floated about the dining room. And, he could hear the sound of pebbles being driven against the large glass windows. Dreams were never so detailed. *And, my ribs ache.*

He would have to move swiftly. Wounded Hawk was the fastest gunman he'd ever seen. The last time they met in battle, John had been wounded badly. Only luck had saved him.

There was no escape from this moment. The reckoning would happen. John would pivot on his left foot and draw both guns from his hips. He'd have to fire hastily then move. Most likely his shots would miss, but they might buy him enough time to take cover behind a table. John mustered control of his limbs for a quick burst of speed. Breath rushed into his lungs as John pivoted and drew the revolvers from his belt. Both hammers cocked before his arms straightened. But the yard was empty. The spot the Indian had been standing only moments ago was vacant. A piece of paper tumbled across the patio and took flight. John closed his eyes and shook his head. *Am I going crazy?* Had the dreams finally made their transition into his waking hours?

With pistols in hand, he moved timidly toward the two French doors that opened onto the veranda. John holstered the gun he held in his right hand and grabbed the handle of one of the doors. With a twist of his wrist, the bolt clicked and the door popped open. The force of the wind nearly ripped it from John's grasp. He eased the door back until it locked into place.

The granite walkway in front of him split a flowerbed that ran the length of the rear wall. The patio extended about fifteen feet to the lawn upon which Wounded Hawk had been standing. John crossed the veranda and knelt before the grass. *Nothing.* There was nothing. There were no tracks or impressions that John could see. *He was standing right here! Is this some kind of a joke, God? Are you finally driving me crazy?* The grass was still wet from the recent snowmelt. Someone standing in it should have left some kind of impression. John rolled his head, popping his neck. He didn't know which scenario was better. If Wounded Hawk were alive, there would be many ramifications to deal with. If he weren't, that would mean John was going crazy. Neither was a preferred set of circumstances. With his free hand, he wiped away a bit of saliva that had crept from his gaping mouth.

Steeplechase Park was empty. Steeplechase Hotel was empty. Ronald Thompson had lied or been given false information. These details pointed to a trap, but he had not been attacked yet. And, he had thought he'd seen Wounded Hawk. But, what could Wounded Hawk have to do with all of this? This was about McCain. What did Wounded Hawk know about McCain? Wounded Hawk was killed long before John had any concrete evidence on the man in the white derby. As a matter of fact, he'd never told anyone about his leads. And why would Wounded Hawk allow McCain to *use* him? There were dozens of answers and none at all, but only one made sense. He had imagined Wounded Hawk. It was only logical that his dreams would eventually exhibit themselves in reality.

John stood, backed toward the dining hall and stopped. His eyes caught the slightest blemish on the granite. How had he missed it? To his right, about ten feet away, a wet smudge stained the walkway. He moved closer, scrutinizing the footprint. His stomach sank. There was no mistaking the track. Modern shoes left two prints, the ball and heel. This track was composed of only one. It was the imprint of soft leather wrapped around a foot. *Moccasins. He's here.*

John rose to his feet and started to head for cover, but noticed more tracks. They followed the pathway to the right and headed for the boardwalk. As far as he could see, the tracks continued in an alternating pattern, one after the other. John started on the trail.

A rush of thoughts swirled through his mind. *How did he survive? Where has he been all of this time? What's he doing here? What does he have to do with McCain?* Question after unanswerable question riddled his mind as he crossed a bridge that spanned a narrow canal. The tracks continued south through the center of the park.

The Indian's moccasins had soaked up much water, leaving an obvious trail for John to follow along the bricked walkway. The tracks continued into the distance. Wounded Hawk *wanted* to be tracked. He would never make such a costly mistake. John was *supposed* to follow. John didn't fear ambush. The Indian was violent and mad, but John's death would be a matter of honor for him. He would meet John face to face and take his scalp when it was over.

To John's right, the giant seesaw teetered in the wind. How many other men were out here? They could have been hiding anywhere. John should have been worried; he should have been cautious. But, he was too drawn—too overcome by a force that beckoned him. His gaze was locked on the wet spots that continued down the walkway. To his right, the great Ferris wheel rotated in its cradle, groaning and popping against the gusts.

The man's face... his white eyeball flashed before John's eyes. Each time, the vision startled him, bringing back ancient memories. John had been the cause for the mask. Wounded Hawk hated him for that. But, it hadn't been John's fault.

Joe had become disgusted with the murderous life Wounded Hawk had chosen to live and cut himself off from him. Enraged, Wounded Hawk had visited and argued with the aging man. Their argument became heated, and, as a result of his rejection, Wounded Hawk attacked Joe. John had intervened and fired a shot at the Indian. The bullet struck a nearby kerosene lamp, which exploded onto Wounded Hawk's face. The Indian fled as Joe died in John's arms. Thunder Crow—the second father John Grady had lost. Wounded Hawk blamed John for his loss. He accused him of stealing the love of his grandfather and said that Joe's death was the result.

As John passed the water tower on his left, an uninhibited wind raged from the ocean. The park opened up and gave way to a vast horizon. Waves billowed and crashed to the shore in foaming blankets of seawater. Ahead, the tracks left the boardwalk and veered into the sand. As John approached the entrance to the long wooden pier, he noticed the smaller rock jetty to its right. The peninsula was formed from a massive pile of boulders that jutted into the ocean. Waves pounded against the side of the jetty opposite the pier. Black clouds churned overhead, attempting to smother the slight orange glow of the setting sun. At the end of the jetty, beneath the swarm of hellish billows, a dark figure stood. The man awaited a life-long reckoning. There was a blood debt to settle.

John stepped off of the boardwalk and into the sand. He holstered the pistol he held in his left hand. It would be a traditional gunfight. Both men would draw from the holstered position. John found it ironic that men developed rules for killing. He supposed every man desired some degree of honor.

Sandy air grazed his face. The jetty was no more than fifty yards away. Each step in the deep sand was labored as John's footing slipped away. The muscle of his wounded thigh ached. There were no words that could describe the significance of this moment. Few people transcended a person's entire life. Not even John's parents had done that— only Anders McCain and Wounded Hawk. In a sudden twist of irony he realized that Wounded Hawk must have felt the same as he did. *Has he hunted me all this time… as I have hunted McCain?* God *did* have a sense of humor.

The solid surface of the jetty offered his legs immediate relief. A concrete walkway led into the ocean, twisted and buckled, rising like tiny mountains in places. Midway down, Wounded Hawk waited. Water rushed past the Indian's feet as a wave struck the jetty. John inhaled deeply through his nose, hiding the action from Wounded Hawk, then marched out to meet him. He stopped thirty paces short. A trembling hand caught the fabric of his mask. He removed the covering and allowed the wind to take it from his fingers and across the foaming waves. He would never wear it again.

For a minute, neither man spoke. Instead, they silently absorbed the moment. Wounded Hawk had aged. He was not the young man that John remembered, though the hatred still burned brightly in his eyes. His graying hair was pulled back on the uninjured side of his face and into a ponytail decorated with two black crow feathers. On the side with the mask, it whipped about his face in loose tangles. His coat was unbuttoned and flapped away from his body, revealing two pistols. One was butt first on his belt; the other was under his arm. *Just the way Joe taught us.*

Something else dangled from Wounded Hawk's belt. It was long, dark, and… *braided.* It was a lock of hair. *Anne.* The savage *had* cut it from her body. And, now, he wore the braid on his belt like a hard-earned trophy. John ground his teeth.

Then, the Indian shouted words from John's dreams. "Hello, Brother! It's been a long time!"

A wave slapped the rocks, sending a spray of salty water through the air. It saturated John's coat and filled his mouth with a foul taste. Water droplets glistened on the surface of his sleeve. John had never wanted to kill Wounded Hawk. He'd never hated him. After all, they had been brothers. He knew, however, that the man would never give up. John understood vengeance. The force that drove Wounded Hawk was unstoppable and had to be dealt with in one of two ways: fulfillment or death.

"Then let's finish it!" John replied, shouting above the roar of the ocean.

Neither man moved immediately, but watched for a sign from the other. There were two approaches one could take—get the jump with the first draw or respond to the move of your opponent. Either way could work. Luck was the major factor, regardless.

Wounded Hawk moved first, drawing both weapons just as they had been trained. John wheeled to his right and drew a single revolver from his hip. Time slowed. And for a moment, the earth stood as a final witness to the reckoning. With blinding speed, Wounded Hawk's pistols moved up and fired two bright muzzle blasts. John's left arm was straight as he pulled the trigger, but his body was turned to the side, offering his opponent a thin profile. Wounded Hawk's bullets blazed by on both sides of John, grazing the shoulder of each arm. Seawater exploded from his coat in millions of tiny particles. Wounded Hawk lurched backward as if hit. A split second later, a giant wave struck the jetty. Water burst into the air and consumed Wounded Hawk in an avalanche of foam.

A moment later, John's feet were torn out from under him.

Thirty-four

John Grady's head smashed into a rock before an uncontrollable force spun his body. The current rolled him over and over again before finally subsiding. He surfaced in waste-deep water only feet from the shore, a pistol still clutched in his hand. A strong rip current pulled his legs toward the open sea. What had happened to wounded Hawk? It seemed as if he'd been blown backward. Where was he? *I won't leave until it's finished.*

John started to clamber up the side of the jetty when the first bullet struck the walkway. A barrage quickly followed. Bullets struck the sand and rocks all around him. His first instinct was to search out Wounded Hawk and end the attack. The shots, however, weren't coming from a revolver, but from some type of machinegun. John scrambled over the rock jetty and took cover on the opposite side. Muffled gunfire rang out from somewhere inside Steeplechase Park. Sparks flew from the jetty walkway as bullets ricocheted just above his head. Shards of rock stung his hands and face. Whatever was being fired at him was a high caliber weapon.

A loud roaring sound approached from behind. John shoved his fingertips between the rocks in an attempt to find a handhold. The wave struck with brutal force and drove him into the boulder, lifting his feet above his head. He held on tight and managed to stay put until the water retreated back to the sea. He had to move. If he stayed next to the jetty, the force of the water would pummel him to death. Before he did anything, though, he needed to know where that gunfire was originating from. *There's only one way to do that.*

He slowly lifted his head above the jetty and scanned the park for the inevitable muzzle blasts. Nothing happened. There were only three structures where the shooter could have been. One of them was a tall water tower, which was the most likely position. John raised himself a little higher, prompting the gunfire to erupt again. Bullets streaked from the water tower, forcing him to take cover. From the height of the tower, the shooters could see anywhere within gun range.

He could make a run for the Steeplechase pier, whose understructure would provide plenty of cover. Or, he could charge up the beach toward the park, then hide within the buildings of the western side. Either way, he had a seventy-five yard run with no available cover. The second option would put a two-story building between him and the gun tower. If John could make it fifty yards up the beach, the building would obstruct the gunman's line-of-sight. With the sound of another approaching wave, John took his cue to run.

Wet sand spun from under his boots and water-soaked clothing tried to pull him back toward the ocean. The machinegun roared to life again, punching holes into the beach around him. John had always been a fast runner, but bullets flew faster. And, these bullets were huge. His legs pumped up and down, driving him through the sand and towards the shelter of the boardwalk. He realized that if he angled left, he would put the building between himself and the machinegun nest much sooner. Shots whizzed by his ears like giant bees. Bullets of this caliber had never been fired at him. He could feel the percussion off of every piece of lead that flew past him. But, there was nowhere to go, no place to hide. No wonder so many men were killed in battle from freezing in the midst of a gunfight. It made a man want to get up and shout, "enough!"

Just when he thought his leg muscles would erupt in flames, the barrage struck the building ahead, blowing red shingles from the rooftop and spinning them into the air. He had reached safety. He slowed his pace and trotted for the boardwalk ahead of him.

Upon reaching the massive wooden walkway, he ducked under it and collapsed against a splintered post. It was time to weigh his options.

For the moment, he was safe. But, before long, men would come looking for him. Or, maybe they wouldn't. Sooner or later though, he would have to leave the boardwalk. Dusk was drawing closer. He pulled the pocket watch and pressed the stem with his index finger. The cover popped open. *Nearly five-thirty.* The freight train would be leaving in an hour. *That should be enough time to get out of here.* Given his current location, the simplest escape route would be along the outer western edge of the park. During

262

his flight from the jetty, he'd noticed that the property next to Steeplechase was largely undeveloped. It wouldn't provide much cover, but it would offer a fast exit. And, if he stayed close enough to the buildings, the men in the water tower shouldn't be able to see him.

John gritted his teeth and rose to his feet. His body hadn't completely healed from his injuries, and he was really starting to feel it. He stretched his leg, trying to relieve his cramping thigh.

John walked the length of the boardwalk, which stretched the width of the park from east to west. Upon reaching the end, he stopped and squatted, then peered around the corner. There was a paved walkway that ran from the beach to Surf Avenue at the north end of the park. Unfortunately, the sidewalk was too far from the edge of Steeplechase and would have been open to gunfire from the tower. *There's my other problem.*

Three men moved along the fence line about halfway up the edge of the park. Normally, a few men carrying pistols or shotguns wouldn't have intimidated John, but he recognized the small rifle-like weapons that the three men carried. The little machineguns were too fast for him to charge. If guards were on the west side of the park, they would roam the east side as well. His only chance would be to maneuver through the buildings on the west. The close quarters would put him at an advantage over McCain's henchmen.

A thought struck him. *Wounded Hawk... where is he?* What had happened to him? John had been so busy trying to save his neck that he'd forgotten about the Indian. It seemed as if he'd been hit, but then that giant wave struck. With the strong rip current, he could have been sucked out to sea. *Or he may be in the park, waiting to finish me off.*

John slipped from the bowels of the boardwalk and pulled himself up and onto its top surface. The building still shielded him from the machine gunner for the moment. Stealthfully, he moved toward the structure and realized, in fact, that it was an open grotto which housed the carousel. He backed against the solid outer wall and scanned the area.

There would be a thirty-yard dash to the next available piece of cover. A circular building was his only choice. The three guards on the west side would be responding to the machinegun fire. Also, the men in the water tower knew his location. He couldn't stay put any longer. His legs were tired and his side ached, but he would have to make the sprint to the building. He pulled two guns from their holsters, just in case, and bolted from his temporary refuge.

The gunners must have been taken off guard because John managed to cover half the distance before they opened fire. The weapon was much louder now that John was only seventy-five yards away from the tower. Chunks of mud blew into the air as the projectiles struck at his heels. A bullet blew through the tail of his coat just as he reached the safety of the building. As he settled in against the curved outer wall of the structure, he happened to catch the name of the attraction. *Holy Land... an ironic place to die.*

From the corner of his eye, he caught movement toward the west edge, just behind a building on the border. He crouched as the monster machinegun quieted. *The men from the border.* They must have been working their way between the buildings and had moved into the park. One of them was easing around the corner of the bathhouse. He hadn't seen John as of yet, but he would within moments.

264

The automatic rifles presented him with a new challenge. Normally, John had only to beat a man before he could fire *one* round. With these guns, though, he had to beat a man who, with the pull of a trigger, had the capability of firing dozens of rounds. If he were going to make it out of Steeplechase alive, he would have to utilize the element of surprise. *I have to catch that train at six-thirty!*

With guns still in each hand, he bolted the ten yards between the Holy Land and the three-story bathhouse. Upon arriving, he jumped the short hedge and flattened against the wall. The Holy Land attraction continued to obstruct the line of fire from the machinegun tower. John holstered one of his pistols as a short black barrel protruded from the north corner of the building. *He knows I'm in this area.* John could choose to be reactive or proactive. With these fast guns, however, it was better to act first. So, he slid along the building, between the hedge and the wall, trying to move as quietly as possible. As he reached the corner of the bath house, his coat snagged on the hedge and caused it to rustle. The shocked guard leveled his gun. John's empty hand caught the barrel and pushed it into the air, then he fired into the man's chest with his unsheathed pistol. The man fell backwards and squeezed the trigger of the sub-machinegun. A burst of shots fired into the air. Windows shattered on the second floor of the bathhouse and a shower of glass careened down. John ducked and covered his head with his coat, but not before a shard nicked his cheek. A hot bead of blood trickled down the curve of his jaw.

From the center of the park, a loan gunshot fired. John reacted in time to see a wobbling cylindrical object fly through the air. Confused, he watched as it landed against the far side of the bathhouse. The wall exploded, blowing mortar and brick outward. Small pieces sprayed John as he dove to the ground. *What was that?!* Another shot echoed from the direction of the water tower and another flying bomb, the size of a soda bottle, wobbled through the air. This time, it was going to land closer. It was time to leave this place or be blown to pieces.

Immediately north of the bathhouse was some type of small train depot. He dashed between the train ride and the Holy Land as the bomb struck the corner where he had been hiding. The concussion of the blast blew him forward and face first into the ground just as a second gunmen fired from between the train depot and another large building. The bullet whizzed over his head. John responded with two shots of his own. The first shot hit the corner of the building, blowing debris into the man's face. The second shot hit him in the gut. Whaling, the man dropped his rifle and fell to the ground. He began to crawl away.

John ran for the rifle, prompting the machinegun to fire from the water tower. Without knowing it, he'd left the sanctity of the Holy Land attraction and found himself protected only by the skeletal structure of the Ferris wheel. Bullets pinged and ricocheted off of the large, metal beams as the wheel spun slowly. Some managed to pass through and impact the concrete around him. More gunfire came from the bell tower, about three stories high and much closer. With his head ducked low, he ran toward the Ferris wheel for cover. Even more shots sounded from behind him. He hustled toward a small alley between the junctions of two buildings at the north side of the Ferris wheel. He dove into the alcove just as another grenade struck the front corner of the building. Dust and debris blew past him, but he remained untouched within his small shelter. The smoke and dust dissipated with hurry in the strong wind currents.

From the corner where he had shot the first gunmen, another man loaded one of the grenade rifles. John watched as the man pulled a cylinder from a satchel, stuck the grenade on the end of the barrel and twisted it into place. He ducked deeper into the alcove and discovered a service door leading into the attraction. He was caught in a horrible position. John was trapped with shooters on both sides of him.

To his left front was the heavy machinegun and grenade launcher. Directly to his left was a gunman in the bell tower. And now, there was another grenade launcher to his right. If he stayed here, they would pummel him to death with the grenades. But, if he ran, he would be fired at from three directions. *I could go into the building.* Inside, though, he would be like a trapped rat.

Another grenade struck. It hit the corner of the larger building, blowing a five-foot section of wall away. A large chunk of bricks tumbled out of the hole and burst on the ground. The concussion blew John against the rear of the alcove, leaving him dazed and disoriented. A sharp tone rang in his ears. He had no choice but to go into the building. He turned and kicked the door with all of his might. It cracked, but did not break, so he kicked again... and again. Finally, the door burst inward and John entered the dim interior.

Thirty-five

The pungent scent of earth overwhelmed John Grady's senses as hanging vines and plants brushed against his face. It appeared as if he were standing in some overgrown forest. He had apparently entered some type of jungle or woodland exhibit. Various species of trees and plants grew throughout the large room. The floor was composed of dirt and moss-covered rock. Diffused sunlight trickled through large windows on the eastern side. *I'll have to stay away from those.* The man in the bell tower would have a perfect shot at him if he got anywhere near those windows.

His first chore was to find a way out of this building, preferably to the north or west. He'd already taken out two of the three men he'd seen patrolling the west side and, at this point, he was getting close to the front of the park. Surely there would be another service entrance in this building.

But, after walking the length of the room, he found that it ended in a door-less wall that had been designed to look like rock. The only exit that he could find was on the eastern wall situated between two of the big windows. The escape route would put him at extremely close range to the bell tower and would offer no protection from the water tower either. *No good.* The building had appeared larger as he passed it on his trek to the ocean. *There must be another room behind this wall.* He would have to find a way around it.

He eased along the wall, straining to see through the maze of vegetation. Finally, his eyes settled on a rock formation that slanted toward the ceiling. As he moved around it, he realized that it was actually a flight of stairs. The stairway had been designed to look like it had been carved from rock. The steps led to a brighter room above. John didn't like his options, but there was nowhere left to go. He placed a boot on the first step and ascended the stairs. His thigh screamed under the pressure of the climb. And as his adrenaline subsided, pain flowed from his rib cage and nearly caused him to collapse. But he couldn't give in. He had to reach Mary. He had to help the people.

John stepped into the upstairs room. A blur flew at him from his right. He ducked just as the ironclad glove of Nick Rocci crashed into the doorjamb, smashing it to pieces. John tried to draw a pistol, but was stopped by the vice-like grip of Nick's other hand. He struggled against the man, but to no avail. Rocci was as strong as anyone John had ever encountered.

With a hard twist of his hips, Nick threw John against the far wall and wrenched the gun from his hands. By the time John bounced off of the wall, he was already drawing another pistol. Nick punched him square in the face with his ungloved hand. John stumbled against the wall and bounced back again. The man's naked fist was almost as hard as the gloved one. As John stepped away from the wall for the second time, Nick grabbed his coat and spun him around, hurling him at the wall once more. John crashed through the partition and tumbled into another room. Upon looking up, his head swooned. Rocci had thrown him onto the ceiling. John held his hands in front of him, expecting to fall onto the kitchen table below.

Nick charged into the room and swung at John who ducked and delivered a punch to his abdomen. Stunned, Nick grabbed a wooden chair that was bolted onto the ceiling directly above. John tried to compose himself, but Nick ripped the chair from the roof and slammed it onto him. The chair smashed into pieces, sending wooden parts skittering around the room. John's vision blurred and his thoughts became foggy. Nick walked over to the disoriented man and grabbed a handful of hair. John groaned against the humiliating pain and grasped Nick's wrist with both hands, trying to relieve some of the pressure.

The Fist cocked his gloved hand and prepared a killing punch. He wrenched the hair on John's head.

"Say 'uncle'," taunted Nick.

John gritted his teeth against the pressure.

"Say it!"

John made no reply. Instead, his hand grasped for the gun on his left thigh. Nick unleashed the coiled fist and sent it flying toward John's temple. Nick's fist met the revolver like the collision of two freight trains. The gunshot tore through the man's ironclad glove. Blood, bone, and metal burst into the air. Nick fell away from John, screaming. The sagging glove had become a formless, blood-soaked mess. He stumbled toward the stairs holding his wrist, slipped in his own blood, and fell. The man sounded like a bucket of bricks as he tumbled to the first level. John slumped to the floor and waited for the room to stop spinning.

He looked around at the strange area, trying to make some sense of everything. Then he remembered a sign he had passed. *The House Upside Down.*

There was no way out from upstairs, only more windows on the east side, which led to certain death. He'd have to leave the same way he came in. At least, the Ferris wheel would provide him with *some* cover. He pulled the pocket watch from his pants and pushed the stem. The cover opened to reveal a fogged glass. *Almost Five-thirty.* It had been close to five-thirty the last time he'd checked back on the beach. He tapped the face with his finger. *Dead!* What time was it? He looked toward the window. It was fairly dark, but had been that way for hours. He had to catch that train. It could have been close to six-thirty by now.

John picked up his guns, limped down the stairway and stepped over an unconscious Nick Rocci. He didn't have enough time to continue this fight. He had to do whatever he could to get out of the park and to that train station. If McCain had somehow teamed with Wounded Hawk, then he may know John's identity. That would mean that Mary and Tim could be in danger, not to mention all of the citizens who were possibly being terrorized at this moment. He had to get back to Upper Brooklyn. He passed through the broken door and exited the protected alcove.

Gunfire immediately flew from the two towers. Two more gunmen had joined the volley and fired from hidden positions beneath the coaster track.

John dove for the operational cavity of the Ferris wheel. The trench was about four feet deep and offered him good shelter. Above him, the giant wheel groaned and shimmied. A piece of the axle housing had broken under the strain of the wind. He ducked into the bunker and the gunfire lulled.

The enforcer with the grenade launcher was somewhere behind him over by the bathhouse. If he could make a run toward him and pick him off, the west side should have been free of threats. But, the enforcer was no longer behind him. John watched him creep out from the front side of the Holy Land and prepare to launch his grenade. John shot him just as he squeezed the trigger of his weapon. The grenade wobbled through the air toward his hiding place. John flattened himself onto the bottom of the trench. With an earsplitting boom, the bomb struck and detonated near the Ferris wheel's axle. The web-work of metal screeched and grinded as the wind pushed at its cars. The man with the grenade rifle was dead. If he could just get to that grenade launcher, he could take out some of those tower gunners. But, the weapon was fifty yards away and in the open. The Ferris wheel popped and shifted above him. If he didn't move, the thing was likely to fall on him. But, his thought came too late. With a slight shift in the direction of wind, the axle mount crumbled, the Ferris wheel wrenched to the side and dropped from its cradle. With a thunderous crash, the monster wheel hit the ground and began to roll down the incline of the boardwalk toward the ocean.

John arose from the pit and ran behind the ride, using it for cover. The tower gunners opened fire, but the spinning beams deflected most of their rounds. Through the whirling shafts, John picked out the two shooters under the coaster track and fired several times. One of them stiffened and fell

272

to his knees. John unleashed another volley of bullets and all gunfire from under the tracks ceased.

As the Ferris wheel rolled, one of its cars was thrown into the air. It crashed with a deafening noise just as John dove for the grenade rifle. He grabbed the rifle and the satchel of grenades. The Ferris wheel struck the edge of the coaster, spun on its axis and wobbled to the ground like a giant coin. Amid steady gunfire, John ran into the carousel grotto and crouched into a sheltered corner.

He reached into the dead enforcer's pouch and found three unused grenades. He took one of the explosives and slid its long tail into the barrel of the gun, then twisted it into place just as he had seen the enforcer doing. *How does this thing fire?* The gun itself looked like a normal bolt-action rifle, so he pulled the bolt back and watched the round load into the chamber. There was no bullet on the end of the cartridge. *It fires blanks and uses the percussion to propel the grenade.* He jammed the bolt forward, loading the round into the barrel.

The shooters had him pinned down. If he tried a shot from where he was, they would be on him too quickly. But, he could walk to the other side of the grotto and pop out on the back corner. That might buy him a few seconds in which to aim. So, he passed by the horse-covered carrousel and stepped through an open arch that looked out upon the ocean.

The sun no longer bled through the clouds near the horizon. The wind, which was unimpeded here, tore at his clothing. He moved to the corner and readied himself to fire. He'd only have one shot before the shooters locked in on him. Peeking around the corner, he examined the water tower for the first time. He could see two men atop the tall structure, positioned on the walkway that surrounded the water barrel. One shooter manned a cannon-sized machinegun and the other held a grenade launcher identical to John's. He steadied himself. The wind was blowing hard, so he'd have to adjust his shot. He fingered one of the spare grenades. It weighed about half a pound and was fairly rounded. It wouldn't drift too much.

John swung around the corner and aimed the rifle. His movement caught the eye of the gunner, who pivoted and took a bead just as John's grenade discharged. The two men watched helplessly as the projectile spun through the air, drifting toward their safe haven. The bomb struck the barrel above them and blew the planks apart. A torrential wave of water fell as the right side of the barrel disintegrated. The men were caught in the wall of water and swept over the side. The machine gunner's screams were drowned as he dropped amidst the pounding waterfall. The other man managed to hang on for a moment before taking the seven-story plunge. His life ended in a muted thud. Water careened down the tower in numerous free-falling streams, creating a river that flowed toward the ocean.

Then, as if waiting for her signal, Mother Nature released her inevitable downpour. Water fell from the sky and joined the force of its sister, the wind. The mixture hit John like a wall and caused him to retreat into the carrousel structure. He looked outside, but could see nothing. There was still a shooter in the bell tower and probably more in the east side of the park. Now, however, he could escape through the west side uninhibited. In the downpour, he was unlikely to be seen at all.

John left the rifle and ran between the Holy Land and the Bath House, where he had originally intended to make his exit. He left the border of the park by way of the miniature train station and climbed the six-foot iron fence. As he ran toward the front of *Steeplechase*, he heard a train whistle blow in the distance. *Six-thirty.* He could make it. It took locomotives a long time to build up any real speed.

John ran as fast as his battered body would allow him and turned the corner of the park onto Surf Avenue. Two hundred yards lay between him and the train station. If he missed the train, he didn't know how he would get back to the city. What would Mary do? What if McCain had already gotten to them? He would return to the church before going anyplace else. He would make sure Tim and Mary were safe, then he'd do whatever else was needed.

John veered left and ran along the outer edge of the train station. He was exhausted. His lungs were on fire. No matter how hard he breathed, he could not satisfy them.

Within minutes, the ground became saturated with water, causing his boots to sink in the fresh mud. Ahead, the light of the locomotive pulled away from the docks. There looked to be several boxcars attached. Two were open. He needed one more burst of speed to match the pace of the train.

John summoned his remaining strength and swung parallel to the cars as they rolled along the track. The train blew another whistle in an attempt to cut the black evening with its shrill sound. John caught one of the boxcars. After a few moments of struggle, he managed to pull himself in and collapsed. The splintered floor offered some respite. He rolled onto his back. His clothing was soaked with freezing water. No strength remained in his body—every ounce had been sapped. In labored gasps, his lungs attempted to regain their precious air. The ride to Brooklyn would take around forty minutes. But there would be no rest. John's mind continued the struggle his body had escaped as thoughts of Mary and innocent people bombarded him.

John stared at the roof of the car, and began to shiver.

Thirty-six

A rain-soaked Charles Kell crept around the front of *The Lunch Room*, a small restaurant on Fourth Street. His hands squeezed the wooden handle of a coal shovel that he'd grabbed as he'd left his butcher's shop.

After the horror that had been committed in his home, Charles had lost all sense of self-preservation. He'd gained consciousness and sent the girls to Mount Zion. Then, he went into his back room and picked up the shovel along with a heavy cutting knife. Charles didn't own any real weapons. He'd never needed to use such devices before tonight. But, now, he wished that he'd owned a gun. No matter, he would confront the rapists anyway. Someone would die tonight, be it him or the enforcers.

He'd been roaming the streets, searching for the attackers when he'd heard glass break. Upon rounding the corner of Fourth Street, an older man had stumbled into him. The man bled from a large gash on his forehead. He told Charles how several armed enforcers had entered his store and beat him without any cause. Afterwards, they had wrecked his place and taken all of his money. Charles had left him and moved along the street until he came upon the shattered window of *The Lunch Room*.

Particles of glass littered the sidewalk before Charles. Inside, he could hear two men speaking loudly. He peeked around the glassless window frame. Two men moved about the restaurant, trashing everything in sight. One of them pounded the furniture with a baseball bat while another dumped an ice cooler full of sodas onto the ground. The bottles broke, spilling their sticky contents onto the wooden floor. The enforcers laughed.

Charles ducked behind the wall. White knuckles tightened around the handle of the shovel. What gave them the right?

"Get on out of here," yelled a panicked voice from within the restaurant. "I'll blow your head off! I swear I'll do it!"

Charles peered through the window frame again. Behind the counter of the restaurant, a tall man stood with a resolute gaze on his face. The man wore long underwear and trousers with suspenders that hung loosely at his legs. He pointed a long-barreled shotgun at the two intruders. Charles recognized the young enforcer who had held him to the floor. He was the same man Charles had chased out of his shop last week. And, the other man… was the leader who'd initiated the rapes. *Mick.* Both men's backs were turned away from Charles. Their hands moved slowly toward hidden weapons.

"Don't do it," said the restaurant owner. "Just back on out of here."

"We can't do that," replied Mickey Henderson.

"You've all had it comin', mister," added Johnnie Roper. "You shouldn't have started actin' stupid."

"This is the kind of thing that happens to you when you don't have *protection*," explained Mickey.

"We don't need your protection," retorted the owner. "You boys have caused nothin' but heartache. Now get on out of here!"

"We told you. You got it comin'," replied Mickey as his hand groped for a revolver that was tucked into his belt.

Charles leapt through the window frame and swung his shovel at Mickey. The tool impacted the back of the man's head with a sickening thud. Mickey dropped to the floor. Johnnie Roper spun, drew a revolver, and pointed the weapon at Charles, who charged toward the young man.

Boom!! The shop owner discharged his shotgun into the back of Johnnie Roper. The look on the young man's face was one that Charles would never forget. He treasured the expression. It was the look of a man who suddenly realized that he'd taken the wrong road and couldn't turn around. His choice had been made and his fate was sealed. Johnnie Roper slumped over and landed face-first on the floor.

"Charles Kell," said Charles, between quick breaths.

"Mac Gentry," replied the man. "Thanks for your help."

"You got more ammunition for that shotgun?" asked Charles.

"Plenty," Mac replied.

"This kind of thing is happening all over town," explained Charles. "There are a lot of people out there who are going to be hurt."

"Well, I don't suppose that we can just sit here, then," Mac replied.

Mac stared at the hunched body of Johnnie Roper. "What do you know? They bleed red."

"We have to get all the men we can find… and get them onto the street," explained Charles. "If we stand together, the gangs will be no match for us."

"Agreed," Mac replied. "Let's go and shake some people out of their houses."

From the front of the restaurant came a low moaning sound. Mickey Henderson dragged himself across the glass strewn floor toward the broken window. Charles stomped across the floor and jammed his heel into the small of Mickey's back. The man grunted.

"How does it feel?" taunted Charles.

Mickey whimpered.

"What are we going to do with him?" asked Mac.

"Tonight may be the only chance we get to send a message to the gangs," said Charles. "And, we have to send it loud and clear. We don't want your protection anymore," he said to Mickey Henderson.

The enforcer's bloody face stared back at him with an immovable gaze. Even in his weakest moment, the man still believed that he owned Charles. Slowly, the colors of the room crept away, leaving only shades of black and white. No mercy remained in Charles; before him lay a rapist and murderer who deserved death. Charles raised the shovel high above his head.

"This is for my daughters, you worthless piece of trash!"

Charles Kell slammed the shovel into the face of Mickey Henderson.

Thirty-seven

Tim O'Hare hurried to the front doors of Mount Zion. Someone had been banging on them for several minutes and caused him to abandon Mary and the Kell girls in the basement boarding room. They hadn't received any word from Charles Kell and Tim was getting worried. Perhaps it was him who was knocking. He was sure that the man must have been consumed with guilt and rage over the rape of his daughters. After all, if he would have controlled his temper, the entire situation may have been avoided. Now, there was this rumor about a citywide shakedown. *God help us*, thought Tim as he padded up the stairs, leaving the basement below him.

By the time he reached the ground floor, the knocking had stopped. Outside, the rain fell in torrents. The wide expanse of the church's sanctuary was akin to a large drum and echoed the unsteady rhythm of the rain as it pounded on the roof. Sheets of water slapped against the windows with near glass breaking force. He couldn't imagine who would be out on a night like this, but, whoever it was they must have had something important on their mind. He nearly stopped and returned to the girls when he noticed a loan figure standing near the front of the church. The man was short, stocky, and wore a long coat that had been saturated with water. A dripping hat cast deep shadows upon the man's face. Tim had no idea who the man was or what he would be doing outside on a night like this.

"May I help you?" asked Tim O'Hare in an uncertain tone.

"I'm appalled, Tim," the man replied. "Would you just let anyone stand at your door and knock on an evenin' like this? Where's your mercy?"

Tim's eyes squinted as he tried to discern the man's hidden facial features. His voice seemed strangely familiar and caused a feeling of uneasiness to surface from the depths of Tim's past.

"I'm sorry," Tim replied. "Strange things have happened tonight."

"Well, take heart," the man consoled. "Things are bound to get stranger before the evenin' ends… Tim."

"I'm sorry… Do I know you?" Tim asked.

The man slowly walked toward him and removed his hat, allowing the dim church light to reveal his notable features.

"Surely you haven't forgotten your old protégé now, preacher."

Tim stood aghast. Though he lived within his grasp, Tim hadn't personally seen the man in over twenty years. Heavy lines now ran from his nose to the corners of his mouth. Gray hair lined his temples, giving the once two-bit enforcer a distinguished appearance. And his blue eyes still gleamed with the undertone of devilry.

"Anders?" Tim questioned, his voice disappearing in the spacious room.

"You *haven't* forgotten me. I'm honored. It makes me feel all warm and fuzzy. You know what I mean, Tim?"

"I'm afraid I don't."

"No, I don't suppose you do."

For the first time, Tim realized that the front doors of the church were ajar and two men stood by them. On the street, several vehicles lined the curb. Raindrops shattered as they impacted the black cloth roof of a royal blue Cadillac.

"It's been a long time since we've talked, Tim," said McCain as he sat down onto the pew and crossed his legs. "Please, take a seat."

"I'm alright standing…"

"Take a seat," McCain demanded, cutting Tim off in mid sentence.

Tim cautiously sat onto the wooden pew. Why would Anders be visiting here? Did he want to keep the Kell girls quiet?

"I'm a reasonable man, Tim… a businessman. Cheap thrills and fame aren't important to me. My bottom line is the dollar. You get the picture?"

Tim made no response.

"I run a fair business. Not everything I do corresponds with the law, but most things that are illegal here are legal elsewhere. And people always want to do what someone says they can't." He uncrossed his legs, leaned over and rubbed his face with his hands. "Take these people, for instance… please, take them," he laughed into the roomy chamber. "No… seriously. They love what I provide them.

Now, you may think that they're all these perfect little angels, but after they leave here on Sunday—it's me they pray to. I'm the one who has what they want, whatever that may be. And I've always given them *protection*. Do you hear what I'm sayin'?" He hammered his next words. "I've always protected them. But, all of a sudden, they don't want my protection anymore! Ten years ago, the Italians were robbin' them blind! So, everybody wanted their own gang. Everybody wanted protection! So, I organized it. You can't imagine the things I had to do, Tim."

"You sold your soul to the devil is what you did," spouted the older man.

"Yes... you might be right. I did horrible things. But, every one of them was necessary because the people needed an organization they could put their trust in. They had to know that their leader would do anything it took to serve their best interests. And, all I asked for in return was their loyalty. That's not so much to ask for, is it?"

Anders stood up and approached Tim, who was still seated. "But what do they do? They stop trustin' me. When we come to collect the money we need to continue their protection, THEY KILL MY MEN!" he spat, screaming the last words. "That makes me angry, Tim. I feel unappreciated," he said in a tone that demanded sympathy.

"Well," Tim replied. "I don't suppose many of them live in a luxury hotel in the center of Manhattan."

McCain snickered. "And none of them have risked what I've risked, now have they?"

"So, you've taken to having young girls raped? Is that one of the things you've had to do?"

"Come on, Tim. I have daughters of my own. Do you really think I'd condone something like that? I can't control everything these boys do. You remember how *we* were."

"*We* were evil. That's what I remember. We were two young men who'd been possessed by the devil. And, we sent many more to meet him. I'm ashamed of who I was."

"Well I'm not," McCain replied with confidence. "In this world, you can work for the devil... or be crushed by someone who does."

"This is madness," Tim said in frustration, rising to face McCain. "One day you'll stand before God, just as I will. What will you tell him?"

"I'll tell him that I *am* what Tim O'Hare *made* me. After all, I was trained by the worst."

"Anders, these people have suffered enough. Please, show mercy."

"*Mercy* is what put me in this situation. These people have forgotten all I've sacrificed for them. But, tonight, they'll be reminded."

"I'm very disappointed in you, partner," said McCain, changing subjects. "You could have stopped this. My mercy was within your reach. Instead you chose to betray me by sheltering the very man who defamed my name. The word is out old man. A preacher of this church was badly wounded... mugged in Manhattan, is the talk. He took a good beating... even a bullet to the leg."

There was no use in Tim trying to deny the truth. "He's not here."

"Of course he isn't. He's on his way back from Coney Island, where he murdered more of my boys. There's your *murderer*! There's your devil. But, you choose to hide *him*. He destroys my home, threatens my life, turns my people

285

against me, and drives me to destructive recourse, but you keep him secret. You've sealed the fate of these people and of your beloved church. You've betrayed me, Tim."

McCain motioned to the men in the back, who left the building and opened the trunk of a black car. The metal containers that the men retrieved appeared heavy and looked to contain some type of liquid. They entered through the doors again, tracking water along the carpeted aisle as they approached Tim and McCain.

"What are you doing, Anders?"

"It's simple," he replied. "…an eye for an eye. You destroyed my home…"

The men poured the liquid around the sanctuary. The pungent smell of kerosene wafted through the building.

"This is a house of God, man," Tim pleaded. "Do you have no respect?"

"That's an ironic thing to say, Tim. Because the only two men I know who live here are both *murderers*. I don't imagine God will be too upset."

Anders turned and strode toward the awaiting downpour. Tim followed behind, begging him to change his mind.

"Please… think about what you're doin'. Think about all the harm you're causin'. Just tell me what to do, Anders. Tell me what to do!"

McCain stopped and turned around, disgusted. "Look at yourself. The Tim O'Hare I knew would have shot me down without a second thought. Now you're beggin' me like some orphaned child? Pathetic…," he chided with the shake of his head.

Tim composed himself. "May God have mercy on you."

"Burn it," McCain commanded the men, who didn't appear too thrilled about the task. "See ya around, Tim," he finished as he marched into the stormy night.

One of the men produced a short, slender stick and rolled it across the back of a pew. The match head ignited in a ball of yellow light. With the flick of a finger, the flame tumbled through the air and landed amidst the pews. Tim ran for the basement.

McCain opened the door of his vehicle and was about to enter, when a navy blue car pulled beside him. The word "Police" was emblazoned on the passenger door in white-stenciled letters. A man wearing a yellow rain slicker exited on the driver's side and rounded the vehicle toward McCain.

"Captain Adams," greeted McCain. "We have to stop meetin' under the worst of circumstances."

"What the hell are you doin', Mr. McCain?" the man demanded.

"Business," McCain replied. "Just takin' care of business."

Adams looked around McCain's shoulder and into the doorway of Mount Zion, where two men exited. A faint orange glow filled the interior of the dim sanctuary.

"Would that business include burnin' churches?" Adams asked gravely.

"It might," McCain replied. "But, my business has never bothered you before."

"You're puttin' me in a tight spot, Mr. McCain. I'm not the commissioner. There is a limit to what I can do. Your boys are causin' trouble all around town right now. We have several reports of burglaries and beatings... even rape!"

"Just delay your response."

"How can I do that? This is no simple thing."

"The weather's horrible," explained McCain. "Surely citizens wouldn't ask their treasured policemen to risk their lives under such conditions."

"Mr. McCain..." Adams hesitated. "I'm sorry, but you're goin' too far... you'll have to stop. Call your men off."

"I'm sorry, Douglas," he replied. "You're right. I have gone too far to stop. I've put you in a terrible situation. My apologies." McCain reached underneath his coat for the Remington .44, which hung on his thigh. As he drew the revolver, Captain Adams fumbled for his own weapon, but to no avail. McCain pulled the trigger and sent a bullet into the forehead of Adams. The man's head jerked back violently. His knees buckled and Douglas Adams dropped into the flooded street. McCain spun the pistol, spraying water into the already saturated air. With a fluid movement, he slid the weapon into its holster and closed his overcoat. There was no turning back. The police wouldn't be able to ignore the murder of one of their own. At this point, however, McCain wanted one thing above all else... the preacher.

"What do we do with him, Mr. McCain?" asked one of the men, as he hovered over the body of Adams.

"Move him. Close the doors so that no one can see the fire. Tell our men to hide themselves in the rear alley."

"Yes sir," the other replied.

McCain looked at Douglas Adams as he lay in the street, his blood flowing into the rain gutters of Brooklyn. As the man died, his facial muscles had tensed into an expression of horror—the look of someone who betrays Anders McCain.

If he only saw that look on the face of one more man… it would be enough.

Thirty-eight

The long ride from Coney Island hadn't offered John Grady much respite. Instead, the trip had afforded him forty-five minutes of agony in which his imagination ran wild. He'd thought of all the cruel things that Anders McCain would wreak onto the people he cared about. Had McCain figured out where he'd been living? Had Ronald Thompson told McCain about his directive to leave a message at Mount Zion? Tim O'Hare had been right. John had brought the wrath of McCain upon the people of this city. He had allowed his personal quest for vengeance to override the safety of the people. *But, McCain has always been a threat to them. It was only a matter of time before he acted.* The age-old battle waged within his conscience.

It seemed that every decision he made in life was always subject to the same process of thought. There were always two sides to his perspective. There was the side of Joe, the

Apache Indian who lived a life of honor and justice, and of his father, who would turn the other cheek until his face was torn off. Or were the voices that of his own and that of God's? This mental war had raged in his mind since childhood. In the end, he chose to do what others feared to do, whether his conscience agreed or not. And, the fact was *McCain would have eventually destroyed these people, regardless of my actions.*

Water splashed around him as he weaved his way between the buildings of Brooklyn. John had chosen to keep to the alleyways until he made it to Mount Zion. He would be of no use to Mary or Tim if he got caught in a shootout.

The train ride hadn't given his body the rest that he'd hoped for. Instead, his muscles had tightened and his legs had nearly locked up on him. He'd spent most of the trip shivering and huddled in the corner of the boxcar... waiting... feeling helpless. Now, as he ran, new life flowed into his battered body. As his blood pumped, muscles relaxed and his body warmed. The deluge was beginning to slack off.

As John finally crossed Seventh Avenue, he glanced south toward Mount Zion, several hundred yards away. Nothing appeared out of the ordinary, though he had heard vehicles drive by. The front of the church appeared normal. Everything was quiet... too quiet... especially if there's a shakedown happening. Then, he noticed a slight tinge of smoke in the air. *It's probably just someone burning wood in a chimney.* But, it wasn't the smell of clean wood burning, but a noxious, unnatural aroma—the kind that occurred when something that wasn't meant to burn was burning.

He crossed the street into the narrow alley between Robinson's Deli and an importer's office. Small rivers of water flowed down drainage pipes from the building rooftops and splashed on his waterlogged boots as he squeezed by. His shoulders scraped the sides of the building as he maneuvered toward the back alley. An uncomfortable tenderness radiated from his left shoulder, alerting him to the fact that Wounded Hawk's bullet had grazed more than clothing. His adrenaline had been too high for him to notice the wound earlier. *There'll be time for that later.* He rounded the corner toward the back of Mount Zion.

John came to a halt in front of two basement doors, set into the ground in the traditional cellar door fashion. Everything seemed normal in the alley as well. In the center of the doors, a large padlock linked the two iron handles. John produced a slender key and inserted it into the lock. Entering through the basement seemed like the best course of action. He could enter from below and immediately get to the living quarters, just in case some of McCain's men had made it into the church. From there, he would have the element of surprise. With the twist of his wrist, the latch popped open. John swung one of the heavy wooden doors up and away, allowing it to flap over the side of the entrance.

Upon entering, he was immediately hit with the smoky aroma he had noticed earlier. Only now, it was much stronger. *The church is on fire!* He had to find Mary and Tim. *The Kell girls!*

A loud snort erupted from the gloomy basement. John extended his hand. "Ash," he commanded into the shadows. "Come here, boy!"

A gray muzzle emerged from the dark room and nudged John's hand. He patted the horse's nose with a reassuring touch. Coarse whiskers tickled the palm of his hand. How he wished he'd have had Ash for the Coney Island battle. But, he couldn't take the risk of allowing the horse to be seen during daylight hours. John had been hiding him inside the enormous unused portion of Mount Zion's basement. The cellar was bigger than any stable Ash had stayed in and allowed him plenty of room to roam around. John would take him out during the middle of the night and skirt the alleyways to Prospect Park, where he and Ash could run free, without the risk of being seen.

"It's all right, boy. We're going to get out of here. Stay here, o.k.? Stay here."

Moonlight drifted from two small windows set into the upper wall of the basement. He hurried across the hay-strewn floor toward the flat, unfinished wall. A single door adorned the partition at its far right. As he reached for the door, a loud bang echoed through the basement. *Someone shut the cellar door!*

John ran to the cellar doors and slammed into one of them with his shoulder. Neither door would budge. They'd been sealed. He'd have to try another route. His gut sank as he thought about the possibilities concerning Mary and Tim. He could only hope that they had somehow escaped.

As he entered the hallway to the living area, he could plainly see smoke drifting down the stairway that led to the first floor. John's focus shifted toward one priority—to get everyone out of this place.

"Mary!" he screamed into the corridor as he ran for the boarding room. John flung the door open with panicked fury. The room was empty. Heavily constructed bunk beds lined the walls. The linen had been disturbed on many of the beds, leading John to believe that Tim had given the Kell girls refuge in the room. But, they had apparently left in a hurry, along with Mattie and *her* children. He ran out of the boarding area and around to Mary and Tim's rooms, screaming their names. Both rooms were empty. *They aren't here! Oh God... please don't let them be upstairs.*

John ran up the stairway into the church. The hallway was filled with light smoke. When he'd left earlier, everyone had been in the kitchen. It seemed like a long shot, but he entered, calling their names. There was no response. He grabbed a dishrag from the kitchen and held it under the faucet, then placed the wet rag over his mouth and continued the disheartening search.

"Mary," he yelled, his voice consumed with panic. "Is there anyone in here?"

He coughed as he moved from room to room, calling their names. The light smoke was taking its toll and caused John to gag. Tears streamed from his irritated eyes. Eventually, he opened the door to the sanctuary.

To his horror, he discovered that portions of the large room were on fire. A wall of heat seared his skin, forcing him to step back from the room. The pews were ablaze in orange and yellow flame, but most of the smoke and heat collected in the expanse of the high arched ceiling. The front doors of Mount Zion were ajar. *Mary and Tim must have made it out, along with the others.* There was no one here, and John himself needed to escape.

As he passed the hallway that led to the back door, he noticed a car through the small window. Someone had blocked the exit with a vehicle. *Tim wouldn't have led Mary and the girls out through the sanctuary, not through the fire.* Then, why were the doors open? Someone had blocked all the doors except the front ones. *They're moving me through a funnel.*

Funneling was a technique used in war and hunting. The goal was to arrange an environment in such a way that it funneled the prey into a prearranged route. The hunter would then sit at the bottleneck awaiting the kill. *They want me to leave through the front doors.* McCain would be waiting.

John grabbed a leather saddle that sat atop a wooden sawhorse and flung it over Ash's back. It no longer mattered whether it was a trap or not, he had to get out. *What about the heat?* Could they make it through the burning portion of the church?

In his journeys, he'd seen men who'd been burned. It was a horrible sight and very painful. As he cinched the saddle down, John noticed that water still dripped from his coat, creating dark spots on the dirt floor. Inspired, he eyed the large barrel that contained Ash's drinking water. *It could work.* He grabbed the tin filler pail and immersed it, then poured the liquid over the horse's flank. Ash shifted nervously as the cool water saturated his hair and ran down his tail.

Anders McCain stood before the open doors of Mount Zion Methodist Assembly. The heat from the burning interior penetrated the chill of the night and brought warmth to his face. The rain, which had drowned the city for over an hour, had been reduced to a light drizzle.

"Is he comin'?" asked one of the men to another.

"He's sure been in there a long time," replied the second man.

Had the smoke overcome him? The sanctuary fire was growing out of hand. At this point, it would be nearly impossible for a man to run through the flames. McCain reveled in the preacher's death under any circumstances, but he would prefer that it happened by his own hand. The Remington .44 needed one last substantial victory before the weapon was retired again.

McCain opened his pocket watch and checked the time. The man had been inside the church for over five minutes. Smoke drifted from the roof of the brick building and rose unobstructed into the calm air. The odor of smoke was strong and wouldn't be ignored. Firemen would respond sooner than later, but not before the neighboring buildings went up in flames as well. Multiple fires hadn't been his intention, but the chain reaction couldn't be helped. McCain supposed it was another bonus to his plan. Not many men had the courage to burn a church. The people would understand that Anders McCain feared no one, not even God.

McCain's men mumbled behind him as he stared ahead into the fiery abyss... waiting... longing for one chance to kill this man who had caused him so much agony. Flames danced before his eyes in a light show of reds, yellows, and amber. The destructive beauty was breathtaking. McCain had set many fires in his life. But, this fire contained a certain unique presence, as if the devil himself had sent one of his angels to carry out his work.

Then, before McCain's eyes, a demon began to take form amidst the inferno. A dark outline morphed from the flames and began to take on the horrid shape of a black rider. A dark cloak, which ended in a deep faceless hood, billowed around his body. The steed upon which he rode snorted, thrusting smoky vapor into the air. Resounding thuds echoed as the creature's hooves impacted the wooden floor. McCain was awestricken. Seconds stretched into eons, time slowed, and Anders McCain absorbed the image of his destroyer. Expletives erupted from the men behind him.

The demon burst forth from the flames, his horrible form still ablaze, and leapt into the air. McCain drew his gun and fired a futile shot into the night sky before dropping face-first into the wet street. The stallion soared across the front end of McCain's Cadillac and with a click of his hooves, landed on Seventh Avenue then galloped away amidst a few panicked gunshots. A burning blanket drifted to the ground and landed before McCain. He watched the smoldering cloth in awe and banged his fists on the pavement.

"Preacher!"

Thirty-nine

John Grady spurred Ash north along Seventh Avenue.
Behind them, car doors slammed. The smell of charred
hair reminded him of how dangerous the escape had
been.

The road was wet, so he'd have to be careful. If Ash
slipped, he would likely kill both of them. Fortunately, John
had covered the horse's shoes in a soft tar upon arriving in
New York. The coated horseshoes gave the animal more
traction on hard surfaces. Still, wet pavement was deadly.

Steam rose from Ash's wet body as the horse galloped
east onto Fourth Street. Upon turning the corner, John
nearly pulled the horse to a stop. Hundreds of people lined
each side of the road. Some hurried in the direction of
Mount Zion, carrying pails of water. A mob of angry men
tore into several other men who were attempting to flee from
them. The men battered their victims with mallets, clubs,
mops, bats—whatever they could get their hands on. John's
first instinct was that McCain's enforcers were attacking the

townspeople. Then, a bloodied Charles Kell pulled away from the fight. He stood on the sidewalk with a shovel in his hand. A strange mixture of pride and sadness occupied his face as he gave John a nod of approval. John's heart broke for the man, but he was also proud. The people were making their stand. New hope flooded into John's heart. McCain had spoken and the people were replying.

"Reverend Grady!" an old woman cheered.

"You get him, Reverend," exclaimed another. Many more shouts rang out from the crowd before McCain's entourage turned onto the street.

Upon seeing the train of cars, some of the crowd ran and for good reason. But, some began throwing trash, rocks, and gravel at the vehicles as they sped past. Various objects pinged against the metal bodies and shattered windows. John's hunters simply ignored them. Their sights were set on a more prestigious target.

John turned onto Eighth Avenue. Cars slid around the corner like savage dogs on the trail of a wounded animal. Engines revved and vehicles lurched forward, shortening the distance between themselves and John. Ash was fast, but cars were faster. As he sped toward the intersection of Third Street, the lead car shot forward and approached from his right rear. The Ford gained on him in steady increments. An enforcer crawled from the passenger side window and brandished a gun over the rooftop of the car. John drew and fired toward the vehicle, forcing the man to duck back inside. The driver accelerated and attempted to ram Ash from the side. John pulled back on the reigns and slowed the horse. The Ford passed them, speeding into the Third Street intersection. An oncoming car attempted to swerve, but crashed head-on into John's pursuers. The force of the moving vehicles detonated like a bomb. The gunner was thrown from the car and rolled into the busy avenue. With a mighty jump, Ash leapt over the tangle of wrecked autos.

The slow rise and fall of a fire truck siren whaled as the pair galloped along Third Street. The red wagon zoomed past with two firemen aboard. One man piloted the machine while the other cranked the handle of the siren. *Good, they should be headed for the church.* John had to get to Prospect Park. If he could just make it to soft ground, Ash could out maneuver the cars.

"C'mon, boy," he yelled, driving the animal into a gallop. John whipped his head around and gauged the situation. There were still five cars behind them and they were gaining speed again. In the rear was McCain's blue Cadillac. Automatic gunfire blazed from two of the cars. John let go of the horse's reigns, drew a second pistol and pivoted at his waist. He opened fire on the closest vehicle, blowing a headlight and the radiator. Steam sprayed from the grill and consumed the front end of the car. The auto slowed, allowing the other vehicles to overtake it. John turned around in time to pass through the entrance to Prospect Park.

He immediately veered from the road and into the trees, hoping his hunters would quit the chase. But, the first vehicle followed directly behind him. The car swerved sharply to miss a group of oaks. The other autos sided next to him on the main entrance road and unleashed a few wild shots as John ran parallel to them in the woods. The terrain drastically slowed the vehicle behind him. The woods thinned and John crossed a large road before re-entering the wooded terrain. The paved road ended, forcing John's pursuers into the woods for a bouncy ride. Ash galloped ahead and entered the vast expanse of Long Meadow, then, veered southeast and ran for the safety of the ravine. He had one objective—lose his pursuers and get back to the city. Mary and Tim were somewhere, lost in the chaos.

McCain's brigade burst from the wooded edge of Long Meadow. The lead car, a black Studebaker, turned abruptly, pursuing John toward the ravine. Wheels spun on waterlogged grass. A Model T Roadster dodged the vehicle, slid to a halt, and tipped onto two wheels before settling back to the ground. Drivers ground gears and jammed accelerators. The vehicles spun back into action.

Three more cars emerged from the woods, hot on Ash's flank. One of the vehicles, a model T pickup, held several gunmen in its bed. The men fired erratically at the horse and rider as their vehicle bumped along the meadow. The pickup hit a hole and bottomed-out, throwing an enforcer into the air. He landed on the edge of the bed with a thud, fell onto the ground and tumbled twice before a trailing car pummeled him.

"Let's go boy," John said, driving the horse. The forested ravine was less than two hundred yards away. A bullet buzzed by his ear. John fought the urge to swat at it. *At least these bullets are small.*

A Ford Roadster pulled beside him to his right. John sent a round of bullets flying into the windows before the shooters could fire. Glass shattered and the Roadster slowed. Ash sprang ahead and dropped out of the meadow and into the wooded refuge of the ravine.

Some of the drivers must have been familiar with the park, because they jammed their brakes. The Roadster, however, was too close and skidded over the edge of the gully. The vehicle tumbled down the ravine behind John, flinging its screaming occupants into the air. John cantered the horse down the steep slope as the crashing sound grew closer. At the last moment, he yanked Ash hard to the right and paralleled Ambergill Creek just as the car tumbled past them. The twisted wreck crashed into the rocky creek bed. Atop the meadow, John could hear the cars speeding off toward the service roads that would offer them passage through the wild terrain.

Ambergill Creek gurgled to their right. John slowed Ash's pace. The rocky terrain of the ravine was no place to hurry. If the horse broke a leg, they would both be finished. They had made it halfway through the park. Once they emerged from the ravine, they would have to traverse the Nethermead, a small meadow in the center of Prospect Park. If they could reach the area fast enough, McCain would never see them slip past.

John cursed himself for allowing McCain to live. The boy had stopped him. He knew the boy would have been scarred for life. But, now, many people were suffering. The Kell girls had been raped because of his choice. It was an age old question of morality—*hurt one for the benefit of many?*

They crossed Center Drive under a high-arched bridge, and then stormed across the widening stream and into the Nethermead. John moved the horse into a canter as they headed south toward the Peninsula. Beams of light splayed across the road behind them. The cars nearly passed them, then lurched left and began their descent through the hilly meadow. Three automobiles still followed. McCain's car was nowhere in sight.

Ahead, the field funneled into a roadway that was wedged between two fingers of forest. John veered left and arched around the expanding watercourse onto the wooded peninsula. Within moments, the speeding vehicles had made up much ground. John was leading them toward the lake and once there, they would have no place to go.

Ash ran along a narrow nature trail that skirted the peninsula's edge. One of the vehicles pulled away from the group and followed them through the woods. The car lurched up and down, shoveling dirt with its front bumper. Wheels scraped the top of the fenders. A gunner emerged from a window and wildly fired an automatic weapon.

Splinters flew from the trees around him as the salvo of bullets struck. The car was so close that its headlights illuminated the road in front of them. John pushed Ash toward a gallop. Ahead, the woods thinned and a shimmering expanse of water waited. The plan was working. A hundred yards and John would lose his pursuers. The gunner ducked inside to reload, but was replaced by another enforcer who fired a revolver. Just as the machine gunner re-emerged, Ash burst forth from the woods. John jumped from the horse as they tore into the lake. A freezing wave of water hit him and stole his breath.

The speeding car attempted to stop, but it was too late. The vehicle barreled into the lake. Water exploded from the grill as the car dove into the icy water. Both men hit the front windshield, shattering the glass. The front of the car began to sink.

John gripped the saddle horn as Ash swam the narrow canal. Freezing water brushed past like the attack of a million needles. John wanted to sink. Exhaustion racked his body once again. He wanted to rest, but *Mary* was out there… somewhere. He had to find her. He had to stop McCain from hurting these people any further.

Ash rose above John as the horse's feet found solid ground. Water poured from their bodies. John looked across the lake to see the remaining two cars stranded on the Peninsula. By the time they managed to drive back through Nethermead and find a road, he would be long gone. But, where was McCain?

He didn't know where McCain was, or Mary and Tim for that matter. The only thing he could think to do was ride through the streets and offer help to any citizen who wanted to take a stand. Against his body's will, he stepped into a stirrup and heaved himself into the saddle. A terrified city waited.

John and Ash rode hard along East Avenue, back toward the Mount Zion neighborhood. The cool air rushed by his wet clothing and he shuddered. He wondered how Charles Kell and the others were fairing. McCain could be nasty. The ride seemed to last an eternity, but eventually they neared the park's main entrance point at the Plaza.

Then, as if God himself had ordained the moment, John glimpsed the taillight of a royal blue car as it left the park headed east on Flatbush Avenue.

McCain was within his reach.

Forty

y the time John Grady made it to Flatbush Avenue, the blue Cadillac had slipped through an alley and was heading toward the train tracks in between the buildings. The avenue was nearly deserted, except for the occasional headlight that pierced the mist. The rain had stopped. Only blocks away, he could see the soft orange glow of Mount Zion as it burned to the ground. Smoke hung close to the street where it mingled with a light fog. The shrill whistle of a train bounced through the cityscape.

Within hours, the storm had come and passed without causing much permanent damage. Ash's hooves clopped on the sidewalk of Flatbush as the pair searched for McCain's vehicle. They eased into the passage through which the car had driven. Yellow lamplight cast hard shadows. John felt uneasy between the two tall buildings. It was like wandering into a canyon after losing site of a deadly outlaw. But, he could still distinguish the glow of two red taillights ahead of them. And then… the red lights vanished.

Within seconds, John could make out the form of the blue Cadillac on the opposite side of the tracks. What would McCain be doing *here*? Could the building have been another one of his warehouses? John squinted, trying to see through the haze. The vehicle appeared to be empty. The piercing light of a train cut through the foggy expanse between the buildings. With every chug of its engine, the iron behemoth filled the area with thunderous sound.

John was preparing to dismount when a clap of thunder caused Ash to bolt. A jolt of lighting racked his right shoulder and slammed the breath from his lungs. John gasped for air and twisted backward as the horse leapt the tracks in front of the steaming locomotive. Before the train passed, John managed to catch a quick look at a figure on the other side of the tracks. Anders McCain held a smoking, long barreled gun. The train flew past, obscuring John's view in a blur of black steel. Pain, like a branding iron, seared his shoulder. He checked the wound with his left hand and pulled away blood covered fingertips. McCain had shot him in his back. Shock gripped him like a talon. His head swooned and he slipped from the saddle.

Anders McCain had watched the pale horse slip across East Drive toward the border of Prospect Park. Could his men do anything right? Then again, it would have been a pity if some 'nobody' had killed the preacher.

He'd watched the dark rider cross the Nethermead and flee toward the lake. After discerning his destination, he'd driven out to East Drive because it was the closest main road. McCain had reasoned that if the preacher were going to cross the water, he would choose this side. Within moments of parking and killing his headlights, the rider had slipped into the road several hundred yards away.

McCain had shifted into first gear, and, with his lights off, eased toward the Plaza. Once there, he'd stopped and waited. Finally, the gray horse had come cantering up the east road. On cue, McCain had turned his lights on and driven onto Flatbush Avenue in search of the perfect ambush site. He'd settled on an urban canyon amidst the jungle of buildings. His empty car had lured the preacher in and the train had trapped his attention. Hidden behind an elevated loading dock, he'd taken aim with his .44 and fired a bullet into the man's back. Timing was everything. Now, the preacher lay on the other side of the tracks wounded, perhaps dying.

McCain's empire was crumbling; there was no denying that. The little worms had even had the audacity to hurl things at his car as he'd ridden by them. Their fear of him had been lost. This *preacher* had embarrassed him. He'd made McCain look like an incompetent fool. He could have lost many men by now. No matter what happened, it would take a long time to get the people to trust him again. But really… what would they do without him? *What will they tell Joe the Boss when he comes looking for his cut? They'll come running back to me.* They always did. People rarely had the guts to take a stand for themselves. That's why they needed men like him. *And they'll need me again… soon.* Until that time, he would have to be satisfied with the death of the man who had planted the seed of rebellion. So McCain stood, waiting with his Frontier model pistol as the train clanked past with its endless line of cars.

John scraped himself off of the gravel and rose to his knees. He'd fallen off of Ash and landed in the dirt. With his left hand, he attempted to wipe the grit from his cheek. A messy mixture of sticky blood and pebbles remained. Any movement of his right shoulder sent shards of lead digging into his neck. The bullet had passed between his muscle and collarbone.

Between the bottom of the boxcars and the elevated track, John could see McCain's mid-section. The man was over there, waiting to finish the job he'd started. John gritted his teeth. He had tried to let the vendetta go. But, this time, McCain had drawn first blood. John *could* have lived without seeing McCain again. Mary had shown him a new way of life. But, he couldn't blame McCain for striking back. After all, John had entered the man's house and threatened his life in front of his family. John understood.

The train stretched as far as he could see. The cars passed by one after the other in agonizing monotony. He thought about trying to shoot between the wheels underneath the freight cars. There was a short interval in which he could take a shot, but that wasn't the way he wanted to end this relationship. Perhaps at one point in his life, he'd have killed McCain in whatever way possible. But, now, he wanted it to end with some degree of honor. This face off would be something he'd remember for the rest of his life. So, he rested on one knee and waited for the train to pass.

McCain watched car after car go by, searching for an opportunity to gun down the man on the other side of the tracks. Had he ever faced an opponent like the preacher? How many gunfighters could claim a victory like the one he was about to have?

Saliva crept into his mouth. Muscles tightened. The end of the train finally came into sight. McCain could see the preacher stand on the other side.

"Come on," he said aloud. "Come on."

Then, McCain saw the flatbed car rolling down the track—a momentary window in the impenetrable wall of steel. At the speed the train was traveling, it would offer him a two second opening in which to deliver a killing shot. But, because the train was elevated, he'd have to attempt a headshot on the man... unless he could get to higher ground.

McCain hurriedly climbed the loading ramp that he'd used to hide behind earlier. He steadied himself, angled the Remington revolver toward the train, and prepared to fire.

Upon seeing the end of the train, John had stood and readied himself for the inevitable gunfight. He knew that McCain would use whatever method possible to kill him. The man had no dignity. But, John hadn't noticed the flatbed that approached. He was caught off guard as the open car passed, revealing the poised assassin on the other side. McCain had been prepared to fire. With his left hand, John drew a pistol with controlled speed. Just as he pulled the trigger, fire jumped from the muzzle of McCain's gun. A bullet ricocheted from the bed of the car and whistled past his ear. John's gun recoiled. McCain bent in half at the waist and stumbled backwards just as the next boxcar rolled by, obstructing John's view.

The passing cars shimmied and creaked in a deafening chorus line. On the other side of this moving barrier, lay the man he'd pursued for so many years. And, this time, McCain had *forced* John to act. A quarter of a mile away, the red caboose signified the end of the train.

Forty-one

After eons, the red caboose passed a shaken John Grady. But McCain was gone. Where he stood, blotches of bright red blood reflected the dim lamplight. John lowered himself onto a knee and examined the blood. The liquid contained particles of partially digested food and reeked of fecal odor. *Gut shot.* He'd hit McCain somewhere in the stomach. An abdominal wound was usually fatal, though it sometimes took days to bleed out.

McCain had left through the same alley they'd entered. And, from the blood patterns, he was walking fast. John tied Ash to the understructure of the loading dock.

"I'll be back, boy. You deserve the rest."

He rubbed the animal's muzzle then started on the trail.

Drops of blood lined the sidewalk in an undeniable connect-the-dots puzzle. McCain was heading back towards Mount Zion. John's best guess was that the man hoped to find some of his enforcers still roaming the area. At the moment, McCain was wounded and needed protection. He wondered if McCain had ignored the sight of the uprising earlier that night. Most likely, his men had left the area long ago.

The sharp pain in his shoulder had subdued, only to be replaced with an ache that consumed the right side of his torso. Above him, the sky was turning a hazy gray. Morning was coming and the clouds were thinning. John kept moving, despite his weariness. The night was leaving, and with it, years of anguish. McCain's organization had fallen and Charles Kell had inspired others to act. Within minutes, John would be a free man. *Will you indeed? Will you ever be truly free?* Could he ever forget about the things he'd had to do? Soon, he would know the answer to that question.

There was a startling change in the pattern of blood. Suddenly, the concrete was smeared with the crimson liquid. It looked like someone had taken a paint brush and dragged it along the sidewalk. McCain had fallen. After walking several blocks, the man had collapsed to the ground and crawled. He'd lost too much blood.

No more than two blocks ahead, Mount Zion smoldered in the twilight. Firemen had managed to save a large portion of the building, but the sanctuary was gone. John could see several fire trucks, including one drawn by a team of horses. Dozens of people worked in front of the church. Some hand carried buckets back and forth from the water hydrant, while others helped salvage furniture and supplies from the damaged building.

But, many people just stood and stared as if in a trance. John could imagine the stunned looks and teary eyes. Sometimes, life changed too quickly to comprehend. In those moments, all one could do was try and make a little sense of the madness.

Ahead, the blood trail made a sharp left turn under the awning of a building that John had passed many times while walking the neighborhood. The old theatre was being renovated and would soon exhibit moving pictures. McCain had broken the glass door and pulled himself through. John ducked through the opening and eased into the theatre. Shards of glass crunched under his boots. The first time he'd met McCain had been amongst shattered glass.

John squinted as his eyes adjusted to the dim interior. All of the linens, tapestries, carpet and furniture were missing. The lobby had been completely gutted. All that remained were concrete floors and bare walls. Two gigantic curved stairways adorned each side of the foyer leading to the balcony. A roost of pigeons was startled and flew from the vaulted ceiling high above. More movement caught his eye. At the back of the spacious lobby, a pathetic shape dragged itself across the uncarpeted floor.

McCain.

Forty-two

Dawn had been eerily quiet this morning. People mulled around in the street outside of Mount Zion. No one spoke. Each person worked through his own thoughts. Police cars had patrolled the area, attempting to restore order. After most of McCain's men had been beaten or worse, the mobs had settled down. It always amazed Tim O'Hare how quickly the ferocity of humans could turn them into the very things they detested.

Plumes of steam drifted from the remains of his beloved church. For the most part, the fire had been extinguished. The pumper engines had been turned off and now people carried pails of water to douse the occasional hot spot. Firemen walked along the inside of the once beautiful sanctuary, digging into smoldering mounds of ash with their shovels and pike poles. The smell of burnt upholstery and varnished wood turned his stomach. Why had it come to this? *Am I still being punished, Lord? Will my sins always follow me?* No matter how hard Tim O'Hare tried, he could never escape the violence of humanity.

Then, from somewhere down the street, he'd heard glass break. He'd initially attributed it to looters. People always found a way to take advantage of others even in the worst of circumstances. But, then, he'd seen the dark figure as he'd stalked the sidewalk in the direction of the church. He'd hoped John was returning—that he'd finally come to his senses, but he stopped in front of the old theatre. The man in black had examined the door for a moment, and then stepped inside.

Tim felt pity for John. His life was a sad story, driven by a quest that could only result in death. Dying wasn't much of a living. Tim knew that first hand. Tim had died long ago, but had been given new life through his faith. But, the memory of his sins remained, along with the faces of those he'd murdered… and the orphans he'd left in his wake.

Beside him, a knapsack rested on the curb. He'd put his most treasured belongings into the bag. Tim didn't own many things that he couldn't live without, but there were several things he'd always promised to keep. Inside the bag was a Bible, a picture of his dearly passed Rosalyn, and a cardboard box—the contents of which he had not looked upon in a very long time. Even now, a force repelled him from the object within. *You don't have to see it again. Why must you do this to yourself?* He placed the cubed container on the back of a fire truck and began to lift the lid. Tim's heart sank.

John Grady aimed his pistol at the back of Anders McCain's head.

"Turn around, so I don't have to shoot you in the back," he said. His own voice startled him as it reverberated in the empty chamber.

McCain halted. He slowly turned to face his executioner and propped himself onto an elbow. His mid-section was saturated with blood.

"Do you know who I am?" he asked McCain.

"Yes. I do."

"Did Wounded Hawk tell you?"

"Some," replied McCain. "What does it matter now?" He spit a wad of blood onto the floor.

"How do you know him?" John asked.

"Be realistic," yelled McCain. "I don't owe you any explanations! You've killed me, you idiot!"

"You don't owe *me* anything?" asked John, incredulously. "You don't owe *me*?! You *made* me!"

"No," replied McCain, solemnly.

"You gunned my father down in front of me! I was eight years old! He was a preacher! Does that help your memory?"

"I didn't kill your father," McCain replied.

"*Do you remember me*?" John asked again through clenched teeth. Jaw muscles rippled under taunt skin.

"It wasn't me," McCain pleaded.

John cocked the hammer of his Peacemaker.

"It wasn't," agreed a familiar voice from behind John. He turned his head, startled to see Tim O'Hare standing in the lobby.

"What are you doing here?" John asked, perplexed.

Tim stepped into a trickle of morning light that found its way through the dust covered windows. The man held something in his hands... something light-colored.

"Anders didn't kill you father, John," Tim said, solemnly. "I did."

John stared at the object in the man's hand. "I don't understand," said John, blankly. His head buzzed from the loss of blood.

"I've wanted to tell you. I haven't known how," Tim explained. "I was the man who shot your father, son."

John couldn't take his eyes off of the thing in the older man's hand. There was something familiar. But, it was too dark to see the object clearly.

"His murder has haunted me more than any other crime I've committed," Tim continued. "That's why you're here. Your pastorate request came across my desk, and I recognized it immediately—John Grady... son of James Grady. I thought I could help you... guide you... I had no idea why you were here... that I was too late."

Tim O'Hare stepped fully into the light. The object within his grasp reflected its brilliant color back to the empty eyes of John Grady. And, from the misty places of his dreams, the thing began to emerge. Through miles of heartache and years of frustration, John Grady had scoured the earth searching for a killer... the man in the white derby. And now, after all this time, it hung in the hands of a man he could not kill. *The white derby.*

"That's impossible!" he screamed.

"I'm so sorry, John. I'm so terribly ashamed!"

McCain began to chuckle and briefly choked on his blood.

"Shut up!" John demanded. He poked his gun at McCain. "He's a killer! He's killed without mercy, over and over."

"As have I," Tim replied.

John lowered his weapon and began to pace nervously. Voices bombarded him. He stepped back and stumbled. What to do? What to say? This was the most ridiculous thing he'd ever heard. The man who had killed his father had become a minister himself?!

Tim O'Hare had looked after John. He'd mentored him. More than anything, John wanted to hate the man right now. He wanted to stick his pistol in the face of O'Hare and pull the trigger. John *wanted* to want that. But he couldn't. He tried. He tried to force the hate from deep within. But he couldn't make himself hate Tim. *Oh God... is this how you work?*

Steaming tendrils crept from his feet and crawled their way toward his gun hand. Inside, his body convulsed at the mixture of feelings. He could no longer contain the explosive power. With a rage beyond his control, John swung the gun toward Anders McCain and prepared to shoot.

"No, John!" Tim exclaimed. "God has used your folly. You've led these people to stand up for themselves. Don't ruin it with this! Don't become like Anders."

The rushing force burst from John Grady's mouth. His cry filled the vast lobby, hurting his own ears. Frightened pigeons flew out of the vaulted ceiling. With all of his strength, he spewed the anger and hate into the dank air. Then, John turned the Peacemaker on Tim O'Hare.

John pulled the trigger over and over again, illuminating the lobby one shot at a time. The white derby flew from Tim's grasp and skittered across the floor as John screamed. When the gun emptied, he pulled another. He blew the hat into the air and shot again. The mangled derby hit the floor and spun. John shot once more before the hammer struck an

317

empty chamber. He dropped the gun, drew a fresh pistol, and aligned the sights toward the shredded derby. But, he didn't have the heart. It was all gone… everything. He was spent. His strength was zapped. His vengeance had been stolen. John Grady dropped his revolver and ambled out of the theater as Tim O'Hare watched. Exhausted, he fell to the curb of Seventh Avenue and sobbed.

"John!" Mary cried. "You're alive! O thank God you're alive!" A small crowd followed behind her, no doubt drawn by the gunshots. She dropped to the curb and held him in her arms. He was glad to see her. He'd spent the entire evening worrying about her. He wanted to tell her how happy he was that she was well… that he loved her… but, all he could do was cry. He sobbed like a baby in her arms.

Tim O'Hare stood over the discarded pistol. "I'm sorry, Anders. I could have been so much more for you."

"Don't patronize me," McCain replied. Blood crept from the corner of his mouth. "You've got it coming. You all have it coming!"

Tim O'Hare picked up John's wood-handled revolver. The butt of the weapon felt strange in his hand. The wood was oddly smooth, like it had been wielded many times. He hadn't held a pistol in over twenty-five years. He'd sworn that he wouldn't. But, he'd left too many sins unattended… too many wrongs that hadn't been righted. With a breath of resolve, Tim O'Hare pointed the pistol at McCain's forehead.

"So, you're still a murderer?"

"Aren't we all?"

Tim cringed as the hammer moved under his thumb.

Outside, the gunshot resounded through the street. John didn't even flinch. Mary rested her chin against his head and rubbed his shoulders. Onlookers backed away as Tim O'Hare exited the building. Without a word, he stepped from the curb and walked through the crowd, south, toward Mount Zion.

In the distance, echoed the wail of police sirens.

"You have to go!" exclaimed Mary.

"No," he replied.

"What do you mean!?"

"I'm just so tired." He pulled away from her and rubbed his eyebrows between his fingers. "I'm finished. I can't live like this anymore."

"Yes, you can!"

"Look at me," he said. "What do I have, Mary? What do I have to show for the effort of my life?"

Mary breathed heavily.

"Nothing," he continued.

"We can build a new life... together." Tears began to fall from her shimmering blue eyes.

"I'd like that... more than anything," he replied. "But I'm no good for you right now."

"John," she replied. "I love you. I was too afraid to tell you... afraid of myself. But, you've shown me how to have courage. And now I'm telling you."

John grasped her delicate hands. "That's why I have to do this. Don't you see? If I'm ever going to be a man that can love you the way you deserve, I *have* to face my consequences. I have to make peace with God. Who else can free me from this life of death?"

"It doesn't seem fair," she said.

A ray of sun warmed his nose. In the overcast sky, the clouds opened, allowing sunlight to trickle toward the damp earth.

As police cars rounded the corner, he released Mary's hands and stepped into the street. Guns began to drop at his feet, one after the other, their heavy steal clanking onto the concrete. With their release, a heavy presence lifted, one he had carried for many years. John Grady raised his hands into the air and dropped to his knees in the middle of Seventh Avenue.

Blue-clad policemen swarmed around him.

Forty-three

1921
Ossining, New York

John Grady gripped the cold, steel bars of his stuffy cell. Across the hall, light flooded through the windows of Sing Sing Prison. He closed his eyes and allowed the warm sunlight to caress his face.

His last meal had been soup… and a cold glass of lemonade, nothing like his mother used to make. Somewhere down the hallway, footsteps echoed on the stone floor. It was time. He was all too ready to be through with this seven by three foot cave he'd existed in. Though he didn't know what lay ahead, he'd made his peace with God. His debts were being paid.

On his neatly made bed, lay a stack of weathered envelopes. He opened one, pulled the letter out, and smiled as he traced the feminine handwriting that covered its surface. Mary's letters had kept him going.

The community had rebuilt Mount Zion, though Tim O'Hare had disappeared. John hoped the man would be able to out run his guilt… that he would find peace. But sometimes, a man had to turn around and fight. Charles Kell had turned around. His bravery had inspired change. Charles had run for city council and won. Things were getting better. Outraged citizens forced investigations within the police department. The Irish mob was in shambles. One man *could* make a difference.

Mary had left Brooklyn over three years ago. The ordeal had been more than she could bear. She'd moved west to a small town in California and had started her own business as a seamstress. He missed her terribly.

A key turned in the lock of his cell door. John folded the letter and returned it to the stack. He took a deep breath and looked around the tiny room. Most everything he knew was in here.

"Reverend Grady?" the young guard asked. "Are you ready?"

"Yes," he replied.

Shiny shoes stepped out of the cell and into the stone corridor. The new suit had been a gift from the warden of all people. He and John had grown close. John had used his remaining time to minister within the prison, giving life instead of taking it. He followed the young guard down the hall. Fellow prisoners watched, their faces pressed against the steel grid of their windows.

"Thank you, Reverend," a prisoner offered. He looked upon John with sad eyes.

"Thank you," affirmed a second prisoner. Mumbles drifted from both directions in the corridor… the voices of men whose lives he'd touched… robbers, murderers, Irish enforcers… guilty men like himself.

John understood the gravity of his crimes when he'd surrendered to police. And he didn't lie about anything. He'd told them about the bombs and the killing... and about Anders McCain. In all, he was charged with three counts of murder, eighteen counts of manslaughter, reckless endangerment, criminal intent to harm, and destruction of private and public property. The jury had gasped collectively.

Ahead of the young guard, a door opened into another corridor. John was led into a short hall flanked by prison guards on both sides. The men nodded and smiled at John as he passed. John returned the courtesy. Most of them were good men. John enjoyed the company of good men, he had known too few in his lifetime.

At the end of the corridor the warden stood. He wore a black suit. Behind him, bright light leaked around a heavy iron door, a door John had thought about many times over the years. Warden Lawes extended his hand to John. "Reverend," said Warden Lawes. John took the man's hand with his own. "We knew this day was coming," he continued with a hint of sadness in his voice.

"You're doing a great work, here," John replied. "Keep doing it." Lewis Lawes was a good man and he was changing lives in this former hellhole.

With a clang, a guard opened the steel door. Blinding light flooded the corridor. John shielded his eyes with his hand and took a deep breath. Warden Lawes placed a hand on his shoulder and ushered him through the door.

"Don't be afraid, John."

But how could he have been anything other than afraid? John had prepared himself for this moment... or so he thought. He'd done everything in his power to make his life right for this time... to be worthy in God's eyes. But nothing can prepare a man to glimpse the remainder of his life. Nothing can prepare him to come face-to-face with his destiny. Tears he had withheld welled into his eyes from depths unknown. And a figure began to emerge from the halls of his dreams and into his waking hour. Would it be another nightmare? Was he still being punished? He stepped forward into the world of illumination.

Strawberry blonde hair glistened in the blinding sunlight.

John had confessed to everything. And as he stood ready to plead guilty to all counts, a strange thing happened. The judge dismissed the majority of charges. The impossible had occurred. John had gotten an honest judge, one who had struggled against the mobs and corrupt police force... one who wanted to do what John had done. McCain hadn't made official reports regarding the incidents. His "bought" policemen had handled the matters privately. Therefore, records were scarce. Any remaining charges were chalked up to self-defense. After all, the whole city had fought back against the mob.

One charge stuck, though. The attack at The Rendezvous was too high profile to be hidden. Anders McCain Junior had identified him, and John was charged with attempted murder. The jury returned a guilty verdict and the judge had given him the minimum sentence—five years.

A refreshing spring wind blew through the graying hair of John Grady as he stood outside the walls of Sing Sing Prison. Behind him, Warden Lawes smiled. It was a gorgeous April morning in New York State. Strong sunlight fell from the clear blue sky, enveloping the landscape in its life giving beams. Standing in front of a lush, ivy-covered wall, was an angel... his angel. Mary's blue eyes beckoned him forward. She was more beautiful than the last time he'd seen her. The wind tugged at her blue dress, revealing contours his eyes hadn't seen in three years.

It had been three years since Mary had left for Fallen Oak, California... where she had been hard at work preparing the old Grady homestead. With the help of the community, she had painted the house, fixed the porch and repaired his mother's white picket fence. A new life awaited them... in a place where he was known as the son of James Grady, the preacher who gave his life for a criminal. And he would use it... He would make the most of everyday he was given. He would give life as his Pa had done.

"Reverend Grady," Mary said with a mischievous nod.

He took her soft hand in his and turned the gold band on her finger.

"Misses Grady," he nodded back with a smile. He leaned in and put his lips to hers. His hands found their way to her face and he caressed her soft cheeks. He had glimpsed the remainder of his life... and it was more than he could ever deserve. *That's how God works.* He pulled away and looked longingly into her eyes. "Let's go home."

She took his hand and led him through the gates of Sing Sing Prison and to a waiting taxi. He raised his face toward the sky and felt the sun on his cheeks. John Grady took the deepest breath he had ever taken in his life... and smiled. And, for the first time in many years...

He *knew* that God smiled back.

About the Author

James Mathews, an author and filmmaker, is passionate about taking readers into a world that they have never experienced, whether it is a time in history or abstract reality. He loves interweaving his real life experiences throughout his stories so that he can better connect with his audience. James is the head of operations at his company, Distant Lands Productions, and resides in Murfreesboro, TN with his wife, Heather, and two children, Aron and Cody.